OUTSIDE THE RULES

Linda Hughes

A KISMET® Romance

METEOR PUBLISHING CORPORATION

Bensalem, Pennsylvania

In memory
     R.A.D., E.D.R., M.F.T.

LINDA HUGHES

Linda Hughes is a native Mississippian who currently resides in Southern California. She is a member of Romance Writers of America, Mystery Writers of America and Sisters In Crime. OUTSIDE THE RULES is her first novel.

ONE

Jamie Royale descended the stairs to the lobby of the Universal Hilton, a grimace tugging at the corners of her mouth. There must be some corollary to Murphy's Law that dealt with out-of-town conferences, she thought darkly. Some axiom about the cancellation of a special pre-conference workshop being in direct proportion to the amount of time, energy and money one had expended in order to attend.

Okay, so she hadn't exactly moved heaven and earth to get there a day early. But she'd had to juggle a few appointments and rearrange her travel plans. And for what? The workshop on marketing strategies had just been canceled because one of the scheduled speakers had missed his flight to Los Angeles. The workshop organizers had apologized, of course, and then advised everyone to "relax, have a few drinks" before the conference officially began the following morning.

Jamie's navy blue pumps sank deep into the plush, rose-colored carpet as she strode across the room. Yeah, right. She had no intention of wasting her time sitting in some smoke-filled room, running up a bar tab on her expense account. This was a working vacation, dammit, and she intended to make the most of it. Fortunately, she'd met several other commercial insurance producers in the hospitality room upstairs. They'd decided to get together for coffee and an impromptu brainstorming session in one of the conference rooms in fifteen minutes.

"Oh, Miss Royale!"

She stopped in mid-stride. The desk clerk who'd checked her in a few hours earlier waved her over to the long marble counter.

"The gentleman was adamant that I give this to you the moment I saw you." He handed her a folded sheet of paper.

Her brown eyes widened with mild surprise. "Thank you."

She opened the note. "Jamie," it read. "Imperative I speak with you a.s.a.p.—Gary Dodsworth." A local telephone number was scrawled underneath the signature.

Gary Dodsworth? Who in blue blazes was Gary—?

She arched an eyebrow as she finally recognized the name. Gary Dodsworth—early fifties, thinning blond hair, wire-rimmed glasses—had been seated next to her on the connecting flight from Dallas. A nice enough man, she supposed, but she really hadn't expected their airborne conversation to lead to a continuing relationship. Nor to mysterious notes being left at her hotel. She frowned. If he was planning to ask her out, he'd chosen a peculiar way to do it.

"Could you tell me if Gary Dodsworth is registered here?"

"Let me check." The desk clerk keyed in the appropriate code and scanned the names displayed on the video screen. "Sorry, I don't see any Dodsworth listed. Is he with the IPA conference?"

"No, he's a commodities broker. At least, that's what I think he said he was." She glanced at her watch. The producers' meeting would be starting in precisely seven minutes. Damn.

She reread the note, but it made even less sense the second time. What could the man *possibly* want to talk to her about? It couldn't be insurance, although the demanding tone of the note struck a familiar chord. They had barely discussed the subject. So why . . . ?

She sighed. "Is there a telephone I can use?"

The clerk pointed to a row of pay phones across the hallway. She murmured her thanks, then turned and walked toward them.

Calling Gary would make her late for the bull session, but she didn't see that she had much choice. He'd asked that she call him a.s.a.p., and she knew she wouldn't be able to concentrate on the meeting if she was wondering what he wanted. Besides, she'd never ignored an "urgent" message in her entire life—from perfect strangers or longtime clients alike—and she wasn't all that sure she could start now. Her father had told her it was a curse, this habit she had of always following the straight and narrow, of obeying the rules, even when they made no sense and were damned inconvenient to boot.

Sometimes her father had a point.

"Excuse me, Miss Royale?"

The male voice came from behind her.

Masking her irritation, she pasted a smile on her face and turned to find herself looking up into a pair of the greenest eyes she'd ever seen. More vividly green, perhaps, because they were framed by long, dark eyelashes.

"Yes?"

"I wonder if you might be able to help me."

His voice was as warm and smooth as Kentucky bourbon, his smile nearly twice as intoxicating. He was tall, just over six feet. She was five feet seven herself, and even with her three-inch heels, she still had to look up to see his face . . . and it was a handsome face. Almost too much so for her taste. But the unruly brown hair, a few shades lighter than her own short, dark mahogany, added a touch of boyish charm she found very appealing.

The smile she gave him this time was genuine. "If I can."

"I understand you were on Delta flight two-oh-seven this morning."

He had the easy, relaxed grace of a man comfortable with his own masculinity. One hand rested casually inside the right trouser pocket of his tan suit as he stood there waiting for her answer. But she'd seen a flicker of something in his sexy green eyes—suspicion? wariness?—that made her suspect he wasn't nearly as nonchalant as he wanted her to believe. Although she wasn't sure why, she suddenly felt nervous.

"So?"

He gave her a disarming smile. "I'm trying to track down a business associate of mine who was also on that flight. His name is Gary Dodsworth. I believe he was your seatmate."

She stared at him for a moment. "But he—" Her fingers instinctively tightened around the note in her right hand. "I'm sorry, but who did you say you were?" She tucked the slip of paper into the side pocket of her already bulging shoulder bag.

"Flynn. Stephen Flynn. Why don't we sit down?" He nodded toward the lobby.

"I'm afraid I really can't spare the time."

"Please?" His face was a mask of smooth professionalism, revealing nothing, but his voice was gentle persuasion personified. "It'll only take a couple of minutes."

She glanced at her watch and shrugged. She was already late for the meeting. A few more minutes would make little difference. "All right."

Most of the groupings of chairs and sofas were already occupied by hotel guests. But Flynn had obviously anticipated their need, because he led her to an empty love seat a discreet distance away from the others. It was half-hidden by a large potted palm and afforded them the illusion of privacy.

"As I was about to explain," he said once they'd settled in, "Gary and I had an appointment this afternoon. When he didn't show up, I became a little concerned."

"But what does that have to do with me?" She crossed her legs, pulling down the tailored skirt that was hiking its way up her thigh.

His gaze flicked to her legs, then back up to her face again. He smiled. "Gary mentioned your name when he called me from the airport."

She opened her mouth to object, but thought better of it.

"When he didn't show up, I thought you might have some idea of what had happened to him. I know how all of this must sound to you, Miss Royale." He leaned forward slightly and she caught a whiff of the crisp, masculine scent of his cologne. "But I assure you I wouldn't be here if it weren't important. Did Gary say or do anything at the airport that struck you as unusual?"

She eyed him curiously for a moment. Forget the airport. What struck her as unusual was receiving an urgent note from a man she barely knew, then being approached moments later by another claiming to be his associate. And just what sort of *business* were they planning to discuss anyway? she wondered, her curiosity kicking into overdrive. Pork futures seemed highly unlikely at this point.

Recent newspaper headlines flashed through her head. Stories about insider trading scams, drug smuggling, even murder for hire. And just as suddenly, she was quite certain she didn't *want* to know what Flynn and Dodsworth had cooking between them. Curiosity had killed the cat, and she, unfortunately, didn't have the luxury of nine lives.

"The desk clerk gave me this a few minutes ago." She removed the note from her purse and handed it to him. "I was just on my way to phone Mr. Dodsworth when I met you."

He frowned. "Do you know what Gary wanted to see you about?"

"I'm afraid you'll have to ask him that, Mr. Flynn—"

"Steve, please."

"I arrived in Los Angeles only three hours ago. Prior to the flight, I had never met Gary Dodsworth. I'm an accounts producer for a property and casualty agency in Baton Rouge, Louisiana. I'm out here to attend a four-day conference sponsored by Insurance Professionals of America." As if to substantiate her claim, she pointed to the name tag fastened to the lapel of her navy blue jacket.

"Now, as for Gary's behavior at the airport—" She shrugged. "I didn't notice anything unusual. and I don't recall his having spoken with anyone else, either. But to be perfectly honest, I really wasn't paying that much attention."

He nodded, obviously satisfied with her answer. "I appreciate your talking with me, Miss Royale." He rose to his feet. "You've been a great help. Do you mind if I keep this?" he asked, indicating the folded note.

"Not at all." She stood, prepared to leave, then hesitated. "Is Gary in some kind of trouble?" It was an impulsive question, and one she wished she could have recalled a moment after she'd asked it.

Their eyes met, and she saw a shadow of worry cross his face. "I wish I knew," he said softly. He tucked the note into an inside pocket of his jacket and smiled, the mask of professionalism in place once more. "Thanks again." He extended his hand. "I hope you enjoy your stay in Los Angeles."

"Thank you."

She watched thoughtfully as he made his way through the lobby back to the adjoining hallway, his tall, well-conditioned body moving easily through the crowd.

With a mental shrug—it really *was* none of her business—she turned away. As she saw it, Dodsworth had probably forgotten about the meeting with his business associate. Flynn would telephone Dodsworth and the two men would sort it all out without her help. As for the note, well, he was probably just planning to ask her to dinner. End of story.

Jamie glanced at her watch. Besides, not only was she

late for a meeting—make that *very late*—she simply didn't have time to stand around speculating on the cloak-and-dagger theatrics of strange men. And with that settled, she smoothed back a strand of her stylishly short brown hair and headed for the conference room, determined to put the entire incident from her mind.

Tony was waiting by the row of elevators at the end of the hallway. Steve could tell by his expression that the investigation had come up with zip.

"Nothing, huh?" Steve asked.

Tony shook his head. "It was clean. I've got security down in the garage doing a search for the car. It may take a while."

Steve looked over his shoulder and watched as the tall brunette walked past. Long, shapely legs taking long, confident strides. Shoulders back, head erect, eyes forward. She looked like a woman who wasn't easily swayed by anything.

Or anyone.

"See what you can come up with on Jamie Royale. Background, financial records, stats. The usual."

Tony nodded. "You still think she's involved?"

Steve slipped his hands into his trouser pockets. "I don't know. But I sure as hell intend to find out."

Several hours later, Jamie returned to her room to freshen up for dinner. The informal get-together with other insurance producers had been a tremendous success, which more than made up for the canceled workshop. For her purposes, it was probably even better.

She had advanced as far as she could at Duval Insurance, a property and casualty agency in Baton Rouge. The simple truth was she was bored silly with her job as an accounts producer. She knew accepting a new position at a different agency wouldn't solve the problem. She needed new challenges. Opening her own agency seemed the natural solution; attending the IPA conference was the first step in her well-thought-out strategy.

Stifling a yawn, she dropped her purse on the bed and walked into the bathroom. She reached for her toothbrush and froze. *Now, that's strange*, she thought. The electrical cord of her blow dryer was dangling out of its travel case. Hadn't the cover been closed when she left?

She then noticed her hairbrush lying at a forty-five-degree angle to the blow dryer. And hadn't she placed it near the edge of the sink? Confusion gave way to apprehension as she made a quick inventory. Cosmetics, hair spray, deodorant. *Everything* on the marble vanity seemed to have been moved. But why?

"I've been robbed!" she breathed hoarsely and rushed into the other room to check her valuables.

But nothing was missing. Her microcassette recorder, an expensive top-of-the-line model, still sat on the dresser. A pair of gold earrings and a pearl necklace that had belonged to her grandmother still lay atop the nightstand.

But the blow dryer's case had been opened.

Hadn't it?

She rubbed her forehead, suddenly unsure. She didn't know what to believe anymore, especially since she couldn't think of one good reason why anyone would want to break into her room and examine her belongings.

In fact, the more she thought about it, the more ridiculous the idea became. "Jet-lag-induced paranoia," she diagnosed wryly and walked back into the bathroom.

All the same, before she left to join the others for dinner twenty minutes later, she rattled the doorknob to make doubly certain the lock worked.

An ounce of prevention . . .

TWO

Jamie awoke promptly at 6:45 the next morning, as she had every morning for the past ten years. Established routines were the backbone of her existence, and they made hotel wake-up calls completely unnecessary. Even if there was a two-hour time difference.

Stepping out of the elevator on the first floor precisely one hour later, she smiled. There was nothing like a good night's sleep to put the world back into proper perspective. Her fanciful imaginings of the evening before now seemed to be—well, just that. Fanciful imaginings. And she was amazed she'd ever thought them otherwise.

She strode confidently down the hall and tossed a quick glance toward the lobby, which was on her right.

She recognized him immediately. But then, Stephen Flynn wasn't exactly an easy man to forget. His tall, lithe form leaned casually against the concierge's desk. When he saw her standing in the hallway, he waved and walked over.

God, he looks awful.

The thought came unbidden as the distance between them shortened. He still wore the tan suit from the day before. Only now it hung wrinkled and limp on his body, looking as tired as he did. Dark shadows smudged the

15

skin under his eyes and a day's growth of beard stubbled his jawline. She found herself wondering if he'd slept at all.

"We've got to stop meeting like this," she said in a deadpan.

He gave her an apologetic smile. "I have a few more questions. A few things I want to get straight."

She adjusted her bulky shoulder bag's straps, temporarily halting their downward slide off her shoulder. "I don't suppose you considered just calling the number he left for me yesterday?"

"It would have been pointless." His voice was laced with weariness. "The number he left was for my office. And Gary never made it there."

"I see." She glanced at her watch. It was 7:50, and the opening ceremonies for the IPA conference would be getting underway at eight sharp. "I really don't know what else I can tell you, Steve. I haven't heard from Gary Dodsworth since I spoke with you yesterday."

"But you *can* tell me about your conversation at the airport—how he acted, what he said."

"I probably could, but I won't—at least, not right now." She was using the tone of voice usually adopted when denying insurance coverage to prospective clients with poor loss histories: pleasant, yet firm. "I'm on my way to a breakfast seminar—for my conference, remember?—and I don't want to be late." She flashed a smooth, professional smile. "It should be over about ten. If you'd like to wait, I'll be happy to answer your questions then. Now, if you'll excuse me." She started walking down the hall.

"Miss Roy—Jamie!"

It was the desperation in his voice more than the hand he placed upon her arm that brought her to a stop.

"I can't wait that long." He reached into his jacket and removed a small leather case. "Please. It's important."

The picture was a bad likeness, she thought. It didn't

show the sexy sparkle of his eyes or the warmth of his smile. Still the ID card seemed genuine enough.

"You're a private investigator?"

He nodded and returned the case to his jacket pocket.

"And I suppose Gary isn't a commodities broker from Dallas?"

"No."

"I see," she said, although she didn't. None of this made any sense, but who was she to quibble over minor details?

"You said you were going to a breakfast meeting." He smiled wryly. "I could do with some coffee myself. Why don't we grab something to eat while we talk?" They were standing outside the hotel's coffee shop, and the tantalizing aromas of freshly brewed coffee and crisp bacon wafted out the open doorway to greet them.

She hesitated. The man certainly fascinated her, and by this point, her usually well-curbed curiosity was threatening to race out of control. (Dead cats be damned.) But talking with him would mean missing the keynote address on future trends in the property and casualty marketplace. It was, unfortunately, a subject she needed to familiarize herself with thoroughly before opening her own insurance agency later that year.

"I'm afraid I . . ." Her voice faded, leaving the thought unfinished. In his eyes she saw worry and frustration, mixed with a kind of frantic hope; in the hard lines of his face, the strain of long hours and little sleep. He needed to talk *now*, she realized with a pang of conscience, not at some later date when it could conveniently fit into her schedule.

She smiled. "Okay." She turned toward the restaurant. "We'll talk over breakfast."

The coffee shop's decor matched the rest of the hotel—muted tones of rose and green in an atmosphere that was cool and airy, relaxed and low-keyed. She could hear the occasional clink of glassware above the subdued murmur-

ings of a group of businessmen near the front as she and
Steve walked across the room to a corner table.

Jamie sat down in a high-backed cane chair and
smoothed out the folds of her skirt, her mind swirling with
a thousand questions. Now that she'd agreed to talk to
him, she could hardly wait to hear what was going on.

"I might as well start at the beginning," he said after
the waitress had brought coffee and left with their order.
"Gary works for Flynn Security."

"*Flynn* Security? Any relation?"

"I own the agency. We're security consultants, Jamie.
Primarily for large corporations. We provide advice, pre-
employment checks, armed protection—whatever is
needed."

"But I thought you were a private investigator." She
stirred a packet of sugar substitute into her coffee.

He smiled. "I am. And so are most of the operatives
at Flynn Security—it goes with the job."

"Including Gary?"

"Including Gary."

She nodded. "Is that why he was in Dallas? To conduct
some sort of investigation for the agency?" She wrapped
her fingers around the warm coffee cup and slowly raised
it to her lips.

"No, nothing like that. Gary was acting as a courier.
His job was to transport the item from Dallas to L.A."

"What was he carrying?"

"That's not important right now. Finding out what happened to him is."

Common sense told her the two were connected, but
she resisted the urge to point that out. "Do you think he
skipped town?" she asked instead.

Steve rubbed his eyes. "That's about the only possibility I *haven't* explored. Gary's got a wife, a family, obligations. He would never have walked away from all that."
He took a long swallow of coffee and shrugged. "I know
the flight was okay because he called on arrival. Agency

rules. But he didn't show when he was supposed to, and I haven't heard from him since."

"But what made you come here? Just how did I get involved in all this?"

"His phone call. He mentioned you when he checked in, and I played a hunch."

"But what did the man *say* about me? What possible reason would a private investigator have for including my name in his check-in report?"

He looked at her over the edge of his coffee cup and smiled, his eyes warm and inviting. "He said you were beautiful. And that I was a fool for not having taken the assignment myself."

His answer surprised her. But not nearly as much as her own reaction to it—a warm, tingling sensation that began somewhere near the center of her stomach.

"But you and Gary had obviously spent some time talking on the flight in," he continued, glancing away. "So when the people at the airline couldn't remember anything unusual, I decided to track you down—you booked your flight through the IPA conference, so finding out where you were staying was easy." He frowned, as if he'd just thought of something that disturbed him. "Anyway, my hunch paid off. I learned Gary drove over here to see you yesterday afternoon." He took a sip of coffee and replaced the cup in its saucer. "His car's still in the parking structure, you know. We found it last night."

The room felt several degrees cooler. "Meaning?"

"Why don't you tell me?" He rested his elbows on the table. The warmth, the openness, were gone from his eyes. It was as if they'd never been there at all. "From where I'm sitting, the facts are pretty clear."

"And they are?"

"Gary phoned me from the airport to say he was on his way to Flynn Security. He came here instead—apparently to see you. And now he's missing."

"I don't think I like what you're implying."

"Do you know what he wanted to talk to you about?

Why he came here, rather than going straight to the agency?''

"How should I know? I just met the man.''

He watched her with the cold, professional detachment of the investigator, seeing much but revealing little. "Then you must've made one hell of a first impression, lady. His note said it was 'imperative' he see you again.''

"I'm well aware of what the note said.''

"Then tell me what it meant. Explain to me why a man you had just met would come to this hotel to see you rather than complete his assignment. What was his motivation, Jamie? Was it because he had no choice? Was it because he *couldn't* complete his assignment until he saw you? Was that it?''

She placed both hands on the table and leaned forward until her face was inches away from his. "I intend to say this only once more, so I suggest you pay close attention this time. I don't like bullies and I don't like being called a liar. If I knew what Gary Dodsworth wanted to see me about, I would have told you the first time you asked me. So back off, buster.''

The waitress chose that moment to arrive with the food, and it forced them to settle back in their chairs, even though the argument was far from over. Jamie folded her arms against her chest and fumed. It was bad enough she had to miss the keynote address, but she'd be damned if she'd sit through another Flynn inquisition. And when the waitress left, she pushed her chair back and stood.

"Jamie, please.'' He rose and took her arm. "Look, I owe you an apology. I usually don't act like a bastard so early in the morning, but the past twenty-four hours have been as close to hell as I hope I ever get.'' He flashed a weak smile and released her arm. "You see, Gary and I go back a long way, almost eleven years. I know him as well as I know myself—maybe even better. He wouldn't have missed delivery without a reason. And a damned good one at that.''

Steve raked his fingers through his tousled brown hair.

"I know you've said you don't know what he wanted to see you about. And I believe you. I believed you the first time, although the way I acted a few moments ago probably made you think otherwise. I'm sorry about that, but I had to be sure my instincts were right—that you weren't keeping anything from me."

She stared at him, but didn't say a word.

"Gary's coming here to see you had something to do with his assignment. It's the only explanation that makes any sense at all. But exactly how you fit . . ." He shrugged and glanced away. "The bottom line is that I need you. You're the only person who might be able to help me find Gary, to figure out this crazy mess." He turned back and met her gaze. "Right now, you're probably thinking I have a hell of a lot of nerve asking you to stay after the way I treated you. But my options are limited. I have to ask. Will you help me?"

She thought of a thousand possible replies, but in the end, she rejected them all. "Your breakfast is getting cold." She sat back down in her chair and took a bite of her whole wheat toast.

He grinned. It was as if the sun had come out from behind a cloud on a rainy day.

"My instincts," he told her in a self-congratulatory tone, "are rarely ever wrong."

Ten minutes later, after the table had been cleared and their third cup of coffee placed before them, Steve asked Jamie to recount everything she remembered from the airport.

"But there's really nothing to tell." She leaned back in her chair. "It was a routine flight, followed by a routine trek through the terminal to get my luggage. I don't remember seeing or hearing anything out of the ordinary. And certainly nothing that might explain what happened to Gary."

He smiled. "Things aren't always what they appear."

"Neither are people." Especially those who profess to be commodities brokers from Texas.

"I know the flight itself was okay," he persisted. "So I'm only interested in what happened *after* you left the plane. Just take your time and tell me everything you remember. We'll worry about its significance later."

She took a deep breath. "Well, we said good-bye in the passenger lounge right after we left the plane—Gary said he had to make a quick phone call. I guess that would have been the one to you." He nodded. "I went straight to the baggage-claims area. There was about a fifteen-minute wait until they started the conveyer belt. And I was still standing there waiting for my suitcases when Gary backed into me."

"Wait a minute. He *backed* into you? You didn't mention this before."

"That's because it wasn't a big deal. One of the skycaps was pushing an overloaded cart through the terminal, and a few pieces of luggage tumbled off the top. Everyone standing nearby had to jump out of the way. When Gary moved back, he bumped into me. End of story."

Steve leaned back in his chair and crossed his arms triumphantly against his chest. "What were you wearing?"

"What was I wearing?"

He nodded. "Yes. What did you have on?"

"Well, a navy blue suit—but you saw what I was wearing when you came to the hotel yesterday afternoon."

He grinned, tiny flames of emerald fire dancing in his eyes. "The tight skirt with the slit up the back?"

She felt the color heighten in her cheeks. "I suppose that's one way of describing it," she mumbled under her breath.

"It's a nice outfit." He took a sip of coffee and frowned. "But not enough pockets and entirely too form-fitting to have been of much use."

What was this, an investigation or a fashion review? She shook her head. "I really don't see what—"

"Were you wearing an overcoat?"

"In June?"

He shrugged. "Well, what about carry-on luggage, a tote bag, anything like that?"

She laughed as his meaning finally became clear. "Afraid not. I just brought two suitcases, and both were checked. The only thing I carried on board was my purse."

He glanced at the item in question. It hung across the back of her chair and bulged out suspiciously at odd angles. "Do you think we could . . . ?"

She sighed and hauled the heavy bag up onto table. She really ought to have her head examined for doing this—the man's eyes were not *that* sexy.

"Do you mind telling me what we're looking for?"

"The reason Gary came to see you yesterday afternoon."

"Couldn't you be a little more specific?" She removed her microcassette recorder and two spiral-bound steno pads and placed them on the table.

"I've already told you more than I should."

Her address book hit the table with a thud. "Uh-huh. Well, whatever it is, we're not going to find it in here. Gary never touched my purse." She pulled a can of Mace and a red quilted cosmetics case out of the shoulder bag and set them on the table beside the address book.

"You may have a point." He pried loose a magazine wedged between her appointment calendar and a small retractable umbrella. "*Popular Woodworking*?" He glanced at her in surprise.

"Furniture refinishing's a hobby of mine," she offered matter-of-factly and reached back down into her purse. She came up with a miniature stapler and a large tin of buffered aspirin.

He cleared his throat. "Do—uh—do you always carry this much stuff around with you?"

"Actually, most of it's for the conference." She removed a half-eaten chocolate bar and a six-ounce bottle of domestic white wine from her shoulder bag. The former had been her lunch one particularly hectic day the week before, and the latter was a souvenir from the flight.

"You're kidding."

She glanced at him, her hand frozen in mid-search. The expression on his face was somewhere between incredulity and amusement as he watched the stack of seemingly unrelated items grow higher. "I believe in being prepared." Then she slapped an unopened pack of thigh-high hose and a hand-held can opener down on top of her wallet.

His eyes met hers. "I'll try to remember that," he said, his voice warm and playful.

She turned the shoulder bag upside down and gave it a good shake. Resisting the urge to say "I told you so," she returned her belongings to the empty purse. When she finished, she unzipped the outside pocket and slipped her hand inside. Nothing. She tried the unzipped pocket on the other side and got the same results. She looked up at him. "Satisfied?"

He looked puzzled. "I don't get it. Why would—?" He took a deep breath. "Okay, Gary bumped into you when the luggage fell off the cart. Then what happened?"

She shrugged. "He apologized."

"And?"

"And my suitcases came around on the conveyer belt about that time, so he helped me get them off the rack." She saw a familiar gleam appear in his eyes, and quickly shook her head. "Oh, no, you don't. They were both locked, and neither one has any outside pockets."

He grinned. "What happened next?"

"I thanked him, he wished me luck with my conference and I left."

"That's all?"

"I told you, nothing happened." She took a sip of coffee, but it had grown cold. She pushed the cup aside.

The smile slowly faded from his face. "So you did." He sighed, then wearily raked his fingers through his hair. "Well, I guess I'd better let you get back to your conference." He reached for the check.

"I wish I could be of more help."

He met her gaze. "You've been a great help already."
He peeled off a couple of bills and dropped them on the
table. "Ready?"

She nodded and grabbed her purse. They walked out
into the hallway.

"If you should think of anything else, give me a call."
He handed her a business card. "It's my private line. I
can be reached there twenty-four hours a day."

"But I've already told you everything I remember."
And her memory had always been infallible. It was one
of the fringe benefits for having a well-organized mind.

He pressed the card into her hand. "Just in case." Then
he turned and walked away.

She watched until she lost sight of him by the elevators.
She looked down at his card and then tucked it into the
side pocket of her purse.

Logic told her she shouldn't have a reason to phone
him. Nothing out of the ordinary had happened at the
airport—nothing she had seen, at any rate—and regardless
of what Steve suspected, she *knew* Gary's reasons for
missing delivery could not have included her.

She adjusted the straps of her bulky shoulder bag and
frowned. But why *had* Gary come to the hotel to see her?

More important, where was he now?

The elevator doors glided open and Steve stepped out
onto the third level of the parking garage, his mouth set
in a hard, grim line. He was no closer to the truth now
than he had been before, and he was running out of leads.

And time.

He walked slowly across the pavement to his black
Acura Legend. What could have gone wrong? he asked
himself for the hundredth time. It was supposed to have
been a minimal-risk operation. A cakewalk, for Chrissake.

Feeling his weariness to the very marrow of his bones,
he unlocked the car door and crawled behind the wheel.
What made it even more confusing was Gary himself. He

was no amateur. Hell, he'd probably forgotten more about running a covert operation than most people learn in a lifetime. If he'd found himself in trouble at the airport, Gary could—and probably would—have done almost anything to prevent the package from falling into the wrong hands. Including slipping it to an uninvolved third party for safe-keeping. In fact, his behavior at the baggage-handling area had all the signs of a hastily improvised handoff.

Steve shook his head. Nice theory. Too bad it just didn't pan out. They'd searched the woman's room, and even her purse, without finding anything. His instincts told him she wasn't lying.

But why else would Gary have gone to the hotel to see her if she *hadn't* been holding the package for him?

Exhaling slowly, he leaned against the warm leather seat and closed his eyes. *Face it, Flynn. You're losing your objectivity about Jamie Royale.*

It was a problem he'd encountered almost from the moment he'd seen her walking across the hotel lobby. He couldn't seem to forget the light floral scent of her perfume. Or her soft Southern drawl—really only noticeable when she became annoyed. Or the way she moved. Smoothly. Self-confidently. With no wasted motion.

He opened his eyes and frowned. But a physical attraction hardly qualified as an objective analysis of the woman's culpability. Right now, he needed facts—not emotions—to corroborate his instincts.

He grabbed the cellular phone mounted to the dash and punched in the number for the office.

"Stephen Flynn's office," came the swift reply a moment later.

"Mona, it's Steve. Has Tony completed his check on the Royale woman yet?"

There was a slight hesitation. "The report's on your desk—there were no red flags. Are you on your way back in?"

He glanced into the rearview mirror and ran his hand

critically across the stubble on his chin. "I was planning on swinging by my place first. Why?"

"I got a call a couple of minutes ago from a friend over at central dispatch."

"So?" He tightened his grip on the receiver.

"A report just came in about a homicide in the Hollywood Hills. . . . Steve, it looks like we may have found Gary."

Shortly after lunch, Jamie hurried up to her room to drop off her souvenirs from the IPA Trade Fair before the afternoon sessions began. It had been a busy morning. She was still carrying all the brochures, pamphlets and audio cassettes, and two hardcover books on the dynamics of selling, that she had somehow managed to accumulate during her various stops. She even clutched a bulky pack of street maps and fliers for local tourist attractions under her chin that she'd picked up from the car rental agency downstairs.

With a skill a contortionist might envy, she inserted the keycard into the lock with one hand while precariously balancing the stack of books and papers with the other. She gave the door a shove with her shoulder and stumbled inside.

The destruction before her was like a physical blow. Clothes ripped from hangers. Dresser drawers upended, their contents strewn about the room. Even the linens had been stripped from the bed and lay in a rumpled heap on the floor.

"Oh, my God!" she gasped, letting everything drop. She'd seen less devastation after a hurricane.

But why? she asked herself, walking slowly around the room. Why had he done this to her? And after he'd said he believed— She sank down on the bed, suddenly afraid her knees might buckle.

She had no doubt Stephen Flynn was responsible for this. His questions had made it only too clear he believed

Gary had given her something at the airport. He had even asked her to empty her purse so he could look for it.

"Bastard."

Her first instinct was to telephone the police. She felt sure his sexy green eyes would have little effect on *them*. Maybe if he spent a few days in jail, he'd think twice before strip-searching someone's room the next time he felt the urge.

But having him arrested would do little to assuage her anger. No, this called for a more personal touch.

She located the telephone—it was half-hidden by the flap of her nylon suitcase—and dialed the number printed on his business card. Seconds later, she slammed the receiver down in frustration. "Mr. Flynn" was out on appointments. But his secretary assured her he would return the call as soon as he possibly could.

"I'll just bet he will," she muttered, reaching for a pair of white linen trousers lying crumpled on the floor.

"Bastard."

Less than an hour later, Jamie left her room. Amazingly enough, the damage had been mostly superficial, and cleanup required little more than the replacing of clothes on their respective hangers and into dresser drawers.

I should've made him do it, she thought, jabbing the button for the elevator. But the time for retribution would come soon enough. Stephen Flynn *would* pay, and pay dearly.

She could guarantee it.

She brushed away a piece of imaginary lint from her skirt and looked around. A tall, blond man—odd, she hadn't noticed him before—stood beside the glass-and-chrome table directly behind her, quietly smoking a cigarette. He wore faded jeans, a black leather jacket and dark aviator sunglasses.

The man appeared to be staring straight at her, the expression on his lean, tanned face unreadable. And then he smiled, a cold, menacing sort of a smile. It sent a chill down her spine, and she hurriedly looked away.

The elevator doors swooshed open and she stepped into the empty car. She pressed the button for the lobby and turned around. The man was gone. Only a spiral of gray smoke rising from the ashtray on top of the table indicated he had ever been there at all. The doors began to close.

Suddenly a black gloved hand slipped between the two converging metal partitions, breaking the electronic beam, forcing the doors to reopen. The man stepped into the elevator.

Jamie backed away instinctively as he moved to the rear of the car. She caught a quick glimpse of short, spiked platinum-blond hair—a color too pale, too stark a contrast with his olive skin tones, to have ever been natural—and a tiny gold hoop earring.

The doors closed and the elevator began its slow descent. She kept her eyes straight ahead, resisting the mad impulse to glance over her shoulder. Still, she *knew* he was watching her. She could feel his eyes boring into her back.

"Where is it?" he asked finally, his voice low and threatening. "What'd you do with the doubloon?"

Doubloon? She tightened her grip on her purse and kept her eyes focused on the floor-indicator panel. Great. Just her luck to be stuck in an elevator with a Captain Kidd wannabe. She decided to ignore him.

There were only five more floors until the lobby.

He sighed. "Don't make me hurt you."

She felt the hairs rise along the base of her neck. *That* comment she couldn't ignore. She glanced over her shoulder and flashed her brightest smile, her right hand slipping casually into her purse to find the can of Mace. "I'm afraid you must have me confused with someone else."

He didn't answer. His only reply was a smile, a smile so completely devoid of warmth it almost made her shudder.

She turned back and nervously glanced at the floor-indicator panel. One more floor.

Seconds later, a bell pinged and the elevator doors opened onto the first-floor hallway—an ominously vacant hallway. She quickly stepped off. His black gloved hand shot out and grabbed her left arm.

"What the—! Let me go!" She tried to wrench herself free. She only succeeded in jerking the straps of her purse off her right shoulder and sending them sliding down her arm. Her left wrist felt like it was caught in a vise.

"Where is the doubloon?" His tone was more insistent this time.

She hadn't been able to find the can of Mace. It was still buried somewhere in her shoulder bag. But the purse itself ought to do the trick. She twisted its straps around her hand and swung the bag like a club. It struck the man square in his chest. He released her arm and stumbled back.

Recovering, he took a threatening step toward her and stopped. They both heard the sounds of voices, laughter, growing steadily closer to the row of elevators. He glanced past her toward the approaching people and cursed softly. "I'll be back," he promised. Then he rushed down the hall, pushing his way past a startled trio of conference attendees.

She stood there and watched him go, too stunned to do much else. First Flynn had ransacked her room, and now this.

Just what the hell was going on around here?

THREE

Jamie dropped her purse on the floor of the Grand Ballroom, leaned back against the green metal chair and closed her eyes. IPA conferences were supposed to be educational, thought-provoking, a chance to broaden one's professional horizons.

So why was hers turning into such a nightmare?

She'd just spent the last forty-five minutes explaining to a rather dense security guard that she had no idea what the man had meant when he asked for a doubloon. The term brought to her mind images of tall masted ships, cutthroat pirates and buried treasure—none of which had anything to do with an insurance conference, nor with her highly structured life back in Baton Rouge.

The guard had eyed her suspiciously—she probably would've done the same had she been in his position—but he'd promised to keep a lookout for the renegade pirate, nevertheless.

She flexed her toes against the tops of her pumps and sighed. At that precise moment, she'd have liked nothing better than to sink into a hot bubble bath. Just lie back, relax. Listen to Harry Connick, Jr. Maybe sip a glass of wine.

She forced herself to sit up straight. Unfortunately, her

schedule called for a workshop on fidelity bonds, and if the activity on the dais was any indication, it was about to begin.

She was in the process of removing a steno pad from her purse when the man seated behind her lightly tapped her shoulder. "You're being paged." He jerked his head toward the exit.

She twisted around and saw Steve near the door at the back of the room, his right hand in his trouser pocket as usual.

"Could I have your attention, please?" came a booming male voice from the podium at the front. "If everyone will take their seats now, we'd like to get started."

Great. She really couldn't afford to miss the workshop. Especially since the little talk with security had cost her a seminar on professional liability, and the breakfast with Flynn had made her miss the keynote address. If the trend continued . . .

Steve inclined his head toward the hallway and walked back outside, seemingly confident she would follow.

Her frown deepened into a scowl. On the other hand . . .

She stuffed the notebook back into her purse and quickly maneuvered her way to the hallway.

Steve stood a few feet away, perusing a brochure at a display booth for a major commercial underwriter.

The change in his appearance seemed almost miraculous. His damp brown hair was combed neatly away from his forehead, except for one strand that curled artlessly across his brow. The stubble along his jawline was gone, as was the limp tan suit—he had abandoned it in favor of a lightweight wool in smoky gray.

"Hello, Jamie." He replaced the brochure on the table and turned to face her. "I'm sorry about your workshop."

The transformation, she realized with a jolt, had only been superficial. The thin lines around his mouth had hardened. There was a new sadness in his eyes, a slump to his broad shoulders. He looked as if he'd aged ten years since breakfast.

It was almost enough to make her forget she was furious with him.

Almost. But not quite.

"I'm surprised you had the nerve to actually show up." Her voice was cool, controlled.

He looked puzzled. "Didn't you call me?"

"But what you did this morning took a helluva lot of nerve. Tell me, Steve, did your associates screw up this time? Or did you decide it was no longer necessary to maintain the charade?"

Guarded green eyes raked across her body like a sensor probe. Seeing, weighing, concluding. He folded his arms against his chest. "Do you want to tell me what this is all about, or am I supposed to guess?"

"It's about my room."

"What about it?"

"Haven't your *associates* filed their report yet? It was ransacked, Steve. And I had to spend the better part of an hour trying to get it back into some semblance of order."

"Somebody broke into your room?" He shook his head. "My people never went near it."

"Then who did? Maid service?" She placed her hands on her hips. "You know, I'm beginning to think the entire world has gone insane. First I get a mysterious note from a virtual stranger, instructing me to phone him as soon as humanly possible. Then you show up, flashing an investigator's license and asking me even stranger questions."

"We didn't search your room this morning." His voice was louder this time, but it might have been a whisper for all the impact it made.

"I miss the opening session for a conference I have waited twelve months to attend. My room is nearly destroyed in your second attempt to find whatever it was Gary *supposedly* gave me at the airport—that is what you did last night, isn't it? Searched my room? And then, as if all *that* wasn't bad enough, I'm assaulted at the elevator by some spaced-out pirate who thinks I have his buried treasure. I'm beginning to wonder—"

"What did you say?" His tone was demanding, forceful.

It stopped her in mid-sentence.

"I said, your people ripped my room apart, and—"

"I don't mean that." He waved his hand. "What did you say about a man assaulting you at the elevators?"

"Oh, that. Some lunatic grabbed my arm when I got off the elevator and starting asking me about his pirate treasure. He was obviously a crackpot, so naturally, I don't blame you for—"

He shook his head. "Pirate treasure?"

She eyed him strangely. Perhaps the stress had pushed him over the edge. "Yes. You know, pieces of eight, doubloons. He wanted to know where the doubloon was."

Steve muttered an expletive under his breath and grabbed her arm. "Come with me."

"Where? What—! Wait a minute," she sputtered as he dragged her down the hallway. She felt the straps of her heavy purse begin to slide off her shoulder, and she struggled to push them back into place as she stumbled after him.

He opened the first door they came to and took a quick peek inside. It was an empty IPA conference room. He drew her inside and closed the door.

"All right." He pulled two chairs out of formation. "Now, start at the beginning and tell me exactly what happened."

She stood rooted to the spot, her hands planted squarely on her hips. She stared at him as if he'd lost his mind. Which, for all she knew, he probably had. "Beginning of what?"

"What the hell have you been—?" He stopped. He took a deep breath. "Look, Gary is dead. He was murdered, Jamie. And I've got a strong hunch that the man who grabbed you at the elevator is one of the bastards responsible."

She felt the color slowly drain from her face. "I don't understand." She sank into one of the chairs with all the animation of a marionette whose strings had suddenly been cut.

"Join the club." He shoved his hands into his trouser pockets. "I told you this morning Gary was a courier. What I didn't tell you was that he was transporting a coin. A very rare, very valuable coin called the Washington Doubloon. We hadn't . . . anticipated any trouble." He sat down wearily in the second chair. "But something went wrong. He missed delivery and tried to make contact with you here at the hotel. A couple of employees from Universal Studios found his body out on the back lot earlier this morning—are you familiar with the place?"

She swallowed hard. "It—it's right up the hill, isn't it?"

He nodded. "That's the entrance to the tour. The studio maintains over four hundred acres of production area farther back—mostly vacant land. That's where they found Gary's body."

She felt a knot form in the pit of her stomach. *Dear God, tell me this isn't happening.*

But one look at Steve's face assured her it was.

"I had assumed they got the coin when they grabbed him," he said, his voice revealing very little emotion. "But since your room was searched and a man approached you about the doubloon, they apparently didn't."

"But why . . . why would they come after me?"

He met her gaze. "Because they think you have the coin. My guess is they followed Gary from the airport and saw him try to make contact with you. When they discovered he didn't have it on him, you seemed the logical candidate."

"But that's ridiculous!" Her well-manicured nails burrowed into her palms. "Why would he have given the coin to *me*?"

"To prevent the bad guys from getting it." He leaned forward until their knees lightly touched. "But we can talk about that later. Why don't you tell me about your room? When did you discover it had been searched?"

She felt his warm hands slip over her tightly clenched fists and closed her eyes. *He's very good at this*, she thought as the panic, the fear, began to subside.

She took a slow, deep breath and opened her eyes to find him watching her. Their eyes locked, his gaze steady and sure. When she was ready, she told him what had happened.

As he listened to her story, his thumb began to stroke the bony ridge along the base of her left wrist, gently at first, with a touch barely perceptible. It soothed, calmed. Without even being aware of it, she relaxed. Her fists unfurled into curved palms; her breathing slowed to synchronize with his.

By the time the topic shifted to the man in the elevator, she had regained her self-control. She found that Steve's gentle caresses, the small concentric circles his thumb made along the base of her wrist, no longer provided the relaxation they once had. They were now delivering a shiver of erotic pleasure she could swear she felt down to the tips of her toes.

Oh yes, Stephen Flynn was *very* good at this.

She pulled her hands away, feeling suddenly flushed. "All I really remember is his hair. He wore it short, spiked. And it'd been bleached a pale platinum blond."

He leaned back in his chair, his expression unreadable. "I see." He reached into his jacket pocket. "What about an accent? Scars, tattoos—anything like that?"

She shook her head, and watched him scribble her vague description into a small spiral-bound notebook. It was the first time she'd seen him take notes, she realized with surprise.

"Is there anything else you can remember?"

She felt her stomach lurch. "Just one other thing. . . . He promised he'd come back."

The pen stopped moving. He looked up.

"I didn't take it seriously at the time because I thought he was a crackpot. But now . . ."

He frowned. "Jamie, I—"

"Do you think he meant it? Will he come back?"

He searched her face for a moment. "It's a possibility," he admitted quietly. "A very *remote* possibility."

"Is that supposed to reassure me?"

"The man is a prime suspect in a homicide investigation. My guess is he's halfway to Mexico by now. You could identify him—it doesn't matter whether you think you can or not," he added in response to the look of protest that crossed her face. "We're talking about what he thinks you could do. If he's smart, he'll realize approaching you again would be tantamount to walking into a trap."

"But the coin—"

Steve shook his head. "He's not interested in the coin, only in the money someone is willing to pay him for it. He's a professional. A hired gun. He'll collect his fee from his employer whether he gets the coin or not, so why buy trouble?"

Jamie drew a sigh of relief and leaned back against the chair. She'd been hoping he would say something like that.

"But if you're still worried, I can make arrangements to have you protected. I'll move you out of here and assign someone to watch over you. You don't have to be afraid."

She shook her head. "The only reason I'm in Los Angeles is for the IPA conference. If I have to leave the hotel, I might as well just go back home." She met his gaze. "I appreciate the offer, Steve, but I'm staying."

He nodded. "Like I said, there's probably no need to worry." He stood up. "But I do recommend you change rooms—just to be on the safe side." He slipped the notebook into his jacket pocket. "I'll talk to hotel security about having your name flagged. Should anyone start asking questions about you at the front desk, they'll notify security pronto."

It seemed a reasonable suggestion. "Okay."

He started for the door.

"But what about the police?" she asked, almost as an

afterthought. "Don't I have to make a statement or something?"

He turned and gave her a smile. "Thanks for reminding me. It *will* be necessary for you to make a formal statement. Just tell an officer exactly what you've told me and then sign the typewritten transcript. But it's something we can do at your convenience over the next week. You're still planning to be in town until Sunday, aren't you?"

She frowned. Since when had her itinerary become public knowledge? "Yes."

"Then you have plenty of time. I'll set up an appointment with the detective in charge. Don't worry, Lou's an old friend of mine. A little rough around the edges, maybe, but otherwise a pretty nice guy. Would Wednesday afternoon be okay with you?"

She mentally reviewed the conference schedule. "Thursday afternoon would be better."

"Then Thursday afternoon it is. I'll even drive you down to the station myself." His smile broadened and he opened the door. "Now, let's go see about getting your room changed."

Shortly after lunch the next day, Jamie stood outside the hotel's front entrance, waiting for her rental car to be brought around. The past twenty-four hours had been blessedly incident-free. She'd encountered no strange characters lurking in the hallway, unearthed no evidence of uninvited guests in her new room—and that was just the way she wanted it.

The glass doors swooshed open behind her. She peered nervously over her shoulder. She saw two men in their late forties exit the hotel, both caught up in an argument over film distribution rights. Following close behind them was a young black man, a folded copy of one of the Hollywood trade papers tucked casually under his arm. Exhaling slowly, she turned back.

Reassuring herself that the nightmare was over, however, couldn't calm the strange queasiness in the bottom of her stomach. She'd been jumpy ever since Steve had told her about Gary's murder, and it would take some time before she felt she was herself again.

The valet drove up to the curb in a dark blue Chevy Nova. Jamie gave him a tip, hopped into the car and took off without a backward glance.

According to her map, the Los Angeles County Museum of Art and the La Brea Tar Pits were adjacent to each other on Wilshire Boulevard at Hancock Park. She slowed the car to a stop at the bottom of the hotel's long curving driveway to wait for a lull in oncoming traffic. She reviewed the itinerary she'd planned back in Baton Rouge when she'd first learned about the free afternoon. She'd drop by the tar pits first, see the exhibit and then go on to the County Museum for a quick tour.

The traffic cleared and she eased the Nova onto Universal Parkway. Of course, she'd have to be back at the hotel by six. Tri-States Insurance, one of the major flood insurers for southern Louisiana, was sponsoring a cocktail party in its suite. It was an event she couldn't afford to miss.

Less than thirty minutes later, she walked into Hancock Park, a stretch of grass and trees running between the La Brea Tar Pits and the County Museum. The area was a hubbub of activity, and she felt her earlier apprehension quickly fade.

A hot-dog vendor had set up shop a few feet away from the exhibit and was loudly hawking his wares. On the steps of the Page Museum to her right, a mime entertained a group of Japanese tourists with sleight-of-hand magic tricks. Up ahead, two old men sat on a bench underneath a gnarled oak and played checkers. Children's laughter mixed with the soulful music of a sidewalk musician's saxophone.

A soft smile playing about the corners of her mouth, Jamie turned left and carefully made her way across the grass to the observation station.

The stench of tar was unmistakable. The asphalt deposits, or "tar pits," were enclosed behind a strip of wire fencing. Inside stood stone replicas of mastodons, the giant elephantlike mammals that had once roamed North America. One of the larger ones was trapped in the tar, unable to escape, while the others watched in horror. Intrigued by the panorama, Jamie wondered if she'd have time to see the exhibits inside the Page Museum.

She glanced at her watch. Maybe if she hurried . . .

Suddenly, a dark-haired little boy raced past her screaming delightedly in Spanish as two larger boys chased after him. She turned and watched them run toward Wilshire Boulevard, her smile deepening into a grin. And then she froze.

Purchasing a soft drink from the hot-dog vendor was the young black man she'd seen exiting the hotel. The newspaper was gone, and he was wearing dark sunglasses and a different jacket, but she was positive it was the same man.

He took a sip of soda and turned toward her. She averted her gaze. *Remain calm*, she ordered herself. *It could be just a coincidence.*

Ever so casually, she looked around again. One hand rested on his hip, his arm brushing the tan jacket aside. She could see a holster strapped across his chest . . . the butt of a gun. And she knew it was no coincidence.

The man looked up and saw her staring at him. He lowered the can of soda and frowned.

Her eyes darted from side to side. She was surrounded by people, but they offered her little protection against a loaded gun. He could shoot her right here and now, and no one would be able to help.

Tightening her grip on her purse, she sprinted across the grass toward the concrete pathway connecting the park with the County Museum. In the distance she could see the zigzagging translucent panels of the Japanese Pavilion rising high above the tar pits. If she could make it to the museum, she'd be able to double back to Wilshire Boulevard and her car.

At least she hoped she would.

Picking up speed as she rounded the corner past the excavation pit, she glanced over her shoulder.

"Oh, God!"

She should never have looked back. The man had followed her—she had known he would. But it was far worse than that.

He had pulled out his gun.

And he was gaining on her.

FOUR

Jamie turned and ran, faster and harder than she had ever run in her entire life. At any moment she expected to hear the gun explode, feel the bullet tear through her flesh.

She raced across a little wooden bridge, her low-heeled shoes tapping a frantic rhythm into the boards. Darting past a group of teenagers gathered on the other side without missing a beat, she sped down the pathway. She concentrated on putting one foot before the other, on putting as much distance between herself and the gunman as possible.

She raced up the incline to the County Museum and tripped over an uneven stretch of pavement. Arms flailing wildly, she landed in the grass bordering the walkway, just missing the hard concrete of the incline by inches.

Wincing in pain, she looked over her shoulder. She pressed her palm to her chest to slow her rapid breathing. And waited.

She saw the man cross the little wooden bridge.

Cursing, she scrambled to her feet, hoisted the straps of her purse over her shoulder and ran.

The ramp led her into the Times Mirror Court, the heart of the museum complex. She stopped. Which way now?

Directly ahead was a small courtyard filled with tables and chairs. On either side, entrances to the segregated wings of the museum. She scanned the crowds. There must be security guards somewhere.

But there weren't.

She turned left, mingling with the people. She shouldered her way past a heavyset Mexican woman carrying a squalling toddler. She tried to ignore the ache in her side and the cramp in her right leg. The man had a gun, her brain screamed. *It doesn't matter that he has no reason to kill you. What reason did they have to kill Gary?*

Ahead she saw a vaulted arch sandwiched between two of the buildings. An exit? she wondered hopefully and picked up speed.

It was.

She ran to the long concrete stairway leading down to Wilshire Boulevard. She took the steps two at a time, her hand skimming along the sun-warmed metal railing. She could overhear snatches of conversations as she thundered past the new arrivals: smatterings of English, Spanish, Japanese. The languages all blurred together, becoming a meaningless drone of disconnected syllables, background noise barely discernible above the frantic beating of her heart.

She glanced back at the museum when she reached the sidewalk. The man stood at the top of the stairs. He saw her and started forward, one hand extended. "Miss Royale!"

"Damn." She turned away and headed for the crosswalk. The sharp pain in her side worsened with each step.

The traffic signal flashed "Don't Walk," but she knew she had to chance it. She jogged across the wide street toward the parking lot, her breath coming in short, ragged gasps. She had nearly made it when the light changed. The traffic started moving again, and she ran for the curb amid the angry horn blasts of the motorists.

She weaved her way through the parking lot to the Chevy Nova, fumbling in her purse for the keys. Her

hands shook as she unlocked the door. She fell into the car
and jammed the key into the ignition, her foot energetically
pumping the accelerator. The engine started on the first try
and she slammed the door.

She could see the man standing by the crosswalk as she
turned onto Wilshire. His hands were planted on his hips,
the gun no longer visible.

Steering with her left hand, she pawed through the side
pocket of her purse with her other. She pulled the business
card free and checked the address. Her memory was correct, as usual. The office was on Wilshire Boulevard, only
a few blocks away.

Steve.

He would protect her, she reassured herself. Keep her
from harm.

She tightened her grip on the steering wheel and glanced
into the rearview mirror to see if the man had followed.

After all, what other hope did she have?

Flynn Security occupied the entire seventh floor of a
glass-and-steel high rise in an upscale business district on
the Miracle Mile. Its neighbors were banks, brokerage
firms and certified public accountants. The area reeked of
money, both old and new; it was probably the last place
Jamie would have expected to find a detective agency.

The elevator doors slid open and she stepped out into a
large, tastefully decorated reception area. She glanced
from the receptionist's empty chair to the long hallway
leading in either direction and, after a moment's hesitation, turned right.

Jamie hurried past several open offices, but didn't see
Flynn. Two men were placing red dots on a large plaster-
board in one office. In another, a man sat behind a desk
and twirled a ballpoint pen in the air like a baton as he
dictated a report. No one paid any attention to her.

At the end of the hall lay a small cul-de-sac holding
two executive suites and a small waiting room. An attractive woman in her mid-forties with graying black hair and

olive skin sat behind a huge oak desk in the center of the room, talking on the phone. She scrutinized Jamie over the edge of her horn-rimmed glasses, then flashed a warm, professional smile.

Jamie glanced at the two doors behind the seated woman. One of them *had* to be Flynn's office, she decided. As if on cue, she heard his voice coming through the closed door on the right.

"Relax, Jim," he said as he opened the door into the waiting room. "I told you, I have everything under control. There's no need for you to worry."

"I don't like delays," the second man said. He was tall. Thin. And extremely nervous. "You promised me—"

"I know, I know. And I *will* make delivery. It just may take a little while longer than we originally thought. Won't you trust me on this?"

"Steve, we have to talk," Jamie blurted out, her voice nearly cracking. "I can't take much more of—"

"Darling!" He slipped his arm around her waist and pulled her close. "I swear, I was just on my way to meet you now." He lowered his head and kissed her full on the lips as he expertly maneuvered her around toward the open door. "Give me one more minute," he urged with a sincere smile, "and we'll go to lunch. Promise."

Then he pushed her into his office and closed the heavy oak door before she knew what had hit her.

Steve turned around to find two pairs of curious eyes trained on him. Mona lowered the telephone receiver and stared at him in openmouthed disbelief, her horn-rimmed glasses perched precariously on the tip of her nose. Rothenberg's bushy black eyebrows shot upward in confusion.

Steve shrugged his shoulders and grinned. "Women."

Mona stifled a giggle and turned away, pushing her glasses back into place.

Rothenberg frowned. "Yeah, well . . ."

Steve put his hand on the other man's back. "Anyway,

like I was saying, everything's under control. I'll let you know when we're ready to make delivery. Okay?''

Rothenberg nodded, and walked away.

Steve watched him go, the smile slowly fading from his face. He'd bought himself a little more time. Three, four days tops. He only hoped it would be enough for what he had to do.

He heard Mona replace the receiver and turned around.

She peered at him over the top of her glasses. "That's some pretty fancy footwork," she said dryly, leaning back in her swivel chair. "Just make sure you don't dance yourself into more trouble than you can handle."

He glanced toward his office and frowned. The warning might have come too late. "Hold my calls." He walked across the waiting room to his office, straightened his tie and then opened the door.

Jamie stood rigid and still in the center of the room. Her short brown hair, usually meticulously groomed, was unkempt, almost windblown. A few curling wisps framed her forehead, and two bright spots of crimson fanned her high cheekbones. Blades of grass and dirt smudged the knees of her light brown pants.

He smiled his most charming smile. "Hope I didn't keep you waiting." He closed the door.

"Is that *all* you've got to say to me?" Her voice was even, well modulated, and had all the warmth of a blast of arctic air in the dead of winter.

He could feel the chill all the way across the room.

"No," he said, sobering. "I also owe you an apology— and an explanation. I don't normally go around shoving people into my office, but the man I was with is a client of the agency. I didn't think it prudent he hear about the missing coin. It—it's not good for business."

"So you decided to *kiss* me?"

"Well, I . . ." Suddenly he wasn't so sure himself why he'd kissed her. At the time, he'd thought it was a reflex action, an automatic response to an immediate threat. Now . . .

"Jamie, why are you here?" he asked, deliberately changing the subject. "Has something else happened?"

Under the fluorescent lights, the soft red highlights in her hair looked like streaks of fire. "You might say that. Someone just tried to kill me."

"Kill you?" He crossed the remaining short distance between them and grabbed her elbow. "When? Where?" He sat her down in the overstuffed armchair in front of his desk, then knelt on the floor beside her.

"When was about an hour ago. Where"—she ran a hand through her hair—"was Hancock Park. I was at the La Brea Tar Pits, and—"

"The *tar pits*? What the hell were you doing there?"

"I was sightseeing. Is there something *wrong* with that?" she asked, her soft Southern drawl deepening.

"Not at all." He'd begun to realize that the arrival of her accent meant she was becoming very annoyed. Just now, he had more than enough to worry about.

"So what happened?"

She eyed him skeptically for a moment. "He followed me from the hotel. It wasn't the pirate, it was someone else. And when I recognized him, he chased me through the park. He had a gun—"

"Did he open fire?"

"No, but . . ." She rubbed her forehead, her fingers slightly trembling, and then told him what had happened. Her account was brief, to the point, and glossed over the terror he knew she must have felt.

"Fortunately, I was able to get a good look at him," she concluded. "He's in his early twenties, tall, slender, black. He was wearing a tan jacket and—"

"What did you say he looked like?" he cut in, his voice suddenly hoarse.

"Tall, slender build, black." She tilted her head to one side and eyed him quizzically. "Why?"

"Son of a bitch," he mumbled under his breath. He scrambled to his feet and hurried across the room to the door. "I'll be right back," he said and rushed out into the waiting room.

Jamie twisted around in the overstuffed leather chair and stared at the closed door.

"What the hell is going on around here?"

First he had kissed her and shoved her into his office, and now he'd run off without so much as a word of explanation. Was he running a detective agency or a lunatic asylum?

She absently swatted at a shock of hair hanging over her brow and tried to rationalize his behavior. Maybe he'd recognized the man from her description. The odd look on his face, his sudden flight—what other explanation could there be?

She smiled. In fact, he'd probably gone to phone the police and have the man arrested.

She glanced around and stared at the black enamel touch-tone phone on his desk, her neat little theory quickly dissolving. Why go into the other room to make the call when he had a telephone in his office?

"Okay, that's it," she muttered.

She stood just as Steve opened the door.

"Well?" She placed her hands on her hips.

"Sorry about that," he said, his voice annoyingly casual. He closed the door and walked over toward her.

"Well?"

A flicker of surprise crossed his face. "I, ah, wanted to check something out." He gave her a well-practiced smile. "The description you gave me sounded familiar." He motioned to the armchair. "Please, why don't you sit down?"

"You know who the man is?"

"In . . . a way." He sat down in a large leather swivel chair behind his desk. "I don't think you have anything to worry about—at least not from him."

She sat down, a wave of relief washing over her. "You mean he's already been apprehended?"

"Well, not exactly." He leaned back in the chair, its soft leather creaking from the weight. "Based upon what you told me, my guess is he was only trying to protect you."

She stared at him for a moment, wondering if she was hearing things. "Excuse me?"

"The man wasn't trying to kill you. He was, ah, trying to protect you."

"The *man* chased me through Hancock Park!"

"I realize that." He pressed his palms together, his fingers interlocking. "Look, I asked hotel security to keep an eye on you yesterday," he admitted cautiously. "One of their men matched your description. He's young and overeager. Doesn't have much field experience. My guess is he took his job to heart and overreacted a little when you started running."

"Overreacted a little?" She wrapped her fingers around the cool leather of the armchair and squeezed. "The bastard chased me with his gun drawn!"

Steve winced. "That's only because he thought you were in trouble. He was trying to save your life, Jamie."

"Oh, is *that* what he was doing? Silly me. What must I have been thinking?"

He took a deep breath. "Look, I've got a call in to the head of hotel security now. The guard will be suspended, and I'll see to it nothing like this happens again. I'll straighten it all out, okay?"

"You damn well better!"

He met her gaze. "I know you're upset," he began, more softly this time.

She laughed. "Upset? Why should I be upset?" She stood up and started pacing around his office, her low-heeled shoes leaving soft impressions in the russet-brown carpeting in front of his desk. "Just because I have men grabbing me in elevators and people ripping my room apart looking for some coin one of *your* employees supposedly gave me? Just because I've been chased through parks by gun-toting security guards who've seen one too many Rambo movies? Just because I've been kissed and shoved into offices like some bimbo who wandered in off the *streets*?''

She stopped abruptly and placed her palms down on the smooth oaken surface of his desk. She leaned toward him. ''I don't think you understand, Mr. Flynn,'' she said, struggling hard to regain her composure. ''I lead a very normal, well-organized life. This . . . *madness* . . . has to stop. And I'm expecting you to make it stop. *Now!*''

She turned, snatched her purse up from the floor and stormed out of his office, not trusting herself to say anything more.

Five hours later, Jamie glided through a sea of dark suits and sparkling dresses at Tri-States Insurance Company's hospitality suite on the twelfth floor of the hotel. She knew from a quick glance into the gilded mirror in the hallway that the dark circles were gone from under her eyes. She looked poised, self-confident, relaxed—all due, unfortunately, to the miracle of modern cosmetics than to an untroubled psyche.

She had returned to the hotel more on edge than ever before. Steve's assurance that the gunman had been nothing more than an overly zealous security guard *had* been convincing—she even had to admit she'd probably overreacted a teensy bit herself at the park—but now that she'd had time to think things through, Jamie couldn't shake the nagging feeling that there was something decidedly screwy about the entire story. Something . . . not quite right.

She grabbed a glass of white wine from the tray of a passing waiter and took a long swallow. Thing was, when Steve had kissed her—odd, how her thoughts kept returning to *that*, she thought with annoyance—and shoved her into his office, she'd been certain he was playing some sort of game.

And *that* made her very nervous.

Shrugging off her apprehension, Jamie scouted the area. She recognized a lot of familiar faces from southern Louisiana. Agents. Brokers. Underwriters. The usual crowd. Pasting on a smile, she walked over to a group of accounts producers from a rival agency and joined in their discussion of a proposed rate increase for flood insurance.

"Well, it's about time you showed up," teased a masculine voice in her right ear a few minutes later.

"Ben?" She turned around and smiled at the bespectacled red-haired man in his late fifties who stood behind her. Ben McCloskey was as short as he was round, and looked for all the world like a benign little gnome. He had the reputation, though, of a troll. And a bad-tempered one to boot. He was a senior underwriter for the insurer sponsoring the party and had the final word on all coverage placed through Tri-States, which according to most people in the industry was usually "no."

"I was wondering when I'd see you." She made her excuses to the producers, then tucked her hand into the crook of Ben's arm and followed him across the room.

"Darlin', I declare, you just get better-lookin' every day," he drawled, giving her the once-over. "How've ya been? I haven't been seeing that much of you the past couple of days."

Considering how she'd spent most of her time lately, she wasn't surprised. "It *has* been a pretty big conference this year, hasn't it?" she said, sidestepping his remark.

He nodded. "Much bigger than the one in Chicago last year. Hell, they just seem to get bigger and bigger every year." He took a long sip of his bourbon and Coke and then glanced at her. He smiled, his blue eyes twinkling speculatively behind his bifocals. "So just what've you been doing with yourself lately? Been seeing the sights, have you?"

"Not as much as I'd like." She moved aside so a couple could walk past.

"Uh-huh." He crossed his arms against his expansive midsection and rocked back and forth on his heels. "Well, I imagine you'll be wanting to stay on for a few days after the conference ends. Maybe even drive up the coast a ways?" He winked. "Spend some time in Sacramento?"

She glanced at the drink in his hand. Just how many of those had he had? "I wasn't planning on it."

Ben grinned, the smile cutting from one side of his chubby face to the other. "I know I shouldn't tease you, honey, but I just can't help myself. I met your friend a little while ago." He looked around the room. "Now, where'd he get off to? He seems like a good ole boy— told me he's from Sacramento. Handles fidelity bonds. Solid future there, girl." He waved his empty glass at her. "You mark my words."

No doubt about it, she decided. Ben was drunk. "*Who* told you he's from Sacramento?"

"Dale Carmichael."

"Dale Carmichael?" She shook her head. "I don't think I know him."

"Now, darlin', there's no need to be—oh, there he is! Dale, come on over. I found her."

Jamie tightened her grip on the fragile wineglass, not all that sure she wanted to be found. Summoning what remained of her courage, she turned around.

"I should have known," she muttered under her breath.

Stephen Flynn, looking more handsome than any man should be allowed to, walked slowly toward them, a glass of wine in his right hand. The white linen dinner jacket molded beautifully against his broad shoulders as he moved, its cut emphasizing his slim waist and rugged physique. His unruly brown hair was slicked back, except for a few stubborn strands that hung over his forehead. She felt her stomach do a flip-flop.

Damn him.

"Hello, Jamie," he said, his voice low and husky. She took a sip of wine to steady herself.

"Why, I was just tellin' her you were looking for her, Dale," Ben offered helpfully. He patted Jamie on her arm and winked again. "Now, I'll see ya'll later," he said and left.

She eyed Steve coolly over the rim of her wineglass without saying a word. She supposed she should give him a chance to explain. Ten seconds ought to suffice. Ten seconds to explain just what he was doing at the Tri-States Insurance Company cocktail party, wearing a name tag for Dale Carmichael.

Then she'd kill him.

He moved closer, his free hand extended in supplication. "Now, don't get upset."

"Why, *Dale*," she said, her voice Southern-saccharine sweet, "whatever do you mean?"

He slipped his hand under her elbow and led her over to a couple of mauve-and-green upholstered chairs that were a relatively safe distance from the mingling guests. "I wanted to talk to you. See how you were after this afternoon." He tapped the name tag pinned to his jacket. "This was the only way I could get in."

"And just how, pray tell, did you know I would be here?"

He leaned forward, his knee lightly brushing against hers. "Simple deductive reasoning."

"Oh?" She took another sip of wine, trying to ignore the pressure of his leg against hers. It didn't work.

"I read the flier pinned to the bulletin board in the lobby," he explained with a smile. "Since Tri-States is a big insurance company in Louisiana, I assumed you'd attend. And I got the name tag from the registration desk so I wouldn't arouse anyone's suspicions."

"You did, huh?"

"Yes, I did." He was beginning to sound annoyed. "It's easier to pass for a sheep if you're dressed for the part."

She swirled the wine around in her glass. "And to think I thought my grandmother was lying about all those wolves in sheep's clothing." She lowered her glass and looked across at him. "You must have been the one she was warning me about."

He frowned. "Jamie, I—"

"Dale, I want you to meet some friends of mine," Ben said, swooping down like a guardian angel. He was accompanied by two middle-aged men. "These boys are a couple of senior underwriters for American Casualty. They're thinking 'bout moving into the California market, and I thought you'd be able to fill 'em in on what's been happenin' out here with that new legislation."

Steve glanced toward her, an emotion closely resembling fear coloring his handsome face. She smiled sweetly in return, placed her wineglass on an adjacent table and stood. "If you gentlemen will excuse me," she murmured and walked away. Flynn had gotten himself into trouble without any help from her. She figured he could extricate himself from it as well.

She returned to her room five minutes later. Her festive mood—if she ever had one at all—had vanished shortly after Flynn's appearance at the party. Whatever he wanted to talk to her about could damn well wait until tomorrow, she decided. All she wanted now was to take a long, hot shower, crawl into bed and pull the covers over her head.

And stay there for about a week.

Yawning widely, she slipped her hands around to her back and unzipped her dress just as the telephone rang.

She eyed it suspiciously. *Now what?* She walked over to the nightstand and lifted the receiver. "Hello?"

"Jamie?" a vaguely familiar male voice asked.

"Yes." She felt the cold fingers of fear tighten around her throat. "Who is this?"

"You have something we want." His voice was low, deep, threatening. It sent a shock wave of recognition washing over her that completely erased her fatigue.

She tightened her grip on the receiver and swallowed hard. "Look, I don't have it, okay?" she said, her voice barely above a rasping whisper. "Gary Dodsworth never gave me anything. I didn't even know the man. If you don't stop bothering me—"

"Didn't you get my message? I taped it to your door so you'd be sure and find it."

She slowly turned around and froze. Taped to the inside of the door was a large manila envelope with her name scrawled across it in blood-red letters.

"I'm running out of patience, Jamie. And you're running out of time. Think about it."

The line went dead.

The receiver slipped from her shaking hand and fell on the bed. She walked to the door and stared at the envelope, almost afraid to touch it. After taking a deep breath, she grasped the envelope and pulled it free. Cautiously she lifted the unsealed flap. Inside were several Polaroid snapshots.

She shook her head in confusion. The pictures were all of her—one at the dinner Sunday night, one at the trade fair the day before, one at her workshop on marketing that morning. Five in total. But why had he taken snapshots of her? Was he crazy?

She pulled out the sixth and final photo and bit back a cry. It was of Gary. Dead. One look at the sightless, staring eyes told her that. The bullet hole in his right temple told her how.

A sharp rap sounded against the door.

She whirled as if she'd just heard a gun blast. She lowered the pictures, her heart pounding.

Had the pirate come back?

FIVE

The knock came again, more persistently this time.

"Jamie?" Steve called irritably. "Are you in there?"

She released her pent-up breath with a sigh. "Steve."

She moved to the door like an automaton and fumbled with the lock. She pulled the door open, then turned and walked back to the bed without saying a word.

"Damn it, why didn't you answer? I—What's wrong?" he asked, his voice gentler this time.

She shook her head, not trusting herself to speak. She could feel hot tears welling up in her eyes, her throat tightening. She knew her prized self-control was quickly slipping away, yet she was powerless to stop it. Her hand trembled as she gave him the snapshots.

A moment later, she felt the comforting warmth of his hand as it encircled her arm. "Jamaica?" His voice was soft as silk. It soothed, caressed.

She turned and looked up into his worried eyes. "He's threatening to kill me, isn't he?"

He pulled her into his arms and cradled her head against his shoulder. "It's all right. No one is going to hurt you."

She felt so safe in his arms, so protected. She wound her arms around him and clung, waiting for the shaking to abate.

He lightly stroked her hair. With each caress, his fingers dropped lower against the nape of her neck. "It's okay. He's just trying to scare you."

"Well, it's working," she said, her voice muffled against his linen jacket.

The steady beat of his heart thudded reassuringly against her ear; the crisp, clean scent of his after-shave enveloped her like a soft woolen blanket. She could feel the warm pressure of his hand against her back where the zipper parted her dress, and she closed her eyes.

"That cuts it," he said gruffly. "I'm not taking any more chances with your safety. You're moving out of the hotel tonight."

"But where can I go? How do I know he won't follow me to Baton Rouge? How do I know—"

"You're not going back to Baton Rouge. You're going to stay with me."

Her eyes flew open. "With *you*?"

His face, inches away from her own, was pale and drawn. "We'll arrange something else later, but for tonight, you'll stay with me." He gently pushed her away. "Pack a few things—only what you'll need for the night. I don't want to tip off anyone that you're leaving the hotel."

She nodded, having no desire to protest. She didn't want to stay in the hotel tonight—not after seeing those pictures. The image of Gary's lifeless body flashed across her mind, and she squeezed her eyes shut, willing the memory to fade.

Ten minutes later, she followed Steve down the hallway to the row of elevators.

"What about the rest of my things?" Her fingers tightened around the thin plastic straps of her shopping bag.

"My people will pick up your belongings tomorrow." He smiled. "It'll be taken care of. Trust me."

Her answering smile was brittle, forced. "I don't have much of a choice, do I?"

The elevator doors opened and they stepped into a partially full car. He pressed the button for the garage.

She scrutinized the faces of strangers, wondering if the pirate's cohorts were among them. She'd begun to believe he and his people could be anywhere. Be *anyone*. Someone had followed her for the past three days and taken her picture, and she hadn't even been aware of it. What if—?

She felt Steve slide his arm around her waist and position himself between her and the other passengers. She leaned back against his chest with relief and closed her eyes.

My God. What is happening to me?

"I need to tell somebody what's going on," she murmured.

Now, that's a laugh, she thought in self-deprecation. How could *she* explain any of this when she wasn't even sure what was happening.

Steve tightened his hold on her waist. "Not now."

The elevator continued down to the lobby without interruption. The door opened and the other passengers debarked, yet he maintained his clasp upon her waist, his breath warm against her neck.

They arrived at the third-level parking garage a few moments later. The doors swooshed open and Steve urged her forward. She got off and had taken a few steps forward when she came to an abrupt stop. She turned to face him.

"I *have* to tell someone what's happening, Steve. Where I'm going. *Something*."

"I can't let you do that." His voice was just as firm. He met her gaze, his face guarded. "It wouldn't be safe."

"But I can't just vanish like this. People will ask questions. Especially Ben—he's an old friend of my boss. He's an old friend of mine. He'll worry and—"

"When Ben doesn't see you for the next few days, he'll assume you're either tied up with the conference or spending your free time with 'Dale.' He won't become alarmed, I assure you." He brushed her cheek with his fingertips. "Now, please." His voice was gentle yet insistent. "We have to leave."

She frowned, but didn't move. "You know, that's another thing. Just why are you wandering around the hotel posing as Dale Carnegie, anyway?"

"Carmichael."

"Whoever. The thing is I resent your lying to Ben and to God knows how many other people you may have run into upstairs at that party. If you'd wanted to talk to me, you could have seen me in my room." She shifted the shopping bag to her other hand and brushed a lock of hair off her forehead. "The masquerade wasn't necessary. Now Ben thinks I'm having some wild love affair with an insurance agent from Sacramento."

He stared at her for a moment, the expression on his face unreadable. A muscle twitched at the corner of his mouth. "Would you prefer I told him the truth?" He took her elbow and guided her forward.

"Of course not. But I don't approve of lying—I have to see that man. Work with him." She jerked her arm free. "Dammit, Steve, I have a reputation to uphold."

"And I'm *trying* to ensure your safety." He stopped in front of a late-model Chevy. "Look, just for the record, I didn't create the scenario about the affair—Ben did. I went along with his assumptions because they added credibility to my cover."

"Well, that's comforting," she said sarcastically.

"You know, I really don't know what your problem is. The only thing that should matter right now is that my cover created a brilliant smoke screen. If your friend the pirate investigates your disappearance, he'll hear the name Dale Carmichael. Which should confuse the hell out of him, since the real Mr. Carmichael never made it to the conference."

"But—"

He grasped her elbow again. "No buts. We have to go. *Now*." He strode across the asphalt with her in tow.

She bit her lower lip, but remained silent.

He led her to a black Acura Legend a few yards away and unlocked the passenger door. She climbed in, her hands trembling as she stashed her shopping bag and purse in the backseat. She heard him open the other door and slip behind the wheel, then the quiet roar of the car's engine.

She took a deep breath and tried to marshal her chaotic thoughts. What she needed was a plan of action, something constructive to focus on.

"So what happens next?" she asked.

"Next?" He backed the car around and shifted gears. "I get you settled in and make a few phone calls about the photographs. Although it's doubtful they'll be much help—the camera is a Polaroid, which will make it impossible to trace."

"Phone call." She felt the knot tighten in her stomach. "He called me, you know. Right before you arrived."

Steve's head snapped around. "You mean the pirate? What did he say?"

"What do you think he said? He wants the coin." She wrapped her hands around her arms to ward off an inner chill. "He told me about the snapshots taped to my door, said I was making him lose patience." She stared out the window at the rows of neatly parked automobiles. "This has gone too far, Steve. I want to talk to the police. They need to do something."

He drove up the garage ramp into the hotel's circular driveway. "I understand how you feel."

How could he possibly know how she felt? she wondered with irritation. She was tired and confused and more terrified than she'd ever been in her entire life.

And more alone.

"But it's best if we go to the police first thing in the morning. You can make your statement, look at mug shots, have it all taken care of. Even work out a temporary living arrangement. Until he's apprehended, you'll need to have protection."

"But why can't we go to the police *now*? Why do we have to wait until tomorrow?"

"Well, for one thing, it's late. And you've just had a shock. Several shocks, in fact." He glanced at her cautiously, as if trying to gauge her reaction to his words. "You need some quiet time, Jamie. Time to get your thoughts together."

Well, that much was true. Right now, her mind was awhirl with a thousand different unanswered questions. Finding the right answers and putting them in order was like trying to solve a jigsaw puzzle with half the pieces missing.

"We'll go to the station first thing in the morning," he promised.

"Okay." She settled back in the seat and stared out the window at the blur of brightly lit storefronts, theater marquees and billboards along Lankershim, then Ventura Boulevard, without really seeing them. A car horn blasted nearby; in the distance she heard the shrill alarm of a fire engine.

She glanced at Steve and absently studied his profile as he drove. Strong chin, though he still needed to shave. Long dark eyelashes—much too long for a man, she thought, with a twinge of jealousy. The smooth, angular planes of his cheek. She remembered the kiss then, and found herself wondering what it would be like if he kissed her and really meant it. What it would be like if he—

She felt the color heighten in her cheeks.

"Something wrong?" He looked over at her.

"Are you married?" she blurted out, then felt herself grow redder. *Of all the asinine questions . . .*

"What I mean," she went on, trying to remove her foot from her mouth, "won't my presence be an imposition on your family?"

He smiled. "No wife. No kids. No imposition." He glanced back at the road. "I'm divorced. Five years. And I live alone, except for Rex. Right now, we're house-sitting a three-bedroom home in the Hollywood Hills for a client who's in France working on a movie. I'm having a sun deck repaired at my own place and Rex was driving the workmen nuts—some people get nervous around nine-ty-pound German shepherds—so we moved into the Fried-man house for a few days. Only my secretary knows I'm there, so it'll be safe." He gave her a smile. "Hey, relax. It'll be okay."

She tried to return the smile. *Yeah, relax. Easy for him to say.*

Twenty minutes later, they pulled into the driveway of a split-level house at the end of a cul-de-sac high in the Hollywood Hills. He pressed the remote control mounted to the sun visor above her head and the garage door swung up.

Jamie crawled out of the car, clutching her shopping bag and purse under her arm, and followed him inside the house to the kitchen. He opened one of the cabinets over the sink and punched in a security code. She glanced at a small rectangular box mounted on the wall above the en-trance to the hallway. A red light flashed a silent alarm, then stopped.

She walked through the kitchen and into the living room. The room was a study in contrasts, a well-blended mixture of the utilitarian with the aesthetic. Hardwood floors and gleaming brass accents showcased a tradition-ally styled, high-backed sofa and love seat in the palest peach leather imaginable. Flynn's influence was easy to spot. Atop the sofa lay the morning newspaper. An empty coffee mug and a half-eaten bagel rested upon the smoked-glass-and-chrome cocktail table, disturbing its thin layer of dust. The whole place could do with a good dusting, Jamie decided, but it was presentable.

"The spare bedroom's just down the hall," he said from behind her. "Come on, I'll take you back."

She followed him down the long carpeted hallway and into the first doorway on the right. The guest room was sparsely furnished. A full-sized bed with a white-painted iron headboard sat beneath the window in the center of the room, bordered by an antique nightstand (walnut, she believed) on the right and a massive chest of drawers on the left. A tall white wicker vase, filled with cane shafts and silk flowers dyed in graduating shades of blue, stood in the corner. As in the living room, a thin layer of dust covered the furniture.

"The bathroom's across the hall. The linen closets are inside." He smiled. "Just make yourself at home."

She heard a low, deep bark that seemed to reverberate throughout the house, then the thud of heavy paws hitting the carpeting of the hallway. A big—*too* big, in her opinion—German shepherd bounded into the room and stopped, his tail wagging, his tongue lolling out the side of his mouth, a mere two feet away from her. They eyed each other carefully for a moment, neither one quite sure what to make of the other.

"Jamie, meet Rex." Steve knelt down and ran his hand affectionately through the dog's fur. "Rex, Jamie."

She tentatively extended her hand. "Hi, Rex."

Rex sniffed her fingers, then she felt him rake his tongue across her palm. Relieved he hadn't taken a bite out of her, she scratched him behind his ear. He sighed and rubbed his big head against her legs, like a cat against a scratching post.

So much for the watchdog theory, she thought in amusement. She had a declawed tabby back home who was more aggressive.

Steve stood up. "Would you like a drink?"

"I could really use some coffee right about now."

He smiled. "I'll put on a pot," he said, edging toward the doorway. "Then I'll see what I can find out about those photographs. Check in with the office. Feed Rex." He nodded back toward the living room. "Come on out when you're ready." He left her to unpack her shopping bag.

Rex stayed for a few moments longer, until they both heard a sharp whistle from the front of the house, followed by the whir of an electric can opener. His body tensed; his ears shot up in recognition. He barked and then bounded out of the room.

Jamie smiled and removed her crumpled clothes from the shopping bag. She'd grabbed the first thing she'd come across, a lightweight tan-and-navy-blue dress with criss-crossing straps and a matching jacket. She shook out a few of the wrinkles and hung the outfit on a hanger in the closet. After placing her gold necklace and her grandmother's pearls on the night table beside the bed, she folded the shopping bag and went back to the living room. She could smell the coffee brewing.

The television was on, and she recognized the voice of Bob Hope. It was an old movie from the 1940s, one of the Road pictures with Bing Crosby and Dorothy Lamour. Steve stood in a den just off the living room that he'd apparently converted into an office. He was peering at the snapshots under the light of his desk lamp.

She pulled out the steno pad from her purse and sat down on the sofa next to the crumpled newspaper. The first step toward making sense of everything would be writing it all down, she decided. Identify the problem, then isolate the solution. She drew two columns on the page, one entitled "Facts," the other "Possible Conclusions."

Steve walked into the living room. "When you feel up to it, I'll need to establish some time frame on the photographs. When they were taken, where you were—that sort of thing."

She nodded but didn't look up.

"The paper is Kodak. He used a Polaroid camera, so it'll be impossible to trace. And since there were probably a lot of photographers running around the conference, it's doubtful anyone noticed him. Still, we can give it a try. I'll have one of my people ask around tomorrow."

The telephone rang in the den. She glanced up. He met her gaze and smiled apologetically. "Excuse me." He walked into the other room and quietly closed the door behind him.

She lowered the pen, the hairs beginning to rise along the nape of her neck. Why had he closed the door? she wondered suspiciously. What was he afraid she would overhear?

I must be worse off than I thought. She shook her head and placed her steno pad and pen on the cocktail table. For all she knew, it could be his girlfriend on the phone. At any rate, he probably had a thousand reasons for wanting to have a private telephone conversation, and not a damn one of them included her. She'd better get her coffee before she lost it altogether.

She stood and walked into the kitchen. Rex was just finishing his dinner and he looked up expectantly, his tail wagging. Ignoring him, she lifted the glass pot and sniffed the coffee. It smelled . . . well, *strong* was as good an adjective as any. And its deep brown color was reminiscent of the tar in the La Brea Tar Pits. She opened the cabinet, found a coffee mug and poured herself a cup. She took a tentative sip and gagged.

The tar would've probably tasted better.

She poured half of the mug down the drain and replaced the dumped coffee with hot tap water. A liberal dousing with nondairy creamer and sugar substitute—both removed from her purse, since the kitchen didn't seem to have the necessary condiments—and the coffee was nearly drinkable.

She returned to the living room and sank onto the sofa. Without waiting for an invitation, Rex joined her and curled up like an oversized cat, his back paws crinkling the newspaper. Frowning, she pried the paper loose, refolded it, then laid it on the table beside the remnants of Steve's breakfast.

Sipping her coffee, she picked up her steno pad and pen and started to work on her notes. She wrote down everything she knew about the case, trying to organize her thoughts about the blond pirate and his telephone call, then collating Steve's comments with her own impressions. Categorizing the data made everything less frightening. More important, it made her feel in control.

By the time she heard the office door open a short time later, she'd drafted a neat listing.

"Sorry about that," Steve said, walking into the living room. "We had an attempted break-in at a jewelry store downtown. Had to talk to the dispatcher. Did you get your coffee?"

She took another swallow and grimaced. "Yes, thank you."

He continued into the kitchen. She heard him lift the glass pot from the coffee maker and pour himself a cup. He came back a few moments later carrying a blue earthenware mug.

He smiled. "So what's all this?" He nodded toward the steno pad on her lap and sipped his coffee.

She recapped the pen. "It's some notes on the case. I've been trying to make sense of everything that's happened, get my thoughts together."

He sat down on the edge of the sofa beside her. "May I?"

She handed him the steno pad and watched as he scanned the sheet of paper.

"Very impressive." He eyed her thoughtfully. "You did all this while I was on the phone?"

She nodded. "Organizing data—and then analyzing it— is one of the things I do best. When I talk to the police tomorrow, I want to be prepared."

His smile began to fade. "I wish to God you hadn't gotten involved in all this, Jamie."

She met his gaze. "I just wish I knew *how* I was involved in all this. Why Gary came to the hotel to see me."

A shadow of sadness, of pain, crossed his face and then was gone. "So do I." He stood up. "Do you think you could go over the snapshots with me now? Give me the time frame?"

She agreed and he went to get them. When he returned, he laid the photographs—minus the one of Gary—out on the cocktail table. After the last one had been identified and an approximate time of day assigned, he scooped up the pictures and his notes and took them into the den to phone the agency.

She drained the last of the coffee in her mug and glanced at the television. The local news was on—funny, she thought, she hadn't even realized the movie had ended—and a silver-haired anchorman was reporting on the crash of a twin-engine Cessna in Palmdale earlier that morning.

Yawning widely, she rose and carried her empty mug into the kitchen for a refill. She could hear the broadcast over her preparations and half listened to the recap of the day's news stories. When she heard the anchorman mention an execution-style slaying in the Hollywood Hills, she froze, her fingers tightening around the plastic handle of the glass coffeepot.

"Police still have no leads in the murder of Gary Dodsworth, whose body was discovered early yesterday morning in the back lot of Universal Studios."

She carefully set the glass pot on the stove and walked back to the living room, the hairs prickling along her forearms.

"Preliminary investigation reveals Dodsworth was abducted from his home in Glendale and driven to the murder site by person or persons unknown," the anchorman intoned. "The Glendale police, in conjunction with the North Hollywood division of the L.A.P.D., have asked for our help in gathering information about this apparently senseless killing that has rocked the quiet community of the nineteen-hundred block of Foothill Drive. If anyone has any information about the killing, please contact either the North Hollywood or Glendale divisions directly or us here at the Channel Ten newsroom."

Jamie shook her head. But that didn't make any sense. Why did the police think Gary had been abducted from his home in Glendale? Steve had said the pirate grabbed him at the hotel. So why weren't the police concentrating their search there instead of in Gary's neighborhood? She frowned. And why hadn't there been any mention of the pirate? Or the coin, for that matter?

She heard the sharp click as the television was turned off and raised her gaze to see Steve standing in the doorway of the den with the remote-control unit in his hand. One look at his hard, unsmiling face told her that he'd heard the broadcast—and that he knew she had, too.

"Steve, what's going on?"

Silence. Only eerie silence as the seconds ticked by.

Why doesn't he answer me? she wondered. And then it hit her. The realization had the impact of a bucket of ice water thrown on a sleeping man. The police were looking in Glendale because they didn't know Gary had been abducted from the Hilton. And they didn't know because Flynn hadn't told them.

She swallowed hard. Flynn hadn't told them. Not about Gary or the coin or even the pirate. None of it. Hell, for all she knew, it was a lie, anyway. She only had his word for it. And here she was alone with him—

She felt a scream bubble up in her throat. *She was alone with him.* And no one knew where she was. He had made damned certain of that, hadn't he? When her body was discovered, no one would suspect Stephen Flynn was involved at all. They'd be too busy looking for Dale Carmichael.

A brilliant smoke screen, he'd called it.

"Oh, my God," she breathed.

Her gaze darted to the sliding glass door off to her right. There was a chance she could make it, she told herself, trying to remain calm. He was bigger, stronger, and her high heels would only slow her down. But a slim chance was better than no chance at all.

"I can explain," he said and took a step toward her.

She bolted for the door.

SIX

She never made it.

His hand clamped down on her arm just as she passed the dining room table. He twirled her around and slammed her body against his, pinning her arms to her side.

"Let me go!" She raised her right foot and brought the sharp point of her heel crashing down on the hard leather of his nearest dress shoe. He winced, but didn't release her. "You lying bastard! Get away from me!"

"Relax, damn it!" He forced his knee between her legs and wedged his foot behind her left ankle. The sudden move threw her off-balance. "I'm not going to hurt you."

Barking, Rex jumped off the sofa. He raced into the dining room area and circled them like a band of Indians surrounding a wagon train, his nails click-clack-clicking against the hardwood floor.

"Let me go!" Her voice rose with her panic. She felt the brush of the dog's silky fur as his tail swatted her leg. Mentally bracing herself for a fall, she threw herself backward and twisted her wrists, hoping to break Steve's hold. She felt his fingers loosen.

"Goddammit!" He brought his calf up hard against her captured left leg until her knees buckled. He then tightened his grip on her arms and yanked her closer.

Heart pounding, breath ragged, she stared up at him, wondering what he would do next.

"Would you just relax?" His face was flushed, intense. A shock of hair tumbled across his forehead. He met her frightened gaze and scowled.

"Please?"

His voice was softer this time. His eyes had deepened to the dusky green of the ocean after a storm, and she found herself staring into them, almost mesmerized. She could feel the heat rising off his body, smell the faint musky scent of his cologne.

"All I want to do is talk to you."

The dog continued to circle them, his barks becoming more agitated with each turn. He skidded to a stop and nudged her stockinged leg with his cold, wet nose.

"Talk to me? Kill me, you mean."

A look of incredulity crossed his face. "Are you crazy?"

Maybe I am, she told herself. Her fear, so all-consuming a moment before, was rapidly vanishing. Standing with her body pressed so intimately against his, close enough to hear his heart beat, close enough to feel his chest rise and fall with each intake of breath, made it hard for her to believe he was capable of harming her. It made it hard to think at all.

Then she felt him tense. His eyes darkened, like paper set too close to a flame, and she knew he felt the same attraction. Time was suspended for a moment. She waited, almost afraid to breathe.

Steve lowered his head and brushed his lips against hers, exploring with such softness that it might have been the caress of butterfly wings. Even so, the kiss sent a shock wave of desire coursing through her. She shivered.

He kissed her again. Slowly. Deeply. The way she'd wanted him to kiss her in his office earlier that day. The way, she now realized, she'd fantasized about his kissing her since the moment they'd met. A soft moan escaped her lips. She leaned against him, trying to align her body with his in even more intimate ways.

Then, inexplicably, he pulled away, letting her arms fall to her side. She nearly toppled over from the suddenness of the release. Gasping like a diver coming up for air, she stared at him, confused, and rubbed her arms. The memory of his touch was burned into her skin, maybe even into her soul.

"I'm . . . not . . . one of the bad guys." His voice was husky, almost unrecognizable. He turned and walked back to the living room. "You're not a prisoner. I brought you here for your own protection. No other reason. If you want to leave, you can. If you want to phone the police, you can do that, too. Hell, it's gone on too long, anyway."

She took a deep breath, trying to get her emotions under control. She felt a flush color her cheeks. "What has? The lies and deceptions?"

He shoved his hands into his trouser pockets. "I never wanted to mislead you, but I had no choice. I was trying to buy a little time—conduct an internal investigation. It was the only way I had of getting to the truth."

"But that's no excuse for *lying* to me."

"And I never lied to you. I just . . . I just didn't tell you the whole truth, that's all."

"What's the difference?" She shook her head. "Look, you could have leveled with me. I wouldn't have compromised your investigation. *My God, Steve.*" Her voice was rough with the fear and frustration wrought by the past forty-eight hours. "Do you have *any* idea what kind of hell my life has been lately?"

Hard lines slashed across his forehead, curved around his mouth; pain—the kind that eats away at a person's soul—shone in his eyes. Stephen Flynn didn't need her to tell him about hell, she realized with a sudden jolt of awareness. He was already living there.

"I'm sorry you had to get involved in all this."

Hearing the utter exhaustion in his voice, Jamie felt her anger dissolve. Maybe she was being too hard—

Now, stop that! she harshly ordered herself. *The man has lied to you almost from the start. Don't be an even bigger fool.*

"You're sorry I got *involved*?" She folded her arms against her chest. "All I did was talk to a man on a plane for a couple of hours about refinishing an oak table. That conversation now has people threatening to kill me because they think he gave me some stupid coin he was carrying. *That's* the extent of my *involvement* in any of this!"

He met the challenge in her gaze head-on, battle-weary green eyes staring into unflinching brown ones. "You're wrong."

"Wrong? But Gary didn't give me the coin. I know everyone seems to think otherwise, but it never happened."

"Maybe *that* was the whole idea. Maybe Gary just wanted it to *appear* he'd given you the coin. You could have been nothing more than a diversion to confuse the people after him."

"A diversion? What are you . . . ?" She sank down onto the edge of the love seat. "Are you saying Gary used me as a decoy to lure away the pirate?"

Steve stared at her for a moment without answering. Then he took a deep breath and shrugged. "It's possible."

Jamie felt an icy numbness settle in the pit of her stomach. What kind of people was she dealing with?

"Look, I've known Gary too long to believe in coincidences. His bumping into you at the baggage-handling area was staged. He did it either to slip you something or to make it *appear* he'd slipped you something. I haven't figured out which."

"But why? What possible reason would Gary have for wanting to . . . to . . . ?" She couldn't bring herself to say the words. The idea that Gary Dodsworth had intentionally made her a moving target was too horrifying to even contemplate.

"Gary involved you because he felt it was his only chance to protect the coin." Steve said it bluntly, without amplification or apology. "He was set up, Jamie. Someone—probably your blond pirate—was waiting for him at the airport when the plane landed. Gary was unarmed. Unprepared." A muscle twitched at the corner of his tightly clenched jaw, and he turned away. "It was supposed to have been a low-risk assignment." He stared out the sliding glass door into the night. Interminable seconds passed. Then he added, "For what it's worth, I'm sure he never would've involved you if he'd known it would place you in danger."

He walked over to an antique mahogany bar set near the patio door and slipped behind the counter. "Want a drink?"

She shook her head.

He set a bottle of Jack Daniels on the counter. "I originally assigned a low-level operative to transport the doubloon, but something came up at the last minute. Gary and I were the only people at the agency on Saturday when the call came in. It . . . it had been a long time since Gary participated in a field assignment. But his wife and kids were out of town for the weekend. He said he was bored." Steve frowned and unscrewed the cap of the liquor bottle. "I had plans, so I agreed."

She eyed him objectively for a moment, refusing to let her emotions cloud her thinking. Parts of his story sounded like they'd been lifted from a Ludlum novel. Operatives. Field assignments. Diversionary tactics. Yet, as farfetched as it all seemed, she believed every word. Years of dealing with clients who'd falsified their loss reports, of evaluating their body language during the claims investigations, had made her familiar with the signs of subterfuge. All her instincts now told her that Stephen Flynn was telling the truth.

"So you think someone told the pirate when Gary was coming in?" She settled back on the love seat and crossed her legs.

"Exactly. Only I doubt they knew it would be Gary. They were probably expecting someone with limited field experience. Gary's presence threw their plans off." He poured two fingers of bourbon into a glass. "My guess is Gary knew he'd walked into a trap and he tried to outmaneuver them—which is probably where you fit in. But his plan, whatever it was, failed. They grabbed him at the hotel. Killed him." He downed the drink in one gulp and grimaced. "He probably gave them no choice."

"Who was the client?"

"Hathaway and Ferris. They're international art brokers. Rare coins, stamps, collectibles—that sort of thing. They're auctioning off the doubloon next week." He refilled his glass. "The agency was supposed to provide the security. We've worked with them for years—the manager of their West Coast gallery is an old friend of mine." He smiled wryly, as if the fact amused him somehow. He screwed the cap back on the liquor bottle. "We play racquetball every Thursday."

"But surely you don't suspect him?"

"Hell, I suspect everybody." His voice was cold, harsh. "Only he and a few people at Flynn Security knew about the coin's arrival time. The information had to come from somewhere." He walked to the peach sofa across from where she sat and slumped down, its soft leather crunching under his weight.

"I see your point," she conceded. "Once you've eliminated wiretapping and any other form of electronic surveillance, an informant's the only explanation that makes sense." She paused thoughtfully. "What about your internal investigation? Did it come up with any leads?"

"Nothing concrete. Just more questions, more suspects." Shoulders slouched, elbows resting on his thighs, he stared down into the amber depths of his drink. "Any way you look at it, Jamie, it still boils down to the same thing. If I hadn't been so wrapped up in other things, I might have noticed what was going on, and stopped it. Then the coin would be in the vault. Gary would still be alive." He took a long swallow of bourbon. "And you wouldn't be in danger."

She felt her heart constrict at the pain in his voice. "I think you're being too hard on yourself. Sometimes things . . . happen . . . that we have no control over."

"I calculated the risk of the assignment. I okayed the substitution. If something went wrong, it was my fault."

No, you're wrong, she wanted to say. *Gary's decision to involve me wasn't your fault. Nor was Gary's murder.* But she clasped her hands in her lap and said nothing. As hard as it was to keep silent, she knew that pointing out the obvious to Steve wouldn't erase his misplaced guilt.

His avoidance of the police, however, was another matter.

"You've *got* to notify the police, Steve," she said, using the firm, no-nonsense tone of voice she employed with difficult clients. "They're trained professionals. Maybe if you just let them handle it, they could sort everything out."

He sighed wearily. "You don't understand."

"But the police have to know why Gary was killed. They're working on his murder, for heaven's sake. If you don't give them all the facts, they can't do their job. If you—"

"He was my best friend, damn it!" His hand was clenched so tightly around the glass, his knuckles were turning white. "And somebody within my own organization could've set him up. That's . . . not something I can just walk away from."

She watched him fight to keep his emotions in check, wanting to help, but knowing she couldn't. "I'm not asking you to walk away from it, Steve. I'm just asking you to play by the rules. If you don't, Gary's killers may never be caught." Her stomach lurched as a new suspicion took hold. "You . . . you're not planning on handling it yourself, are you?"

He looked up and met her worried gaze. "You mean, am I planning to track down the bastards and kill them?"

His mouth curved in a half smile. "The thought crossed my mind a few times. But I'm no murderer. I want them put away. *Legally*." He set the empty glass on the cocktail table. "I'm not out for revenge, Jamie. The only reason I've been stalling for time is so I can find the leak. Plug it." He raked his fingers through his hair. "Hell, if I can't secure my own agency, how can I promise to do it for anybody else?"

He leaned forward, his expression growing serious. "Look, I'm sorry I didn't level with you from the beginning, but I just didn't feel I had much choice. I hope you can understand that."

"And now? What do you intend to do?"

He shrugged. "Like I said in the car, I'll go to the police first thing in the morning and tell them everything. The detective in charge of the investigation is an old friend of mine. I've been dodging him since Monday and I don't think I can put him off much longer, even if I wanted to."

He held her gaze for a moment, then looked down and frowned. "I guess the next move is really up to you."

She considered her options. But in the end, she knew she had only one. Regardless of how it had all begun, she *was* involved now. And she knew she would stay involved until the investigation was over, like it or not.

"In that case, I propose we both get some sleep." She stood up and rubbed the tense, aching muscles bunched along the nape of her neck. "It's late. And I, for one, am exhausted." She picked up her purse from the cocktail table and forced a tired smile. "Let's say we just tackle it all tomorrow, okay?"

Then, not waiting to hear his reply, she turned and went back to her bedroom.

A loud, raucous screech broke through the silence of the morning. Cursing under his breath, Steve reached out and fumbled for the alarm. His fingers wrapped around the soft foam rubber of the baseball-shaped clock, and he hurled it across the room. It hit the wall with a thud and the alarm stopped.

His arm fell back exhausted on the bed.

A moment later, he heard scratching at the door, a low growl and the thunder of heavy paws pelting the carpeting, scurrying around the room. Then . . . silence. Blessed, sweet silence. He smiled and felt himself drifting back to sleep. A few minutes more, he promised himself; then he'd—

Suddenly a ninety-pound bundle of coarse fur and taut muscle leapt onto the bed, jarring him awake.

He groaned. "Go away."

Rex dropped the alarm clock on the pillow beside Steve's head. It rolled down and struck his bare shoulder, bringing with it the unpleasant odor of dog breath and a warm stickiness whose origin he would rather not speculate on.

"Aw, hell." Eyes still closed, he grabbed the baseball and hurled the blasted thing across the room, with Rex in hot pursuit.

Refusing to give in to the inevitable, Steve turned over and pulled the covers over his head. He heard Rex growl another warning, then felt a tug on the comforter. Gentle at first, the tugging became more insistent, until a final jerk yanked the comforter completely off the bed.

"What the—?" Steve sat up. Shafts of daylight crept through the cracks of the drawn shades, nearly blinding him. He raised his hand to ward off the glare and squinted.

Rex stood at the foot of the bed, the comforter in a heap beside him, the alarm clock back in his mouth. Steve could've sworn the dog was smiling.

The alarm sounded again.

Rex dropped the ball and barked.

Steve crawled out of bed. It was the same routine every morning. Not even a change in living arrangements altered it. The alarm would go off, he'd throw the clock, then Rex would hurtle into the room to find it. By the time they'd played a few rounds of toss and fetch, Steve would be awake.

Pissed, but awake.

He bent down and grabbed the clock. The LCD crystals read 7:07. Yawning, he shut off the alarm and tossed the ball onto the beside table. Coffee. He ran his hand across his stubbled chin and frowned. He needed coffee. So badly, he imagined he could smell it brewing.

He pulled on a pair of gray sweatpants, then stumbled down the hallway toward the kitchen, hearing the rush of running water coming from the guest bathroom as he went past. Jamaica must be taking a shower, he thought. He arched his back and flexed his shoulder muscles in a morning stretch.

Jamaica. Damn funny name for a woman, if you asked him.

He walked into the kitchen and stared transfixed at the freshly brewed pot of coffee sitting in the coffee maker. Shrugging, he poured a cup, wrapped his fingers around the warm mug and lifted it to his lips. He took a tentative sip and sighed. Delicious.

Rex barked, nipped Steve's pant leg and backed across the linoleum toward the patio with Steve in tow.

"Okay, okay, I get the message." He shook his leg free, shut off the burglar alarm, then dutifully marched to the sliding glass door, feeling the cool planks of the hardwood floor against the soles of his feet. He reached through the drapes, released the lock and slid the door open far enough for the German shepherd to get out.

Yawning again, he pulled out a chair from the dining room table and slumped down. He then propped his elbows on the oak table and sipped his coffee, wondering how anyone could be expected to function so early in the morning.

Minutes later, he heard footfalls on the hallway carpeting and looked up. Jamie walked into the kitchen, towel-drying her short brown hair. She wore his football jersey.

(The damn thing was too big for her, he thought. It hung clear down to her knees.) He remembered the embarrassed flush that had colored her cheeks when she'd asked him for an extra pair of pajamas the night before, and smiled at the memory. The jersey had been the closest thing to pajamas he'd brought with him.

She saw him sitting at the table and stopped. Then she smiled. "Good morning."

"Morning." At least she was half right.

He watched as she poured her coffee, then opened the red cosmetics case she'd brought with her and removed packets of sugar substitute and nondairy creamer.

"You really are prepared, aren't you?"

She glanced over her shoulder. "I always carry a few extras with me. Good thing, too. You're out of everything, you know."

He shrugged and drained his mug. "Yeah, well, the Friedmans didn't exactly leave the larder well stocked, and lately I've been spending most of my time down at the agency. We'll have to stop at the market tonight."

He pushed the chair back and walked over to where she stood at the counter. He caught a whiff of the soft floral scent of her perfume as he refilled his mug. The fragrance surrounded him, filling his senses. He closed his eyes, remembering the kiss, savoring the memory as if it were a fine wine to be sipped slowly.

When he opened his eyes moments later, he couldn't help but notice how the fabric of the jersey clung to the small of her back. How her skin still had a sheen from the shower. She looked soft and fragile. Vulnerable. He wanted to reach out and touch her skin, to see if it felt as soft as it looked. He wanted to . . .

She looked up and their eyes met. Held.

"Good coffee," he mumbled. He brushed past her and walked down the hallway to take a shower.

A *cold* shower.

God, he hated mornings.

* * *

An hour and forty-five minutes later, Jamie followed Steve down a bustling corridor of the North Hollywood precinct house to a small office with "L. Abrams" stenciled across the smoked glass of the upper door. Steve paused briefly, as if to brace himself, then rapped once and turned the doorknob.

A man in his late thirties sat in a high-backed swivel chair and talked on the phone, his scuffed black leather shoes resting on a stack of files atop a cluttered metal desk. His curly brown hair lightly brushed the collar of his pale blue shirt. A loosened tie hung a few inches below the open collar.

"What? You nuts or something?" the man was saying in a thick East Coast accent. Probably New York, Jamie decided. Or New Jersey. "Do I hafta come down there and kick somebody's butt or what?" He saw Steve and Jamie standing in the doorway and stopped. "I want the report by three." He slammed the receiver down and swung his feet off the desk.

"Hello, Lou." Steve smiled.

" *'Hello, Lou'?* " The man pressed his palms against the desk for leverage and stood up. "What kind of remark is that s'posed to be, huh? How 'bout just telling me where've you been the past three days, Flynn." He walked around the desk, stuffing his shirt back in his trousers. "You give one of my people some half-assed story about researching Gary's case files and leave. You don't return my phone calls. You don't tell me nothin'. Now you come waltzing in here saying 'Hello, Lou.' " Abrams slammed the door shut. "I ought to run you in on charges."

Jamie winced and moved away from the two men.

"I had my reasons." Steve sat down in one of the two scarred wooden chairs facing the desk and crossed his legs, seemingly unconcerned by the lieutenant's anger.

"Reasons?" Abrams placed his hands on his hips. "Oh, I'll give you reasons. Impeding a police investigation. How's that for a reason? Withholding evidence. Another good one. Obstructing justice. You want I should go on?"

He gestured at Steve with his right hand. "I got myself quite a list here."

"He was set up, Lou."

Abrams stared at him for a moment, then frowned and sat down on the edge of the desk. He pulled a crumpled pack of cigarettes from his shirt pocket and lit one. "What was he working on?"

"Simple courier assignment."

"Try it again."

"He was transporting the Washington Doubloon for Hathaway and Ferris. They're having the auction next week, and we're providing the security."

The lieutenant's face was impassive. "Yeah, I heard about it. So why was Gary transporting it? You expecting trouble?"

"Last-minute substitution. The assignment was supposed to have been routine."

"Hmm." Abrams took a long drag on his cigarette, the lines deepening along his forehead as if he were concentrating. "Somebody grab the coin?"

"They tried. Apparently Gary didn't have it on him at the time." Steve glanced at Jamie. "Lou, this is Jamaica Royale."

She stiffened, her fingers digging into the arms of the wooden chair. *Jamaica?* Had he actually called her Jamaica?

She gave herself a mental shake and relaxed. "The name is Jamie, Lieutenant Abrams. *Jamie* Royale."

Abrams shook her extended hand. "Pleased to meet ya."

"Uh . . . Jamie . . . was on the flight with Gary," Steve cŏntinued. "She's attending an insurance conference at the Universal Hilton. Gary was trying to contact her at the hotel when he was grabbed."

"Oh, yeah?" Abrams looked at her speculatively over his cigarette. "Why'd he want to do that?"

"We're not sure." Then Steve filled Abrams in on what

had happened: the pirate, her ransacked room, the photographs.

Everything.

Well, almost everything, she amended, casting a furtive glance in Steve's direction. He'd somehow neglected to mention the hotel security guard who'd chased her through Hancock Park. She couldn't say she really blamed him for leaving that out, though. Considering his current status as persona non grata with Lieutenant Abrams, Steve had probably made a wise move.

Abrams stubbed out his cigarette in an overflowing ash-tray on his desk. "You should've been here sooner. You know as well as I do there ain't much we can do once the trail gets cold. We might've been able to catch the guy. Now . . ." He shrugged.

"Look, she couldn't provide a positive ID, and I wasn't too sure he would even come back. I had one of my people keep an eye on her just in case, but I felt my priorities lay with finding the leak. It was a judgment call. Simple as that."

"A poor judgment call," Abrams corrected coldly. "And one that could have some serious long-range consequences."

Steve frowned, but didn't say anything.

"So is there anything else you haven't told me?" Abrams asked, his voice regaining its cutting, sarcastic edge. Steve shook his head. "No? Okay, then. Now, you"—the lieutenant nodded toward Jamie—"need to make a statement and work with a sketch artist to see what kind of a picture we can come up with on this blond pirate of yours, while Sam Spade"—he indicated Steve with a jerk of his head—"and me step out in the hall and have a nice little chat about proper procedure."

She shifted her position in the uncomfortable wooden chair. She'd be willing to bet their "nice little chat" out in the hall would be anything but. She glanced at Steve. Eyes downcast, shoulders slumped, he was rubbing his forehead with his thumb and index finger as if he felt the same way.

Abrams picked up the telephone receiver and pressed a couple of digits. "Ruiz? Get in here. I want you to take a statement."

Moments later, a young Hispanic officer hurried in with a clipboard, nervously shuffling sheets of paper into position.

"Get Peters down here a.s.a.p. to work up a composite," Abrams instructed the officer. The young man nodded, glanced quickly at Jamie and Steve, then moved behind the desk and picked up the receiver.

Abrams slid off the desk. "Once you give Officer Ruiz your statement and a description of the guy who accosted you, Miss Royale, you'll be free to go." He slipped his arm affectionately around Steve's shoulder as the latter rose to his feet. "You, on the other hand, may get to stay a while. It'll all depend on your answers—*and my mood.*"

Steve looked back when he reached the door and met her worried gaze. He winked. "See you outside," he whispered.

She frowned. She wished she could feel as confident about that as he did.

Steve took a last swallow of coffee, crumpled the paper cup in his hand and dropped it into the basket in front of the vending machine. Lou stood off to one side, arguing—loudly—with a cop about another case. The officer finally threw up his hands and walked away. Sensible solution, Steve thought. Walking away was the only way to handle an argument with Lou Abrams.

"And to think I moved to the Valley to reduce my stress level." Lou removed the crumpled pack of cigarettes from his shirt pocket. "This place is worse than the Bronx."

"Yeah, but at least the weather's nicer."

"Can the crap, Flynn." Lou lit another cigarette, eyeing Steve over the flame. He flicked the cap of the lighter closed and exhaled a ribbon of smoke. "You realize I could pull your license for this, don't you? Even charge you with obstruction?''

"Lou, it was Gary. Put yourself in my place. What would you have done?''

A muscle twitched at the corner of Lou's jaw. "Same thing.'' He turned and watched two uniformed officers walk past them. From farther down the hallway came muffled laughter and the incessant ringing of a telephone. "How's Chris holding up?''

Steve felt a cold knot tighten in the pit of his stomach. He hadn't been able to face Gary's widow since he'd told her the news. Truth was, he didn't know if he ever *could* face her. Just what were you supposed to say to a woman when you felt you were responsible for her husband's death?

"Pretty well, I guess. The services are this afternoon.'' He shoved his hands into his trouser pockets. "Forest Lawn in Glendale. Three P.M.

"Tell her if there's anything I can do . . .'' Lou took another drag on the cigarette, then turned back to meet Steve's gaze.

"So you got any idea who this leak of yours is?''

"I made a list of who it isn't. That was a lot easier.''

"And?''

"And not counting me and Gary, there's Tony Robinson—he's the one who was supposed to transport the coin. And Mona, of course.'' He shook his head and muttered under his breath, "Hell, I'd rather suspect my own mother than Mona.''

"Robinson?'' Lou repeated with interest. "He new?''

"He started about six months ago. He's okay, though. His wife went into premature labor two hours before he was to leave for the airport. No way he could have planned that.''

Lou grinned.

"Which means everyone else is a suspect. Along with Jim Rothenberg and the people in his office. Tony's been helping me weed out the possibles. So far, nothing.''

Lou nodded, but didn't say anything. He flicked ash toward the trash can and missed. "You ready to tell me the real story about that little lady in there?" He jerked his head back toward his office.

"You mean Jamie? You've already heard the real story. Whoever killed Gary thinks she has the coin and now they're coming after her. At first I thought Gary might have slipped her the doubloon for safekeeping. Now I'm inclined to think she was just a diversion."

"Nice guy, old Gary. Why didn't he paint a bull's eye on her back while he was at it?"

Steve tensed. He balled his hands into fists in his trouser pockets. "I'll never believe he deliberately set out to endanger her, Lou. It wasn't Gary's style."

"Hell, he was with military intelligence for fifteen years. Don't kid yourself."

Steve stared at his reflection in the shiny chrome finish of the vending machine. He knew better than anyone what Gary Dodsworth would've been capable of if he'd thought the coin was in danger. But to *deliberately* place an innocent bystander at risk? He didn't like to think it was possible. Besides, Gary had been trying to contact Jamie when he was grabbed—if he'd set her up as a decoy, he would hardly have followed her to the hotel. He would've continued with the delivery.

Wouldn't he?

"Look, the important thing is that she *is* in danger." Steve glanced back at the lieutenant. "And until I plug the leak, Flynn Security can't really protect her."

Lou took a long drag on his cigarette. "Where's she staying?"

"With me. I'm staying at a client's house in Hollywood Hills while the workmen finish the sun deck. Remind me to give you the address. I've got the phone on Call Forwarding."

"So what's the problem? She can just keep on staying there with you until we nab the guy or it blows over."

"But she can't stay with me. How am I supposed to

conduct my investigation with her tagging along?'' Hell, for that matter, how could he concentrate on anything *but* her when she was around? Last night had proved that. But the attraction, powerful though it was, wasn't merely physical. Jamie touched a chord deep inside him, unlocking emotions he hadn't felt in a long time . . . and wasn't all that sure he was ready to start feeling again.

"There *has* to be another solution," he muttered.

Lou dropped a couple of quarters into the vending machine and pressed the button for coffee with sugar and cream. "Well, it ain't gonna be the L.A.P.D. So far, all the guy's done is make a couple of threats and take her picture." He took a sip of coffee and grimaced. He swirled the contents of the cup around as if that might improve the coffee's taste.

"And what's this investigation crap you were talking about?" he asked. "If it's Gary's murder, you can forget it. I won't allow it."

Steve frowned and removed his hands from his pockets. "I was talking about the doubloon. The agency's insurance policy only covers seventy-five percent of its value. I'm responsible for the rest." He met Lou's gaze. "I have to find the coin, Lou. Otherwise I'll lose the agency."

Lou took a long sip of coffee. "What's it worth? Couple hundred grand?"

"Try a million."

Lou whistled.

"I haven't told Jim Rothenberg the doubloon's missing yet. He's been pressing me for answers for the delay in delivery, but I wanted to find out exactly what I was dealing with before I said anything to anybody. I know it's bending the rules a little bit''—he smiled ruefully—"but if you could hold off the press for a couple of days, I'd really appreciate it."

Lou eyed him for a moment, then flicked another cigarette butt into the ashtray. "You got forty-eight hours. Any longer than that and the chief'll be breathing down my neck."

"Thanks, Lou. I owe you one."

The lieutenant shrugged. "You just make sure you don't step out of line this time. Hey!" He tapped Steve on his shoulder and glared. "I'm serious, Flynn. You interfere with my investigation once more, and I'll bust your ass. Friends or no friends. *Capeesh*?"

Steve grinned. "Capeesh."

The door to Lou's office opened, and Officer Ruiz and Jamie walked out.

Lou nodded. "Good. Now get the hell out of here before I change my mind."

It seemed like good advice, so Steve grasped Jamie's hand and did just that.

When they arrived in the parking lot several minutes later, he slid into the car seat and reached for the cellular phone. He punched in the number for the office as Jamie stashed her purse on the floorboard. Mona answered on the second ring.

"It's me," he said. "Any messages?"

Papers rustled in the background as if she was shuffling phone messages. "The usual. Rothenberg has already phoned twice, and Abrams called several times late yesterday afternoon—you know you can't keep dodging him forever, Steve."

"So he told me. Among other things." He undid the top button of his shirt and loosened his tie, quickly plotting his next move. "Send Tony to the Hilton to pick up the rest of Jamie's things. She's moving in with me at the Friedman place for the time being."

He heard the scrunch of leather as Jamie twisted around in her seat to stare at him. He glanced at her and smiled.

"Tell him it's a Priority One." His voice dropped lower. "I don't want any interoffice communication on this, Mona. Miss Royale's whereabouts are to remain strictly confidential."

"You don't have to say it," she assured him and rang off.

He leaned over and replaced the receiver in the cradle

mounted to the dashboard just inches from Jamie's knee. When he raised his head, he found her studying him, her mouth turned downward in annoyance.

He flashed a bright, reassuring smile and straightened. "Ready?"

"For what?" she asked suspiciously. "Just where are we supposed to be going now?"

"Oh, didn't I tell you?" He inserted the key into the ignition. "We're going to Chinatown."

SEVEN

"Chinatown?" she repeated in confusion. "Whatever for?"

He glanced into the rearview mirror and backed the car up. "To talk with an old friend of mine. He may be able to give me a lead on the coin."

"But I thought . . ."

He met her gaze, his hand resting on the steering wheel. "I know I told you we'd make different living arrangements," he said, misinterpreting the reason for her disappointment, "but the police department can't spare any personnel right now. They're short on manpower and tall on caseloads. Lou and I agreed it would be best if you continued to stay with me at the Friedman place, under my protection, until the pirate is apprehended. No one knows I'm staying there—except my secretary and now Lou. There's no way the pirate can find you."

Fine, but the pirate might be the least of her problems, she thought, remembering the kiss she and Steve had shared in the living room the night before, the gentle caress of butterfly wings that had turned into fiery passion. The intensity of emotion it had unleashed had taken them both by surprise. Living with Steve under one roof, if only for a day, would be flirting with danger.

"Normally, I wouldn't drag a client all over town," he said, giving her an apologetic smile, "but I've got to investigate the coin's disappearance. So, for the next couple of days, I'm afraid it'll just be you and me, Jamaica."

She felt her skin crawl, as if someone had raked fingernails down a chalkboard. "Will you *please* stop calling me that! My name is Jamie." She spelled it for him. "Not that, that . . . what you just said." She waved her hand in the air.

He cast her a sidelong glance. "I, ah, take it you don't like Jamaica?" His bottom lip twitched as if he were finding it hard to keep a straight face.

"I have nothing against the island. It's being called the name half my life that I object to."

"Hmm. I don't know." He tilted his head to one side and regarded her with mock seriousness. "It's beautiful. Exotic . . . I think it suits you."

You would.

"You sound just like my father. 'Now, Jamaica, stop being such a self-righteous prig. It's a beautiful name.' " She rolled her eyes. "Do you have any idea what it's like to be saddled with an idiot—hey, wait a minute." Her eyes narrowed. "Just how did *you* know about it, anyway? No one except my parents has ever called me Jamaica. Even my boss doesn't know that's my real name, and I've worked with him for ten years."

He shrugged and glanced back at the road. "Good instincts."

Instincts, my foot! There's no way he could have guessed my given name. No way at all. Unless . . .

She took a slow, deep breath and ran her palms along her thighs, brushing out the wrinkles in the skirt of her navy-blue-and-tan dress. Checking into her background, she reminded herself, was a sensible move. A *necessary* move. A move she undoubtedly would've made herself, had she been in his position. But even so, she couldn't help feeling an eerie chill at realizing that strangers had been poking into the private aspects of her life.

"So why'd your parents name you Jamaica?" he asked, breaking into her thoughts. "Old family name?"

"Hardly." She shifted her position in the seat. "I got the name because they spent their honeymoon in Kingston, Jamaica."

"No, seriously."

"Yes, seriously. I was born nine months later." She looked over to find him staring at her. From the expression on his face, she could tell he was having a little trouble believing her explanation. "I suppose you could say it was their way of commemorating the occasion."

"You've got to be kidding."

"Remind me to tell you about my brother, Dallas."

He laughed.

She'd expected as much. Disbelief, quickly followed by ribald laughter. It was the reaction most people had to her parents' eccentricities, which was precisely why she never used the damned name in the first place.

She shrugged and gazed out the window at a group of pedestrians crossing the intersection. Still, as names went, she supposed hers wasn't *that* bad. In fact, it did seem to have a certain charm—especially the way Steve said it—but no one, absolutely no one, ever took "Jamaica" Royale seriously.

And she had worked too long and too hard at *being* serious to have people think her otherwise because of a stupid name.

Thirty minutes later, they turned into a side street off Broadway. Chinatown, she deduced, gawking at the ornate red-and-yellow signs attached to the storefronts along the busy street. Steve parked the Acura in front of an herbalist shop.

Moments later, Jamie followed him down the crowded sidewalk toward Broadway. She felt as if she'd walked into an alien world: red pagoda roofs as far as the eye could see, and strange odors that brought to mind images of decaying fish and burning incense. A radio blared from an open doorway with the sound of a rap band. Two wary

Asian-American teenagers leaned against the doorjamb and sized them up as they walked past.

"Do, ah, you come here often?" She tightened her grip on her purse straps.

He smiled and slid his hand around her waist, the simple gesture sending a comforting warmth through her body. They walked to a whitewashed, single-story building sandwiched between a discount clothing store and a Szechwan restaurant half a block away. The sign above the door read HARRY'S GYM; the wording underneath was in Chinese.

Steve pushed the door open. The large room was divided in half by a strip of worn red carpet that led back to the rear of the building. To the right were rows of weight-lifting equipment: bench presses, barbells, weight pulls. Most were vacant, except for the set of barbells being used by two muscular young men.

On the other side of the room, ten boys—most looking no older than fifteen—were going through an intense, yet exaggeratedly slow, workout on a tan-colored pallet. Eyes straight ahead, each boy extended his right arm, palm outward, then slowly shifted forward in a silent reflection of the instructor's movements.

"Tai chi," Steve explained. "It harmonizes the body and spirit."

Jamie nodded, too fascinated to comment further.

Steve tapped her arm and she reluctantly turned away. The clank of barbells being returned to the metal stand seemed a strange accompaniment to the graceful, fluid rhythms of the tai chi, Jamie thought as she followed him down the strip of carpeting to the rear of the gym.

A young Chinese woman sat on a high-backed stool behind the sign-in desk. Her long black hair was gathered on top of her head in a clumsy knot, mystifyingly held in place by a green, butterfly-shaped clip. Seven gold earrings, ranging in size from small hoops and studs to a cross an inch in height, adorned the lobe and outer rim of her left ear. She wore only one earring in her right earlobe—a long black exclamation point.

The girl looked up from reading a magazine and broke into a broad smile. "Flynn!"

"Hiya, beautiful." He leaned over the counter and gave her a kiss on her cheek. "Is he in?"

"Yeah," she said, giving Jamie a casual once-over, which Jamie returned with one of her own. "He's probably going over the books. Just go on back."

"Thanks."

He slipped through the bamboo curtains hanging behind the check-in desk. Jamie cast another speculative glance at the girl before following. Granted, Flynn's personal life was none of her business, but just then she was more curious about his relationship with the punked-out China doll on the stool than the mysterious "he" in the rear of the gym.

Steve moved through a cluttered storeroom to a small office, partially obscured by a tall metal shelf. A gray-haired Chinese man in his late fifties sat at a wooden desk in the office, frowning at the ledger spread out in front of him. On the floor lay a large Siamese cat, her tail wrapped gracefully around her curved body. When Steve tapped on the open door, the feline raised her head and eyed both him and Jamie with regal disinterest.

"Yes?"

"Hi, Harry," Steve said.

Harry's head snapped upward. "Steve! Well, I'll be a—!" He rose to his feet and lithely skirted the desk to greet them. "Come on in." He slapped Steve affectionately on his back and beamed. "What's it been? Six months?"

"More like seven."

Harry grinned. "So what brings you to Chinatown?"

"Business. I need some information, Harry."

The older man's face grew solemn. His gaze darted to Jamie, then back to Steve again. "Sit down." He nodded toward a couple of folding metal chairs in front of the desk. "Let's talk."

Jamie walked forward, stepping over a stack of weight-lifting magazines.

"Harry Chung, meet Jamie Royale," Steve said as she brushed past him.

"Jamie." Harry nodded and smiled.

She murmured a greeting in reply and sat down in the chair farthest away.

"Harry's a retired cop," Steve explained with a grin. "Vice. He used to work with my father back in the bad old days."

"Your father's a policeman?" She glanced at the row of framed photographs affixed to the wall behind Harry's desk. One of them showed a much younger Harry Chung and a tall, broad-shouldered man who bore a remarkable resemblance to Steve. The two men, both wearing police uniforms, were holding a wooden plaque and smiling broadly into the camera.

"Was." Steve's face clouded for a moment. "He was killed in the line of duty about ten years ago. Harry was his partner." He smiled. "Then Harry quit the force. Moved to Chinatown. Opened this gym for area youths."

Harry shrugged. "I got tired of busting them, so I decided to give them something better to do with their time." He went behind his desk and closed the ledger. "But you didn't come here to discuss my altruistic nature." He sat down in the worn leather chair and looked across at Steve. "You said you needed information. What can I do for you?"

The cat stretched her long body and walked over to rub herself against Jamie's legs. Jamie absently dropped her hand down to scratch the short, coarse fur behind the feline's head. The answering purr had the decibel level of a DC-10.

Steve sat down in the other chair. "Flynn Security was hired to transport a coin to L.A. for an upcoming auction," he said, coming straight to the point. "Before the courier could make delivery, he was abducted and killed."

Harry frowned and leaned back in his chair. "So Gary was transporting the Washington Doubloon. I was wondering . . ." He saw the look of surprise on Steve's face and explained. "I heard about the auction. Gary's murder. I just put it together." Harry regarded Steve for a moment, then asked, "How are you handling it? I know you two were pretty close."

Steve shrugged. "I'll be a lot better once the people who did it are behind bars—*and* I find the doubloon."

"Didn't they get it when they grabbed Gary?"

"Looks like he stashed it somewhere first." Steve quickly filled Harry in on what had happened. "I'm not having a lot of luck flushing out the informant, so I thought I'd try to track down the buyer instead." He leaned forward and rested his forearms on his upper thighs. "Which is why I'm here. I know you collect coins. And you've got more contacts on the streets than the entire L.A.P.D. If anybody could help me create a best-guess scenario on what the killer planned to do with the coin, I figured it'd be you."

The cat leapt into Jamie's lap and curled into a furry ball of contentment. She continued to stroke the animal, feeling a twinge of homesickness for her own cat, K.C.— not that K.C. had ever been so loving, mind you. The overfed tabby's usual sign of affection was to sink her sharp teeth into her mistress's hand whenever the latter was foolish enough to try petting her.

Harry shook his head and frowned. "The Washington Doubloon's not just any coin, Steve. It wouldn't be easy to unload."

"At a cool mil, I guess not."

"That's a conservative figure. For most collectors, the doubloon's priceless."

"But why?" Jamie asked. "What makes the coin so special?"

"Its historical value, for one thing," Harry said. "The doubloon was minted in the late 1700s, shortly after the Revolution and before the States had an official treasury department. Spanish gold. English pounds. It was all legal tender. Some shopkeepers even minted their own tokens. It didn't matter, as long as the gold content was kept standard.'' Harry leaned forward, his eyes sparkling as if the story were one he enjoyed telling.

"In the summer of 1782, a goldsmith named Nathan Webster thought the U.S. needed an official coin. So he made one. He put George Washington's face on the front of the coin—dressed him as an emperor with a wreath of olive branches around his head. The obverse was an eagle soaring above the mountaintop, with the Latin phrase 'One Nation Under God' inscribed below it. Records indicate Webster only made a dozen. The coins were never adopted by the U.S. government. After the break with England, the thought of Washington as an emperor was too much for most people to contemplate.''

"So where do the pirates fit in?" Jamie asked curiously.

"Pirates?" Harry looked puzzled.

"It's called a Washington *Doubloon*. That's what they call pirate treasure, isn't it? Doubloons?''

Harry laughed. "Oh, I see what you mean. But there weren't any pirates. The coin got the name because it's roughly the same size as a Spanish doubloon. Collectors like to give coins nicknames based upon their size or appearance. Like the Buffalo nickel or the Indian Head penny. But the Washington Doubloon . . . only one coin is still known to exist from the original dozen. A collector would do almost anything to own it.''

"Including kill?" Steve asked.

The room grew silent for a moment. "That all depends on the collector.'' Harry shifted in his chair, causing a squeak of chair coils and rested his arms on the desk. "Like I said, the Washington Doubloon's the premier piece. Only one of its kind. There'll be museums bidding for the coin at the auction.''

"Provided there is an auction.'' The worry lines deepened along Steve's forehead. "Any idea who'd be interested in buying the coin from a fence?''

Harry frowned. "You haven't been listening. The Washington Doubloon's not the kind of thing you take to a fence. You'd need to have a client already lined up. A client with a great deal of money and a strong desire to own the doubloon." He glanced down at his desk thoughtfully for a moment. "Offhand, I can think of only four collectors who fall into that category. They've all dealt with black-market sources for their acquisitions in the past, and they collect Early American coins."

Steve pulled out his notebook and flipped to a clean page.

"There's Jonathan McCabe," Harry began. "He's the CEO of McCabe Industries. Spends most of his time traveling between his estate in Santa Barbara and the corporate offices in San Francisco. Second on the list is Evelyn Von Zant. Local socialite. Old family, old money."

"You don't mean Mother Teresa?" Steve said.

"Mother Teresa?" Jamie repeated uncertainly. She looked from Harry to Steve for an explanation.

"She's a local do-gooder," Steve offered. "Always involved in charitable causes. A few years ago she spearheaded a fund-raiser that netted close to a million dollars to feed the homeless. The press dubbed her the Mother Teresa of Los Angeles."

"And you think she did it?"

"There's a lot more to that woman than charity fund-raisers, Jamie," Harry interjected. "She's an avid collector of Early American coins, and has bent the rules more than once in her search for pieces. From what I hear, she's one tough broad."

He glanced back at Steve. "Third is Marcus Saritsky. His collection is *supposed* to be one of the best in the world. Supposed to be, because he won't let anyone see it. He's as crazy as Howard Hughes was and probably has twice as much money." Harry frowned. "And finally, there's Kwon Liu Chin."

Steve stopped writing and looked up. "Liu Chin? Isn't he involved in the Chinese underworld?"

Harry smiled. "He's a businessman, Steve. Like all the other drug dealers in L.A. Anyway, he's been collecting Early American coins for a few years now, even before he moved here from Hong Kong. He has both the interest *and* the money to acquire the doubloon. He wouldn't have any qualms about killing anyone, but I doubt Liu Chin arranged the heist."

"Why?" she asked, puzzled. Of all the collectors mentioned, Liu Chin seemed the most likely suspect.

Harry turned toward her. "You said the man in the elevator had bleached blond hair. That he was either Hispanic or Anglo. Liu Chin only employs Chinese."

Steve said, "Maybe he just brought in some outside talent to throw off the police."

"Believe me, Liu Chin's not that smart. But he'd buy the coin if it were available—just like the rest. And he wouldn't ask any questions about the legality of the sale, either."

Steve nodded and jotted the information down in his notebook. Suddenly the cat jumped off Jamie's lap and padded across the floor to the open doorway.

"If you think it would help," Harry said, "you can borrow my copy of the doubloon. At least it'll give you a better idea of what you're looking for than a photograph."

"You have a copy of the doubloon?" Jamie asked, intrigued.

"The Washington Doubloon's one of the most counterfeited coins in the world, Jamie. Scams have abounded since old Nathan first minted the damn thing. Mine was made by Jimmy Morales back in the early sixties. You're probably too young to remember Jimmy," Harry said to Steve, "but he was a master craftsman. One of the best counterfeiters around till he got sent up to Quentin for trying to dupe some treasury plates.

"The coin's solid fourteen karat," Harry continued, "worth about three hundred dollars on the open market. Unless you run a few tests, it'll pass for the genuine article. I'll have Kimmie drop it by your office this afternoon."

Steve smiled and stood up. "Thanks, Harry."

Jamie retrieved her purse from the floor and rose to her

feet, brushing off the cat hair that clung to the front of her dress.

"No problem," Harry said. "And I'll make a few inquiries. I haven't heard any rumors on the street about a private auction, but if they're planning one, word will get out. Especially if Liu Chin is involved." He smiled. "It's a small neighborhood."

"I'd appreciate it," Steve said from the door, lifting his hand in farewell.

Minutes later, Jamie settled back against the sun-warmed leather of the Acura and fastened her seat belt, trying to ignore the persistent growl of her stomach. Breakfast had been nothing more substantial than a toasted bagel and—she glanced at her watch—it was already past twelve. Steve either heard her stomach growl or felt the same hunger, because he suddenly suggested they get some lunch.

At a Burger King a few blocks away, she quickly ate her cheeseburger and fries, glancing furtively at him between bites as the silence between them lengthened. What dark thoughts were swirling around in his head now? she wondered with concern. Although he hadn't brought the subject up with either Lieutenant Abrams or Harry Chung, she doubted if his mistaken belief in his own culpability had vanished overnight.

Especially since Gary Dodsworth had been his best friend.

Running the tip of her index finger down the side of the perspiring plastic cup, she allowed her gaze to be drawn to the smooth curve of his cheek, then up to the shock of tousled brown hair tumbling across his forehead. She felt her stomach do a familiar somersault. Almost against her will, she found herself wanting to reach out and brush his hair back into place, but resisted the impulse. Such tender feelings, she tried to remind herself, were as counterfeit as the coin Harry Chung had told them about. They weren't based upon shared character traits or common goals or even mutual respect, but rather on a fleeting physical attraction. An attraction momentarily heightened by the threat of danger and her compassion for a guilt-ridden man.

She took a deep breath and closed her eyes. Yet what she'd felt last night in his arms was stronger, more powerful, than anything she'd ever experienced before. Counterfeit emotions or not, she *had* wanted him. And wanted him with a hunger that shook her to the core of her being.

She opened her eyes and frowned. "So what happens next?" she asked, forcing her thoughts back to business. She dropped her crumpled napkin on the plastic tray.

He glanced at his watch. "I want to run a background check on the names Harry gave me, see what comes up."

"You think one of them is the buyer?"

"Seems reasonable. And if we find the buyer, we may be able to find the seller. I also want to track Gary's movements on Sunday afternoon to see if we can figure out where he dropped the coin." He drained the soda from his cup and frowned.

"But right now I've got to go to Gary's funeral." Weariness began to color his voice. "You're welcome to come if you like, or I can swing by the station and have Lou watch you for a couple of hours." He met her gaze. "The choice is yours."

Her answer was immediate. "I'd like to go to the funeral."

Though if her decision was more out of concern for Steve than a reluctance to see Lieutenant Abrams again, she couldn't say.

It was probably safer that way.

Forest Lawn was almost too beautiful for a cemetery, Jamie thought, casting a quick look around. Rolling green hills dotted with marble statues of winged angels. Flowering azaleas and bougainvilleas. Shady elms.

She heard a muffled sob and turned back to face the gravesite as the minister slowly opened a leather-bound

Bible. "Loving husband. Devoted father. Trusted friend. Gary Dodsworth was all of these . . ."

From beside her, Steve drew a sharp intake of breath, his body tensing. Impulsively, she reached for his hand, feeling his fingers wrap around hers and squeeze.

Then the sob came again, softer this time, but just as heartbreaking.

She glanced to her right. Gary's widow stood beside their two teenage children. She was in her early fifties, Jamie guessed; thin, with short auburn hair, wearing a black suit, a black pillbox hat and dark sunglasses. Gary's daughter, blond and fair-skinned like her father, cried softly against her older brother's shoulder, while the boy, his auburn hair gleaming in the afternoon sun, struggled hard to keep his emotions in check.

Jamie felt like an intruder and quickly turned away. It had been a closed service, with less than twenty people in attendance. Mostly the immediate family and a few close friends. She scanned the faces of the mourners as the eulogy continued, stopping when she came to a tall woman with graying black hair and horn-rimmed glasses. *Mona*, her subconscious supplied. *Steve's secretary*. The woman was dabbing at her eyes with a white linen handkerchief. Jamie was about to look away when she saw a flash of light from over the woman's shoulder.

Curious, she craned her neck and saw a man, almost obscured by a row of oleanders near the parked cars, taking pictures of the services. A second person stood beside him, but all Jamie could make out was an arm. The oleanders hid the rest.

She frowned. A couple of reporters were all they needed right now. Maybe she should ask one of the attendants . . .

Steve tightened his grip on her hand, and she saw that everyone had bowed his or her head in prayer. She followed suit. Moments later, the mourners began moving toward the family to pay their last respects.

Steve and Jamie walked back to the car in silence, still holding hands. She noted his ashen complexion, the rigid set of his jaw, and felt a twist of pain. He'd spoken briefly with Gary's widow when they had first arrived, the traditional murmuring of condolence offered and accepted.

From what she'd observed, Jamie didn't think Chris Dodsworth blamed Steve for her husband's death. Not that absolution from Chris was what Steve sought, she reminded herself. It wasn't that simple. He wanted absolution from himself, and that would take a long time in coming.

If it ever came at all.

She squeezed his hand and felt his fingers tighten around hers in response.

Trusted friend.

Forty-five minutes later, the elevator doors swooshed open onto the reception area of Flynn Security, and Jamie and Steve stepped out. A tall, thin black woman in her late twenties sat behind the counter at the telephone console. She looked up and sighed in exaggerated relief at the sight of Steve.

"Am I glad to see you," she said, rising to her feet.

"What's up?"

The woman handed him a stack of pink message slips a half inch thick. "Jim Rothenberg's been phoning every fifteen minutes for the past couple of hours. Says he has to speak with you. Today, if possible. I swear, the man's about to drive me crazy."

Steve frowned. "Anything else?" He shuffled through the phone messages.

"The rest are self-explanatory. Nothing urgent as far as I can tell. You did get a delivery, though." She reached under the counter and removed a small brown envelope. "Kim Chung dropped this off for you about an hour ago."

"Thanks, Yvonne." He took the envelope and started walking back toward his office with Jamie beside him. "Is Tony here?"

The telephone rang. "He just stepped out a few minutes

ago,'' Yvonne said, raising her voice. "Should be back soon—said he was working late.''

"I need to talk to him,'' he called back.

Jamie followed him into his office and closed the door. He crossed the room to his desk, slipping his index finger under the sealed flap of the envelope. He shook out the coin, examined it, then handed it to her.

"I'd better call Rothenberg before we get started,'' he said. "Sounds like the man's coming unglued.''

She nodded, running her fingers over the smooth gold surface of the doubloon. Harry was right, she thought. The coin looked as if it could've been minted two centuries earlier. Most of the soaring eagle's feathers had been worn away, and the wreath of olive branches around Washington's head was barely visible. She shrugged and slipped the coin back into the envelope as Steve was replacing the receiver.

"Busy signal,'' he grumbled. He pulled open a desk drawer, removed a heavy manila file and passed it over to her. "Most of what I've got is in here. Mona's still working on a few reports, though. We can get them in the morning.'' Then he picked up the telephone receiver again.

"Okay.'' She sat down on the edge of the desk.

After the funeral, Steve had decided to drop by the office and run the background checks on the list of collectors they'd gotten from Harry Chung. Because he also wanted to review the case file and start tracking Gary's movements, Jamie had volunteered to help wade through the paperwork, organize the data. Surprisingly, he had accepted her offer.

She skimmed through the file, making a mental note of its contents. The passenger manifest from the flight. Statements from the flight crew. Even a written transcript of her conversation with him in the hotel coffee shop on Monday morning. She smiled and closed the file. Incredibly well organized. She doubted if she could have done a better job herself.

She heard him replace the receiver and looked up. He was transferring the collectors' names from his notebook to a legal pad.

"I think the easiest way to do this is to make a chart," she said. "We could use a piece of poster board and map out Gary's movements from the airport in chronological order, based upon your records."

"Good idea. We'll grab whatever materials we need from the supply room on our way out." He capped the pen and glanced at his watch. "I'll have Tony begin working on these names first thing tomorrow. It's nearly six now. What say we go home and start on the chart after dinner?" He stood and walked around the desk. "You like pizza?"

"I love it as long as it has pepperoni and black olives with extra cheese." She slid off the desk.

"My kind of woman. I can see we'll get along fine."

Deciding to let the comment slide, she tucked the envelope containing the coin into her purse, then grabbed the file and followed him to the supply room. When they arrived at the front office a few minutes later, Yvonne was replacing the receiver.

"When Tony gets back, tell him I want a background check started first thing tomorrow." Steve handed the receptionist the folded sheet of paper. "I want a preliminary on my desk by ten, and a completed report in seventy-two hours. He can call me at home if he has any questions."

Yvonne nodded, jotting down the instructions in a spiral-bound assignment book. "What about Rothenberg? He was insistent that he speak with you today."

He punched the button for the elevator and glanced at Jamie. "Look, his office is over on Beverly, about twenty minutes away. Would you mind if we swung by there on our way home?"

She shrugged. "Okay with me."

The elevator doors slid open.

Moments later, they stepped out into the subterranean parking lot. The Acura was parked less than twenty feet away in one of the spaces assigned for Flynn Security. They walked quietly toward the car, the click of her high heels on the concrete echoing through the nearly empty parking structure. From farther back in the garage, a car engine started.

"The trip to Rothenberg's office shouldn't take long. The auction's a week from tomorrow, so I still have a little more time under our contract before I *have* to produce the doubloon. I'll just remind him of that, make a few excuses and leave."

"You can't stall forever. Rothenberg will have to know sooner or later that the coin's missing."

Steve frowned. "Yeah, well—"

They both heard the screech of rubber on the concrete and turned. A long black limo sped forward, the front passenger window slowly opening. When the car got even with the Acura, a gunman extended his black, gloved hand. Steve cursed.

Before Jamie could react, she heard the sharp report of a gun blast, followed by the shattering of glass. Then Steve fell against her, knocking her to the pavement.

She felt his dead weight crushing against her, his head resting unmovingly against her shoulder.

She screamed.

EIGHT

Jamie screamed again. She frantically pressed her palms against Steve's chest but couldn't budge him.

Oh, God, no! she prayed. *Please don't let him be dead.*

Then he groaned. He slowly rolled off her to the concrete, his eyes squeezed shut as a spasm of pain crossed his face.

Relief gave way to instinctive action. She sat up and tugged at his brown jacket. She had to find the gunshot wound. Stop the bleeding.

"Just lie still. I'll call an ambulance, and—"

"Has anyone ever mentioned you have a scream that could shatter concrete?"

She stared at him for a long moment, unable to comprehend what she'd just heard. Then she relaxed her grip on his jacket. "I take it this means you're okay."

His eyes opened. He met her gaze and flashed a crooked smile. "Other than a ruptured eardrum and a few bruises, yeah." He sat up and gave her a quick once-over. "How about you?"

She glanced at her torn hose, the grease stains on her dress. Under the circumstances, she was just fine. She nodded.

He stood and walked around the car, assessing the damage. As far as he could tell, the bullet had shattered the rear window of the Acura, sending bits of glass flying over the backseat. By now, the limo was long gone, the parking garage eerily silent. The stench of burning rubber hung in the air.

He raked his fingers through his hair. "Damn."

"That's putting it mildly." She struggled to her feet and walked over to where he stood. "Tell me, do these kinds of things happen to you often?"

He glanced at her in surprise. "You didn't see him, then?"

"The gunman?" She shook her head. "I just caught a glimpse of a black, gloved hand, that's all. Did you?"

"Briefly." He paused, then met her gaze. "He was blond."

A chill ran down her spine. She grasped his arm. "The pirate! He's knows I'm with you."

"Obviously." His voice had acquired a hollow, defeated tone she'd never heard from him before. "And his message is pretty clear. He wants me to back off the investigation." He stared down at the car. "Maybe I should listen to him."

"You can't be serious. You can't give up now."

His jaw tightened. "Looks like I don't have much choice. The risks are getting too high."

She continued to stare at him, too surprised to do much else. A few hours before, he'd been determined to continue the investigation no matter what the risk. The pirate took one potshot at them and Steve was willing to walk away. The abrupt turnabout didn't make any sense.

Then just as suddenly it did. He wanted to back off because he knew *he* wasn't the gunman's target.

She was.

She swallowed hard, fighting down a wave of nausea.

"So that's it?" she asked. "You'll just let him get away with it?"

"He won't get away with anything. The police'll find him. Just as they'll ultimately find the informant. I'll concentrate on protecting you and figuring out where Gary stashed the coin.''

And spend the rest of my life blaming myself for Gary's death, she silently added.

She looked him square in the eye. "Funny, I never thought you'd be the kind to turn tail and run.''

He stiffened. "I'm not running.''

"Aren't you?''

"Damn it, Jamie! Don't you think I've jeopardized your safety enough for one week? If I don't back off, it may get you killed.''

"Look.'' Her voice was equally as harsh. "If the pirate wanted to kill me, I'd be dead.'' She opened the car door and brushed off pieces of pebbled glass from the front passenger seat. She saw the bullet lodged in the dashboard and blanched. "The shot was a warning. Like the snapshots. This was just his little way of reminding me that he wants the doubloon.''

"And what if his . . . *reminder* . . . takes a more serious bent next time?''

"Who says we have to give him another opportunity? I think it's high time we started kicking some butts and taking down some names.'' She climbed into the car and folded her arms against her chest. "All I want to know is, are you coming with me or do I have to go alone?''

He stared at her for a moment, his expression guarded.

Then he relaxed, a slow grin crossing his face. "*Definitely* my kind of woman.''

It was seven o'clock when Steve parked in the small lot directly behind Hathaway and Ferris Galleries in Beverly Hills.

"You think Rothenberg's gone home for the day?'' Jamie glanced around the nearly vacant parking lot with concern.

"His car's still here.'' He nodded toward a brown Jaguar parked to their left. "We'll have to ring the buzzer to announce our arrival, though. The doors are locked after five."

Minutes later, she followed him to the rear door of the two-story brick building. He pressed the intercom buzzer and waited. Twenty seconds passed. Thirty. No reply. He pressed the buzzer again, his brow lowering in a puzzled frown.

"Maybe he went home after all," Jamie suggested.

Steve grasped the doorknob and twisted. The door popped open. He shot her a skeptical glance. "Without locking the door?"

Feeling a knot form in her stomach, she stepped inside the small entryway after him. A closed door lay directly ahead; a narrow staircase, to their right.

She followed him up the steep flight of stairs to the second floor. He turned left into a waiting room adjoining an executive suite, then stopped. Slowly he scanned the area, his cautiousness adding to her own uneasiness. But nothing seemed out of place. A stream of air from the cooling vents gently moved the leaves of a six-foot ficus placed next to a cream-colored sofa in the corner of the anteroom. The secretary's desk was cleared for the night, the typewriter covered, a stack of papers neatly arranged beside it. All was as it should be.

A light shone through the partially open door of the office beyond. Steve frowned and slowly moved toward the door. "Jim? It's Stephen Flynn. I rang the buzzer, but you didn't answer." He pushed the door open.

Jamie took two steps into the office and ran full tilt into Steve. Then his arm came around her and he turned, pushing her back toward the waiting room.

"What's wrong? Isn't he in there?" she asked.

"Wait for me in the other room." His face was ashen as he met her gaze. "You *don't* want to come in here."

"Why? Steve, let go of me." She struggled out of his grip and looked past him into the office.

A man was slumped over a huge oak desk in the center of the room. Matted blood covered the side of his head.

She drew a sharp breath. "Rothenberg?"

Steve walked over to the desk. "Yeah."

"Is he . . . dead?"

He checked for a pulse in the man's throat. "Very."

She swallowed hard and looked away. When she glanced back, Steve was examining Rothenberg's desk, carefully moving sheets of paper around with the tip of a pencil.

"What are you *doing*? We have to phone the police!"

He nodded, but continued with his examination nonetheless. "I will, just as soon as I've completed my search." He glanced back at her. "Why don't you wait for me in the other room?" he suggested with concern. "You look a little pale."

Pale? She almost laughed. She was standing less than ten feet away from a dead man. Just how did he *expect* her to look?

"I'm okay." She tried not to stare at the hideous sight slumped on the desk, even though she felt strangely compelled to do so. Something about the corpse looked familiar, but she couldn't place him. Where could she have . . . ?

Then it hit her. Rothenberg was the man she'd seen leaving Steve's office the day before. The man who'd seemed so nervous.

She took a deep breath and forced her gaze away. She caught a glimpse then of something protruding from behind the desk and took a closer look. It was a marble paperweight.

A decidedly *nasty-looking* paperweight.

The knot in her stomach tightened. "There's, ah . . . something over there I think you should see. It looks like it's covered with blood."

Steve walked behind the desk and knelt by the paperweight, careful not to touch it. "Probably the murder weapon," he said matter-of-factly, then stood and visually examined the telephone receiver dangling at the end of its long cord over the side of the desk. The bottle of scotch and the empty glass sitting next to the phone. Then he stared intently at Rothenberg's right hand.

"Jesus," Steve breathed, turning a little pale himself.

"What is it?"

"His watch. It's been shattered . . . along with most of his wrist."

"Shattered?" she echoed hollowly.

"Yeah." He reached for a cube-shaped memo pad a few inches away from the dead man's hand. "Looks like the killer used the paperweight on Rothenberg's hand." He peered at the top sheet for a moment, then carefully peeled it off and slipped it into his jacket pocket. "Wonder why."

She groaned. Great. Just great. Now he was removing the evidence altogether.

She closed her eyes and leaned against the door, feeling the metal doorknob press painfully into the small of her back.

"Hey, are you all right?" Steve asked softly moments later. Without waiting for her answer, he slid his hand around her waist and led her into the waiting room. "No arguments this time, Jamaica. I want you to stay put."

"Stop calling me that. I'm fine. Or I would be if you'd stop tampering with the evidence and call the police like you should have in the first place."

He looked surprised. "*Tampering with evidence?* What happened to 'kicking butts and taking down names'?" A trace of amusement colored his voice. "I thought you wanted me to continue the investigation."

"I do want you to continue, but I meant by the rules. And removing evidence from a crime scene"—she gestured toward the open office—"is a definite no-no."

"Hey, relax. Trust me. I know what I'm doing."

"So do I. That's the problem." She stared him down. "Are you going to call the police or do I have to?"

His smile slowly faded. "I'll call them." Then he walked over to the secretary's desk and lifted the receiver.

She sat on the edge of the cream-colored sofa and eyed

him warily as he punched in the number, not at all sure if he was phoning the police or the corner delicatessen. The man was incorrigible. First he lied. Then he removed evidence. Lord only knew what he would do next.

He hung up the receiver a moment later. "A squad car's on the way."

"Thank you."

"You know, there's really no need for you to . . ." He glanced down at the open pages of the appointment calendar and smiled. "Well, what do you know about that?"

"What?"

"Rothenberg had an appointment with Evelyn Von Zant tonight around six." With a familiar gleam in his eyes, he reached for the appointment calendar.

"There is no way I'm letting you leave with that thing, Flynn," she quickly warned, rising to her feet. "*Trust me*. The police will notice the book's missing."

"I'm not planning to take it, Jamie, I just want to check—ahh. Just as I thought."

"What is?" She walked over to the desk and scanned the page for Monday.

"Rothenberg had appointments with both Marcus Saritsky and Jonathan McCabe this week—Saritsky on Monday and McCabe yesterday afternoon. They were on the list Harry gave us."

"But they're all legitimate collectors. They could have wanted to discuss any number of acquisitions."

He picked up the appointment book. "But what do you want to bet they all wanted to discuss the Washington Doubloon?" He walked out into the hallway.

"Where are you going now?" she asked suspiciously, trailing after him.

He stopped across the hall in front of a photocopier and placed the calender facedown on the machine. "I'm photocopying evidence, if that's okay with you."

They heard the wail of the police siren in the distance, and he cursed softly. From the speed with which he moved, she deduced that Steve thought the police wouldn't approve of his unorthodox investigative techniques any more than she did.

Once the appointment book was restored to its original position on the secretary's desk, he grabbed her hand. "Come on, we'll meet them downstairs." He folded the photocopies with his free hand and stuffed them into an inside jacket pocket as they headed for the main stairwell.

That was when Jamie noticed the closed-circuit TV camera installed near the juncture of the wall and the ceiling. The lens was pointed straight at the doorway to Rothenberg's office.

"Security cameras usually operate around the clock, don't they?" she asked, an idea slowly forming in her mind.

"Yeah, why?"

"Well, there's a camera installed near the doorway. Maybe it caught Rothenberg's murderer on tape."

Steve cursed under his breath.

Stopping at the edge of the stairwell and releasing her hand, he turned and walked over to a closed, unmarked door across the hall without saying another word.

She frowned. "Where are you—*Steve*?" She went after him.

He stood inside a room no larger than a broom closet, examining the row of high-tech video equipment lining the metal shelf. The front of the center machine had been pried open, a cluster of multicolored wires dangling out of the hole. "The recorder's been tampered with," he said. "The tape's missing."

"Missing?" She looked at the broken video equipment with confusion. "But how would the murderer know where to find the tape? For that matter, how did *you* know where to look?"

He ran his hand along the rim of the metal shelf. "Easy. Flynn Security installed the security system."

"Oh." Then the impact of his words sank in. *"Oh, no."*

He met her gaze and frowned. "My sentiments exactly."

When they arrived back at the house two hours later, all Jamie wanted to do was take a hot shower and fall into bed. No more evidence analysis. No more police interrogations. And *definitely* no more dead bodies.

In fact, she felt quite sure she'd had enough mental stimulation to last her for a lifetime. Any more, and her brain would probably short-circuit.

She shrugged out of her jacket as Steve telephoned Lieutenant Abrams to fill him in on the shooting in the garage and their discovery of Rothenberg's body. Since both incidents had occurred in other police precincts, Steve felt—uncharacteristically so, in her opinion—that his detective friend should be apprised of the developments.

While he made the call, she went to her room to change. Her two suitcases, she noticed with relief, sat beside the bed.

Fifteen minutes later, after a relaxing hot shower, she checked on Steve one last time before retiring for the night. She found him sitting at a desk in the den, huddled over the sheet of paper he'd lifted from Rothenberg's office. A wide array of noxious-smelling chemicals sat in vials nearby. He was mixing chemicals together in a small dish like some mad scientist from the late-late show.

Now what was he up to?

On second thought, she probably didn't want to know.

"I thought you had turned that over to the police."

He smiled. "And I thought you had gone to bed."

She tightened the sash on her terry-cloth bathrobe. "I am going, in a few minutes. What . . . ?" She gestured at the desk.

He returned his attention to his experiment. "The sheet I took from Rothenberg's notepad had indentations on it from an earlier notation. I'm trying to reconstruct the wording."

"Why don't you trying rubbing a pencil across the surface?"

He shook his head. "The indentations are too illegible for that. Might not work. Besides, Rothenberg used a felt-tip pen, and he didn't exert a lot of pressure."

"Felt tip? How do you know *that*?"

"I saw the open pen on his desk. Anyway, I figure we've got two possibilities." He added a few drops of iodine to the compound. "Either Rothenberg wrote a note while the killer was in the room, as a means of identifying him, and got caught in the act, or"—he peered at the compound curiously—"the memo's not related. It could be nothing more than a reminder to himself to pick up the dry cleaning on the way home." He set the vial of iodine back on the desk.

"Personally, I think the first alternative is more viable, since the note looks unfinished and the original's missing. My guess is Rothenberg was writing the note when he was struck. He raised his arm to ward off the attack. The paperweight hit his wrist, shattering the watch along with the bone." He slowly swirled the dish.

Jamie felt her stomach lurch. Steve's analysis of Rothenberg's murder was so cold, impersonal. She knew the two men had been friends—friendly enough for a weekly game of racquetball, at any rate—so how could he just turn off his emotions like they were a household appliance? She hadn't even known Jim Rothenberg, but the memory of having seen his lifeless body would haunt her for a long, long time.

"So what's that stuff you're making?" she asked, focusing her attention on the strange concoction in the dish.

"This? It's just a little technique I learned in chem lab at UCLA. It restores indented writing."

"What course was that? Dirty Tricks One-oh-one?"

He laughed. "Close. Criminal Investigations—Documentation Handling. What this should do," he said, lightly brushing the mixture over the sheet of paper, "is highlight the alterations in the fiber structure." He held up the sheet to the light. "In other words, make the writing reappear. Like so."

She glanced at the paper. Almost like magic, a series of numbers appeared. Underneath them, in less legible script, was the letter *Y*. Or *V*. She couldn't be sure which.

"What is it? The combination to a safe?"

He shook his head. "Don't think so. It's got seven digits. Probably a phone number. The prefix looks like East L.A."

She yawned. "You planning to call the number tonight?"

He looked up at her, his face softening. "Nah. It'll wait till morning. Why don't you go get some sleep? You look beat."

She nodded and went to bed.

Steve sat in the leather swivel chair staring after her, a soft smile lifting the corners of his mouth. Why did he feel as if he'd known her for years, instead of just a few days? That having her at his side, in his life, was the most natural thing in the world. They fit. Meshed. Blended so beautifully.

He glanced at the sheet of paper in his hand and frowned. But he had other obligations at present. The drive-by shooting had illustrated the danger Jamaica was still in. The danger *he* was ultimately responsible for having caused. Pursuing a relationship would only intensify that danger. Yet . . .

Yet he couldn't stop thinking about her. Couldn't stop remembering the way she'd felt in his arms. So soft. So right. And he couldn't forget the raw, aching need she'd aroused in him with a single kiss.

Which, once he thought about it, was probably far more dangerous than anything the pirate could throw at them.

NINE

Jamie awoke at a few minutes after seven the next morning, her mind already awhirl with plans for the day. They needed to establish Gary's itinerary. Follow up the names of the collectors they'd received from Harry Chung. Investigate the telephone number Steve had lifted from Rothenberg's office.

The sooner they started, the better.

As she walked into the hall, tugging on her bathrobe, an alarm clock went off in Steve's bedroom. She heard him mumble a curse; fumbling noises followed as though he were groping for an object on a bedside table.

She glanced toward the partially open door at the end of the hall and smiled, picturing his tousled hair and little-boy-lost expression. Flynn was damnably attractive at any time, but he had an early morning sexiness she found difficult to resist.

Suddenly a foam rubber baseball—an unusually noisy baseball, she thought with surprise—hurtled past her, just missing her head by inches. It landed with a thud on the carpeting three feet away.

"What in the . . . ?" She placed both hands on her hips, then glanced from the ball to Steve's bedroom.

Heavy paws pounded on the carpet from the direction

117

of the living room. Rex raced past her, the baseball in his mouth, and burst into Steve's bedroom, pushing the door all the way open. She waited. All she could see was the edge of a bureau and a pair of shoes lying on the pale blue carpeting. Seconds passed. Then Steve cursed again—more emphatically this time—the dog barked and she heard someone hit the floor.

Stifling a laugh, she turned and walked toward the kitchen to make a pot of coffee.

Something told her Steve was going to need it.

An hour later, Steve sat in the swivel chair in his make-shift office and reviewed the chart Jamie had started while he was taking a shower. She'd drawn a graph, blocking out time in twelfth-of-an-hour intervals, and was now transferring the information from the case file on Gary's movements to the poster board resting on an easel a few feet from his desk.

"So he phoned the office at 12:21," she said, penning the item on the chart.

"Right." Steve took a long swallow of coffee, savoring its dark, rich taste. He'd begun to think the only thing bearable about mornings these days was Jamie's coffee.

He casually glanced over at her. She was wearing the tight blue skirt again, he noticed with approval. The one with the slit up the back that showed a mile and a half of legs.

He smiled. Better make that *two* things that made mornings bearable.

"Okay, so, according to the desk clerk, Gary delivered the message to me at 2:35. How could he be so precise?"

"The clerk said Gary asked the time when he left the note." Still smiling, Steve forced his gaze back up to her face. "It's an old trick. Gary knew I'd be questioning the hotel staff if something happened. By asking the time, he assumed that the incident would stand out in the clerk's memory when I came by."

"Very clever." Jamie turned back to the easel. "So where was he for the two hours in between?"

"Don't know. It would've taken him about forty-five minutes to get from LAX to the Hilton. Maybe less, since it was a Sunday. How long were you with him in the baggage-pickup area?"

"Not long. Maybe ten, fifteen minutes."

Steve rose and walked over to where she stood. "Okay. Giving him about five minutes to walk to the baggage area after calling the office, then fifteen minutes to talk to you, brings us up to 12:40." He took the pen from her hand and scribbled the additional guesswork on the board. When he finished, the result still left an hour unexplained. An hour during which Gary could have done almost anything with the coin.

"Still no good," she said, reaching for her coffee mug on the desk behind them.

He reviewed the chart, then glanced down at the case file. He knew the answer to the missing hour had to be there. The only question was which seemingly unimportant detail about Gary's movements contained the vital clue.

"If we could just figure out why Gary went to the hotel."

Jamie looked surprised. "I thought he was trying to see me."

"Yeah. But why? He didn't give you the coin, so he wasn't trying to retrieve it." Steve frowned as an idea began to form, nebulous at first, then slowly becoming more concrete. "Gary *could* have followed the pirate to the hotel." He began pacing around the small office, one hand in his trouser pocket, the other tapping the pen against his thigh. "Knowing the pirate was following *you* because of the faked handoff at the airport. Maybe Gary realized it was out of control, that his plan had backfired, and he wanted to warn you."

"Maybe, but considering what happened next, I doubt it."

He glanced at her for clarification.

"If the pirate thought I had the doubloon, why grab Gary?"

Steve came to an abrupt stop in front of the easel, his shoulders slumped. "I guess he wouldn't." He sighed, dropping the pen on the desk.

Jamie drained the last of her coffee. "Want a refill?"

He nodded and handed her his half-empty mug. She left for the kitchen.

He walked to the other side of the desk and picked up the sheet of paper he'd taken from Rothenberg's office. He studied the number again, although he'd already committed it to memory. Glancing at his watch to establish the time, he lifted the receiver and pressed the digits. He gave up after the seventh ring. Chances were they could spend most of the morning calling the number and get the same results. Time was one thing he couldn't afford to waste right now.

Especially since he had other options.

Brightening, he pulled the Rolodex toward him and flipped to the entry he wanted. Then he picked up the receiver again and punched in the number, mentally rehearsing his approach. The line was ringing when Jamie returned with the coffee.

Minutes later, he had the information. The number was listed to an Ynez Miranda at 154 Arguello in East Los Angeles.

"Do correct me if I'm wrong," Jamie murmured disapprovingly as he replaced the receiver, "but isn't impersonating a telephone repairman against the law?"

He grinned. "Probably. But I needed to get the name and address to go with this number. Normal channels would've taken too long." And they would have required his explaining to Lou Abrams exactly *how* he'd come by the number, a little fact he wasn't ready to divulge.

Not yet, anyway.

He studied the scrawled initial on the sheet of paper, the downward slant of the right bar of the squiggly *V*. It could be a *Y*. A *Y* for Ynez. Although he'd assumed Jim's killer was a man, there was no reason a woman *couldn't* have struck the death blow. Wielding the small paperweight wouldn't have required much strength—only determination. He tossed the idea around in his head for a moment. Nothing clicked. He slipped the paper into his notebook.

"So what do we do now?" Jamie asked.

"We go to the office and check it out." Then he shrugged into his jacket and headed for the door, Jamie fast behind him.

When they arrived at Flynn Security thirty minutes later, the preliminary background checks were waiting on Mona's desk. Steve retrieved them, gave Mona a slip of paper containing Ynez Miranda's address and telephone number and instructed her to run a background check.

He gave a cursory glance to the computer printouts on the collectors as he and Jamie walked into his office. Most, with the notable exception of Kwon Liu Chin, were the stereotypical pillars of their respective communities. But if Harry was right—which he usually was—the complete background reports should prove to be very interesting reading.

After handing half of the printouts to Jamie to review, he picked up one of the remaining two and settled back in his chair. Evelyn Von Zant. Single. Born October 12, 1942. Only child of industrialist Peter Von Zant, now deceased. His gaze dropped lower. The rest of the bio read like a request for canonization. Founding member, Southern California Society for Environmental Conservation. Chairperson, Mayor's Committee on the Homeless. Patron of the arts and humanities.

Frowning, he reached for the phone.

Seconds later, a woman answered.

"Good morning," he said, trying to insinuate every ounce of charm he possessed into the simple greeting. "Would it be possible to speak with Ms. Von Zant?"

A few minutes past ten, Steve parked the Acura in the curving driveway of Evelyn Von Zant's Bel-Air home.

Mindful of the pebbles of glass from the shattered rear window still dusting the front seat, Jamie climbed out of the car. She gave the estate a quick appraisal as she straightened her skirt.

A well-manicured lawn swept for several hundred yards in either direction. Neatly trimmed hedges about two feet high bordered the front of the Tudor-style brick house. Directly across from the four-car garage, luxuriant green vines climbed a wooden trellis attached to the left half of the house. Impressive, Jamie thought. The price of maintaining the front lawn alone probably cost more than her monthly rent.

Steve lifted the brass knocker on the stately double doors and rapped once. He and Jamie waited a minute; then he rapped on the door again, louder this time.

"She did say come right over, didn't she?"

"Yeah, that's what she said." Frowning, he looked down the front of the house toward the edge of the vine-covered trellis and the garage beyond. A brick pathway leading around to the rear of the house was partially visible between the two buildings.

"Come on, let's see if she's around back." Then he set out for the path before Jamie could convince him otherwise. She hoisted the sliding straps of her purse and followed.

When they got to the stone patio near the rear of the house, the cloyingly sweet scent of roses rushed out to greet them. The smell was overpowering, making the air itself seem stifling, closed. Row upon row of well-tended roses of every imaginable shade lined the grounds for several hundred feet past the patio. Farther back, a short, stooped figure in a floppy hat and an oversized jacket was kneeling over a flowering crimson bush.

"Hello," Steve hailed, stopping at the threshold to the patio.

The figure turned to look in their direction, a pair of pruning shears dangling from one hand. "Good morning," a female voice called back. She dropped the tool, dusted her heavy work gloves against each other and began walking toward them.

When she came closer, Jamie could see that the woman was around fifty, plain—though pleasantly so—and tending toward plumpness. She was, Jamie decided after a quick perusal, the kind of woman you'd pass on the street every day and never notice. Self-effacing. Quiet.

Ordinary.

The woman drew off her gloves and smiled. "Mr. Flynn?"

"Yes."

She removed the large, floppy hat to reveal soft, graying curls. "How do you do. I'm Evelyn Von Zant." She extended her hand. "I apologize for not greeting you at the door, but Thursday is the servants' day off and," she said, smiling warmly at Jamie, "I usually tend to my roses then. Please, won't you sit down?" She nodded to a wicker-and-glass table and matching chairs a few feet away on the stone patio.

"I appreciate your seeing us on such short notice," Steve said as he followed the woman to the table. He nodded toward Jamie. "This is my associate, Miss Klindsmidt."

Klindsmidt? Jamie felt like kicking him, but somehow resisted the urge. "How do you do," she murmured politely instead.

Von Zant smiled. "Would you care for some tea?" She sat down and indicated the pitcher of iced tea and the four tall glasses sitting in the heavy silver tray atop the table.

"Thank you." Steve took a seat across from her.

"Do you take lemon, Miss Klindsmidt?"

"Yes, please," Jamie said, sinking into the thick floral cushions on the wicker chair.

Von Zant passed the glasses of tea around, then leaned back, her chin at an upward tilt. Her hands were folded demurely in her lap, her expression one of studied politeness. She reminded Jamie then of a Southern grande dame holding court—the epitome of genteel refinement and good breeding.

But those ladies, Jamie recalled with a sudden chill, often had another trait far less laudable—the frightening ability to wield power with a single, soft-spoken word.

She shifted her position in the chair, smoothing out the folds in her navy blue skirt.

Von Zant smiled. "So how may I help you, Mr. Flynn?"

He stirred sugar into his tea, then set the spoon aside. "I wanted to talk to you about Jim Rothenberg. I understand you were one of his clients."

Her face grew somber. "Poor, poor man. I received a call this morning from Chief Bernsen about Jim's death." She shook her head. "He should have taken more care to guard against thieves. I understand the back door wasn't even locked."

"You think Jim Rothenberg was killed by a *thief*?" Jamie asked, taking a sip of tea.

"What other possibility is there? It's well known that Hathaway and Ferris keeps valuable stamps and coins in the gallery. A thief must have come in hoping to steal something, ran into Jim and was forced to kill him." Von Zant picked up her linen napkin from the table and spread it across her lap.

"Then he must have been a very eccentric thief." Jamie's voice held a trace of sarcasm. "The only thing he took was the videotape from the security cameras."

Von Zant's eyebrows rose. "Did he really? How odd."

Steve shot Jamie a warning glance, then said, "I understand you had an appointment with Jim yesterday evening."

The woman drank some tea and carefully set the glass on the table before answering. "That's correct. Unfortunately, he canceled our meeting sometime that morning."

Jamie watched the woman, feeling unaccountably suspicious.

Steve smiled. "Were you by chance planning to discuss the Washington Doubloon with him at that meeting?"

Von Zant looked surprised for a moment, but quickly recovered. "How very clever of you to figure that out, Mr. Flynn," she murmured, glancing down. "But then, my collection of Early American coins is well known, as is my interest in the Washington Doubloon." Her fingers moved self-consciously along the length of the linen napkin. "Jim had agreed to grant me a private showing of the coin before the auction next week. The purpose of my meeting yesterday was to view the coin."

Steve's face was an expertly controlled mask. "Did he offer any explanation for the cancellation?"

"He said there were problems, difficulties. But he didn't offer any specific reasons, no."

Jamie took a long swallow of tea, glancing from Steve to the woman and then back again. She recognized the look in his eyes. It was the same one he'd had the day in the hotel coffee shop when he'd grilled her about Gary Dodsworth. Unless Jamie missed her guess, he was about to do the same with Evelyn Von Zant.

"Do you know if Jim was planning to show the coin to any other collectors?" Steve asked.

"Not that he mentioned. But clients of the gallery could always arrange a private showing before an auction."

"Ah. And who might some of the others be?"

Von Zant folded her hands in her lap, the linen napkin tucked under her left hand. "Well, there's Marcus Saritsky and Jonathan McCabe. They're both interested in the doubloon. And I imagine Paul Murphey of the Metropolitan Museum would be as well." She smiled. "The Washington Doubloon is one of a kind, Mr. Flynn. There's none other like it in the world."

"So we've heard," Jamie interjected dryly.

Von Zant glanced at Jamie, then at Steve. "But surely you don't believe Jim's death was related to the doubloon?"

He leaned forward, resting one arm on the table. "It's

certainly beginning to look that way," he said in a con-
spiratorial whisper. "In fact, it appears Jim may have been
involved in a plot to steal the coin."

"Steal it!"

Steve nodded, then settled back in his chair. "Fortunately, he didn't succeed."

Von Zant appeared to relax. "I see." She leaned forward slightly. "Do you have the coin, then?"

Despite Evelyn Von Zant's light, facile tone, Jamie suspected that the woman's interest in the doubloon was far
from casual. Her pale blue eyes had a glitter in them, a
sheen. Her hands tightly clutched the napkin.

Steve folded his napkin in half. "Let's just say Flynn
Security is prepared to proceed with the auction next
week. Whether the gallery feels the same way . . ." He
shrugged.

The woman smiled weakly.

"I want to thank you for your time, Miss Von Zant,"
he said, rising to his feet. "But Agnes and I must be
going now."

Agnes?

Jamie's eyes narrowed as she bent down to retrieve her
purse from the stone patio. This time he had gone too far.

Von Zant rose and walked around the table. "I hope
I've been of some help to you, Mr. Flynn."

"Oh, you've been enormously helpful. Thank you
again."

Jamie forced a tight smile, then followed Steve down
the pathway to the front of the house. She knew the older
woman was watching them and didn't dare say anything
to him.

When they reached the Acura, it was another story.

"Just what is it with you and my name?" she demanded
once he had slid into the seat next to her. "First you call
me Jamaica, then Agnes Klinderhoff!"

"Klindsmidt," he corrected her with a smile. "Agnes was
my third-grade teacher. She had a killer smile and a great
pair of legs." He inserted the key in the ignition and

started the engine. "Personally, I thought it was a pretty good cover."

"But why did *I* need a cover?" She settled back in the passenger seat and fastened her seat belt. "You know, that's your biggest problem. You fabricate tall tales when the simple truth would suffice. Society has rules, regulations, that everyone must obey. Even you. Removing evidence from crime scenes, impersonating telephone repairmen, even lying about my name. These things go against the very fabric of our society. They—"

"And what if Evelyn Von Zant is involved in the plot? Until we identify the players, it's not a good idea to advertise that Jamaica Royale is traveling with me."

"Did you forget the little incident with the limo? The pirate already knows."

He frowned, the worry lines deepening on his forehead. "He may not be the only one we have to be concerned with."

She glanced at the bullet hole in the dashboard, then back at the missing rear window. She turned to him. "Okay, what are you keeping from me, Flynn?"

"Jim Rothenberg was killed by a blow to his head around 6:15 yesterday evening. His wristwatch was broken at the time of the attack, which fixed the hour. I'm sure the coroner's report will substantiate my calculations."

She nodded. "What's your point?"

He slowed the Acura to a stop at the end of the drive. "That's about the same time the limo paid us a visit in the parking structure. Jim's office is a good twenty minutes from Flynn Security. No way the killer could have been in both places at the same time."

She felt a shiver of apprehension creep along her spine. "Which means the pirate didn't kill Rothenberg?"

"Right. It could be we have two factions of the same group at work here—or two groups. I don't know. But with two people already dead and the pirate taking potshots at us, I didn't think it made sense to tell Evelyn Von Zant your real name."

When he put it that way, it was hard for Jamie to disagree with his logic.

"So why didn't you question her thoroughly, instead of smiling and making polite inquiries?"

"Because I'm not a cop," he said dryly. "Using strong-arm tactics would only get me arrested. Hell, the woman's a leading member of the community—didn't you hear her casual reference to Chief Bernsen? Besides the chief of police, she's friends with the mayor and half the elected officials of the state."

"And she's also a liar. Reading people, analyzing their body language, is something I've gotten to be pretty good at."

"I always suspected you were a lady of many talents."

She ignored him. "Point is, she *was* lying to you. I don't know about what or even why. It could be nothing related to the case at all, but she was lying."

"I know."

"You do? Then why didn't you—?"

"What good would that have done? If I'd confronted her, she would've thrown us out and not told us anything at all. At least now we know her appointment with Rothenberg yesterday evening was to view the Washington Doubloon."

"So? She said it was standard practice of Hathaway and Ferris to provide pre-auction showings to major clients."

"Right, but we were supposed to deliver the coin to the Bank of America in Beverly Hills first thing Monday morning. Plan was, due to the doubloon's value, it would stay in the B. of A. vault until the auction. The only time Rothenberg would've had access *outside the bank* was on the day of the auction. Yet, according to Von Zant, he'd set up at least one appointment—probably more, since both Marcus Saritsky and Jonathan McCabe were listed in his appointment calendar—to view the doubloon. If you ask me, it looks like Rothenberg knew the doubloon would never make it to the bank."

"Meaning he was the leak?"

Steve's smile faded. "Meaning he was the leak."

*   *   *

As soon as they got back to Flynn Security, Steve deposited Jamie in his office, then went to check on Tony's progress at the other end of the suite.

Jamie sat down on the overstuffed armchair across from Steve's desk and reviewed the notes she'd scribbled in the car. If Rothenberg had been planning to steal the coin and sell it in a private auction, why hadn't Harry Chung heard about it? His contacts on the street were without parallel, yet he'd heard nothing about an underground auction. And what was Evelyn Von Zant hiding?

She tapped her pen against the notebook and frowned. Coming up with hard questions was the easy part. It was finding the answers that gave her a problem.

Sighing, she closed the notebook and stood, stretching her cramped muscles. She checked her watch. It was a few minutes past eleven. If she were back at the hotel, she'd be getting ready for the closing banquet at the IPA conference right about now. And probably thinking about the intensive two-day workshop on agency management she was scheduled to begin tomorrow.

It was funny how things could change, she thought with amazement. How your priorities could shift almost overnight. A few days ago, attending the IPA conference was the most important thing in the world to her. Now she was dodging bullets, tripping over dead bodies and assisting in a murder investigation.

Even so, the rent on her one-bedroom apartment back in Baton Rouge still had to be paid. *And* her boss still thought she was coming to work on Monday morning. Steve had cautioned her not to let anyone know where she was, but surely one phone call couldn't hurt.

She pulled out her telephone calling card from her purse and lifted the receiver on the desk. She punched in the number for her office.

"Good afternoon, Duval Insurance," came a familiar voice moments later.

"Barbara? Hi, this is Jamie. Is Ed in?"

"Jamie?" the woman drawled. "Is that really you? Well, how are you? You know, you sound so clear, almost like you're in the next room instead of halfway 'cross the country. You're still out there in Los Ang'lus, aren't ya?"

Jamie rolled her eyes. Barbara Fontenot was the human equivalent of an assault rifle—instead of bullets, she fired off questions, and far more quickly than the average person could ever answer them.

"I'm fine. Look, is Ed in? I really need to speak to him."

"Well, he's not in right now, sugar. He had an appointment with Glesby Glass and won't be back till tomorrow mornin'. I know he's gonna be real sorry he missed your call."

That would make two of them. "Then I need you to give him a message. I want to take some more time off—say a couple of weeks. I have the vacation time accrued, so there shouldn't be a problem. Oh, and could you call Mr. Patarias, my building super?" she added as the image of a ten-pound tabby flashed into her head. "His number's on my Rolodex. He's been feeding K.C., so he needs to know I won't be home for another two weeks. There should be plenty of food in the pantry, but I may be running low on kitty litter. Tell him I'll reimburse him for any expenses."

"Will do," Barbara said, scribbling the instructions down. Then she lowered her voice. "Now, honey, you don't have to answer this, but I'm gonna ask it, anyway. Are you looking for a job out there in California or something?"

"No. What makes you think I'm looking for a job?"

"Well, what else are we s'posed to think? Ed got a phone call a few days ago from someone out in Los Ang'lus, wanting to check you out, see how long you've worked here. If you had any relatives or friends in California. That sort of thing. The only thing we could figure was that you were looking for a job."

Jamie felt an icy tremor, the kind caused by an internal

coldness rather than by an external temperature. "Do you remember who the person was?" She tried to make her question sound casual.

"Well, the first one—"

"How many have there been?"

"Two. The first one came Monday morning. 'Course, that was someone from the IPA—said your reservations were all screwed up. Wanted to know when you were expected out. I talked to him—he seemed real nice, too. I gave him your flight schedule and told him you should already be at the hotel."

Jamie frowned. Good old dependable Barbara. "And the second?"

"Well, that came yesterday. Ed talked to him. I don't remember the name. Something like Jefferson or Washington . . . well, it was some dead president, anyway. Ed had me phone the hotel, but they told me you'd checked out."

Her fingers tightened around the receiver. "Did they?" She took a deep, steadying breath and closed her eyes for a moment. "Well, I had a few problems with my room, so I had to make different accommodations."

"With Dale Carmichael?" Barbara asked slyly.

"What?"

"When we couldn't find you, Ed called Ben McCloskey. He told us you'd met this guy. Said y'all gone all moon-eyed over each other. We found out Dale wasn't registered, either, so Ben thought y'all must've slipped off somewhere together."

The office door opened slowly, and Jamie looked up to meet Steve's gaze. One hand rested in his trouser pocket, his arm casually pulling the tan jacket to one side to display his trim, flat abdomen. The other hand leaned against the doorjamb, his long, bronzed fingers gently splayed against the woodwork. As happened every time Jamie saw him, she felt her stomach do a somersault.

Damn you, Ben, she thought with a sudden flush. *Why don't you stick with analyzing insurance risks?*

She quickly averted her eyes. "Look, I've got to go," she said into the telephone. "Just give Ed my message and tell him I'll keep in touch. Oh, and, Barbara, if anyone else should call about me, would you *please* tell them you haven't heard from me?"

"Honey, something *is* wrong, isn't it?"

"No, nothing's wrong. Well, nothing that I can't handle. Just do this for me, will you?"

She replaced the receiver and looked up at Steve. He still stood in the doorway. His expression was closed, unreadable.

"That was my office," she explained and slipped the calling card back into her wallet. "I needed to arrange for more time off, make sure someone fed my cat. Like I told you the other night, I can't just vanish into thin air."

"Did you tell them where you were?"

"Of course not." Then she added worriedly, "Steve, two people have called there asking about me." She relayed what Barbara had told her.

He frowned. "The first was our office."

"*Your* office? Whatever for?"

"I had to be sure that you were who and what you appeared to be. Tony phoned your job to check."

"So he was the IPA representative."

He nodded.

"But what about the second one? The Washington person."

He met her gaze. "We only made one phone call, Jamaica. And considering the name he used . . ."

She felt her throat tighten as the chilling sensation returned. The caller had to be either the pirate or one of his cohorts. But as terrifying as that realization was, the message was even more so.

Until the case was solved, she couldn't go home.

On their way to the market to buy groceries, Steve swung by his house in Malibu to check on the workmen's progress. He was pleased to find that the repairs to the sun deck, weakened by several seasons of high winds and rain, were nearly completed. He was also pleased by Jamie's response to the ramshackle two-story Victorian he'd bought three years before and was slowly refurbishing.

She'd wandered from room to room, voicing her approval at his choice of moldings and his decision to go with natural woods whenever possible. He'd explained his plans for the house, how he envisioned it looking in five years or so, and she'd offered several suggestions on wood-varnishing techniques for the shutters—just to prove, she'd told him with a grin, that her subscription to *Popular Woodworking* wasn't a wasted investment.

They'd both begun to relax, almost forgetting the circumstances that had brought them together. And as they walked past the contractor's pickup in the driveway, on their way to the street, he reached for her hand as though it were the natural thing to do.

A gentle sea breeze wafted toward them from the Pacific Ocean a few blocks away, tumbling strands of Steve's hair across his forehead. Squinting from the glare of the afternoon sun, he reached into his jacket pocket for his sunglasses as they reached the Acura. In the distance, a car engine sprang to life. He casually glanced toward the sound.

Twenty yards down the quiet residential street, a black stretch limo was pulling away from the curb and out into the sparsely moving traffic.

He froze.

Uneasiness prickled the nape of his neck. *It's probably just one of the locals out for a special celebration*, he told himself. *No need to panic.* Then the limo began to slow its speed as it moved closer to the Acura. Closer to Jamie.

"Son of a—!" Steve whirled around. "Get down!" He pulled Jamie to the concrete.

"Steve, what—"

Head down, he scurried toward the asphalt just off the curb with her in tow. The car would provide little defense against a shower of bullets, but it was the best protection they had.

Knees bent, his back leaning against the car, he slid the Beretta from its holster. He checked the clip, then glanced once at Jamie, seeing her grow pale.

"Steve . . ." She reached out for him, shaking her head in terror. "Please, don't."

Turning around, he raised himself up slowly, feeling her fingers slide down the lapel of his jacket, and peered over the hood of the car. The limo had stopped alongside the Acura, less than six feet away. He leveled the Beretta at the front window and waited. Seconds later, the rear passenger window slid down.

"Mr. Flynn?" A Chinese man in his late thirties flashed an amused smile. "If I've come at an awkward time, I do apologize." The accent was clipped, precise and unmistakably British.

His gaze flicked to the gun in Steve's hand, and his smile grew wider. "Please allow me to introduce myself. I'm Kwon Liu Chin. If you and the lady could drag yourselves away from your amusements for a short while, I would like to speak with you."

TEN

Jamie leaned back against the soft upholstery of the stretch limousine and stared in fascination at their host. Kwon Liu Chin's exotic good looks, suave sophistication and Oxonian accent seemed at odds with his reputation as a leading figure in the Chinese underworld, yet she had read his computer profile. Drugs, extortion, prostitution. Even murder. The list of his suspected crimes was extensive and no doubt highly accurate.

Liu Chin issued a brief order in Cantonese to the driver, and the glass partition slowly rose. Then he smiled. "I told Chang-Soon to circle the block whilst we discuss our business."

"And just what business do we have to discuss?" Steve asked.

His thigh pressed lightly against her leg; his upper arm brushed her shoulder. Even though she felt strangely at ease with Liu Chin, she was grateful for Steve's presence. His very nearness promised comfort, reassurance.

Safety.

Liu Chin arched a delicately curved eyebrow. "Why, the Washington Doubloon, what else?" He clicked a button on the sidebar. A panel slid upward, revealing a bottle of Pouilly-Fuisse chilling in a bucket of ice. "Would you like some wine, Miss Royale?'' he inquired lazily. "It's an excellent vintage. Nineteen-seventy-five.''

"No, thank you,'' she murmured. Then she realized he'd called her by name, a peculiar act since they'd never been formally introduced. She cast a worried glance at Steve and felt his warm hand slip over hers and squeeze.

"Mr. Flynn?'' Liu Chin extended a crystal goblet.

Steve shook his head. "About the doubloon . . . ?''

Liu Chin shrugged and set the bottle back in its ice bucket. "Well, it's missing, for starters,'' he said dryly. "Your courier was abducted in transit and killed. The men responsible for the heist now think Miss Royale has the coin and they've threatened to kill her.'' Liu Chin took a slow sip of wine, eyeing Steve over the rim of the goblet. "Does that about sum it up?''

"Pretty much,'' Steve said stonily.

Liu Chin smiled and swirled the wine in its glass, the heavy gold ring on his right hand catching Jamie's attention. On the crest was a winged dragon, its exquisite workmanship unlike anything she'd ever seen before. Two tiny ruby eyes flashed crimson fire whenever his hand moved.

"And for all intents and purposes, your investigation is at a standstill. Multiple suspects, of course, but few with sufficient motive for murder.'' He smiled, revealing even, white teeth. "That's why I've decided to offer you my assistance.''

"Assistance?'' Steve repeated.

Liu Chin nodded.

"But why would you want to help us?'' Jamie asked in disbelief.

"My dear Miss Royale, why shouldn't I? Acquiring the Washington Doubloon will be the culmination of a lifelong fascination with Early American coins. And it would provide me with certain . . . opportunities . . . I might not have otherwise. You see, I have every intention of purchasing the doubloon at the auction next week, but shan't be able to if it's not available.'' He tilted the goblet back and drained the wine. Then he set the glass on the sidebar.

"To put it bluntly, I've decided it's in my own best interests to see that you both succeed."

Two hours later, Jamie dropped a brown paper bag filled with groceries on the kitchen counter to the sound of Rex's barks of joy. The dog circled her once, then nudged his head against her legs, his tail thump-thump-thumping against the lower cabinets.

"And I'm happy to see you, too." She scratched him behind his ear. "Now go away."

His tail drooped. He stared at her with wounded brown eyes.

"Jamaica doesn't have time to play right now." Steve set the last two bags on the counter. "She volunteered to cook dinner, and I think the pressure's getting to her."

"Funny, Flynn." She removed a package of tomatoes from the first bag. "Just for that, you can go away, too. The last thing I need right now is a couple of males underfoot."

He grinned. "I was planning to check in with the office, anyway, and see if the report's ready on the Miranda woman." He called the dog, and they both headed for the living room.

Forty-five minutes later, the groceries had been put away and the chicken was stewing. Jambalaya. It was one of her mother's specialties, and Jamie knew the recipe by heart. She smiled and chopped an onion, feeling unaccountably content cooking for Steve. Odd, she thought, that she'd feel this way about a man she'd known for less than a week. Odder still was that sometimes she felt more comfortable being with him than with any other person she'd ever known. And closer.

So much so, it frightened her.

She lowered the knife to the cutting board and frowned. As much as she wanted to believe otherwise, she knew what she felt for Steve was much more than a physical attraction. It had depth, intensity.

Which was why it was so dangerous, she reminded herself. It made her think about their future, when she knew they didn't have one. How could they? He was a modern-day Magellan who circumnavigated the rules rather than the globe. She was a conformist who thrived on the very bureaucracy he seemed to take such delight in defying. Besides, sooner or later the case would be solved.

And she would go home.

"Something smells wonderful," he said, coming up behind her. She felt a rush of warm air as his breath caressed her neck.

She shivered. "It's, ah, chicken jambalaya." She moved to the stove, putting a little distance between them, and added the chopped onion to the tomatoes and peppers already simmering in the pot with the chicken. "Was the report ready?"

"Yeah." He leaned against the counter, next to the cutting board. He'd removed his jacket, along with the leather holster and gun he'd worn all day. His silk tie was casually loosened. "The Miranda woman's clean. No priors. Turns out she's a data processor for a temp agency downtown."

"Then why'd Rothenberg scribble her telephone number?"

"Don't know." He popped a radish drying on a folded paper towel into his mouth. "Tony's following up an angle now."

She nodded. "Did you call Lieutenant Abrams? Tell him about Liu Chin's offer?"

"Wasn't in." He rolled up the cuffs of his powder-blue shirt and turned around. He started tearing lettuce for the salad. "He's gonna love it, though. One of the biggest crime bosses on the West Coast offering to help ferret out information on the heist. And just so he can *purchase* the missing doubloon at the auction next week."

"The man seemed sincere, Steve."

"Yeah, and he probably was." He dumped the torn lettuce leaves into a large wooden salad bowl. "Looks like Harry was wrong about Liu Chin's motives. It's not the dream of owning the coin that drives him. It's the prestige of ownership itself.''

"So you don't think he hired the pirate?"

He picked up the knife and sliced the leftover green peppers into long, thin strips. "At this point?" He shook his head. "I think it's safe to assume he didn't.''

She stirred the bubbling jambalaya. She'd reached the same conclusion about Liu Chin herself. "So that leaves one of the other collectors. Or Rothenberg.''

"Jim is the most likely suspect for hiring the pirate. He knew about the flight schedule and the courier's routine. And he'd been arranging showings of the doubloon for special clients even though he knew the coin was supposed to have been stored in the bank until the auction.'' Steve dropped the pepper strips into the salad and frowned. "Looks like Rothenberg was going into business for himself. If so, it'd explain why Evelyn Von Zant seemed so nervous when we talked to her this morning.''

"Or she could be more deeply involved than we thought." Jamie checked the rice and turned off the heat. "How's the salad coming?"

"All done.'' He tossed the vegetables and carried the bowl into the dining room.

"Good.'' She walked over to where he'd been standing at the counter and removed a couple of plates and salad bowls from the upper cabinet. "Then dinner is ready.''

She turned around to find him standing in front of her. His broad-shouldered presence seemed to fill the small kitchen, blocking sight of all else. Caught off guard, she moved back, feeling the counter press against her backside.

He smiled. "Why don't I set the table?"

His fingers brushed against hers as he grasped the china. The brief contact sent a tingling warmth rushing up her arm and she shivered again. With a deliberate casualness—almost, she thought irritably, as if he knew the effect he had upon her and was enjoying it—he leaned forward to remove flatware from the drawer beside her, then sauntered back to the dining room.

She breathed deeply, her eyes fluttering closed for a moment as she tried to steady herself, then walked over to the stove. When she carried the chicken jambalaya to the dining room minutes later, he was lighting the two tapers in the center of the table. An open bottle of chilled white wine sat next to them; two filled goblets were in front of each place setting.

"Candles? Wine?" She tried to keep her tone light. "What's the special occasion?"

"Do we need a special occasion?"

She slowly placed the serving dish on the table and sat down as he hit the light switch, sending the room into semidarkness. Through the drawn drapes over the sliding glass door, she could see the unmistakable shape of Rex lying forlornly on the patio.

"This is much better, don't you think?" he asked, slipping into the chair across from her. "Cozier. After the week we've had, I thought we should relax, take our minds off the case for a while."

She regarded him quietly for a moment. The candlelight softened the lines on his face, deepened the green of his eyes. His smile was warm and inviting. Would it really be so wrong to have a romantic candlelit dinner with a handsome man? To acquire temporary amnesia for a couple of hours, forgetting both the investigation and the warnings of the little voice inside her head, and just enjoy his company?

She knew the answers even as she asked the questions.

And she decided to do it, anyway.

She returned the smile and lifted her wineglass in a toast. "Excellent idea," she murmured.

She felt her earlier tension vanish as they ate dinner. They talked and laughed and talked some more, yet they discussed nothing of great importance. It was as if they were trapped in a time bubble. No past, no future. Only the moment.

And she never wanted the moment to end.

"So tell me about your family." He leaned forward, his forearms resting nonchalantly on the table. "You said you got your name because your parents spent their honeymoon in Jamaica. Were you serious about that, or just teasing me?"

"Oh, I was serious. The year after I was born, they went to Dallas, which is how my brother got *his* name. I guess you could say my parents are a little . . ."

"Eccentric?"

" 'Crazy' is more accurate. But they're lovable. And Dallas assures me they're harmless, even if they do act irresponsibly at times." She drained the wine from her glass. "They live in Metairie, a suburb outside New Orleans. At the moment, my mother's making New Age jewelry—you know, crystals on chains, that sort of thing—and taking a course on channeling. Last year she was into origami. She changes hobbies every year."

He refilled their wineglasses. "And your father?"

"He's had the same hobby for years—searching for Jean Laffite's pirate treasure. That's how he spends his summer vacations from Tulane, where he teaches Medieval Lit—trekking through the bayous and backwoods of southern Louisiana."

"And you disapprove?"

She shrugged. "It seems such a waste of his time and energy, but it's harmless enough, I guess. I don't know. My parents have always been a little 'out there.' I guess that's why I'm such a control freak."

"You do like your rules and regulations, don't you?" His tone was somber, yet his eyes held a mischievous twinkle. "Maybe you should have joined the army instead of going into insurance."

"Funny you should mention that," she said, her voice soft with amusement. "Mom swears I was a general in a past life." She lifted her wineglass. "She, ah, was into reincarnation a couple of years ago, you see. Analyzed the entire family."

He laughed then, the flickering candlelight dancing in his eyes. "I can't wait to meet your mother, Jamaica. She sounds delightful."

She sipped her wine, feeling a warm inner glow at his words. Now wasn't the time to remind herself that she shouldn't take his lighthearted comments too seriously. For the moment, she would just enjoy the feeling.

Sometime later, they strolled into the living room and sat on the sofa. Jamie slipped out of her navy pumps and flexed her toes, feeling deliciously languid. Her jacket lay across the back of the love seat. The rich leather of the sofa felt cool against her sleeveless silk top as she leaned back. She turned her head and gazed up at Steve, who sat two feet away. The short distance between them seemed like miles.

"Now it's your turn," she said. "Tell me about yourself."

He smiled, a smile warm and soft and oh-so-intoxicating. "What do you want to know?"

Everything. She wanted to know about his family. His childhood. A thousand and one details of his life.

"How long were you married?" she asked, surprising herself with her first question.

"A year and a half." He took a long sip of the wine and placed the glass on the table. "Marie worked for a toy manufacturer out in the Valley. They suspected one of their people was selling the schematics for a line of robotic toys to the competition. I went undercover to find out. We met, fell in lust and married less than six weeks later."

He smiled wryly. "When the dust settled shortly after the honeymoon, I think we both realized we'd made a mistake. We had different goals, different dreams. She, ah, disliked my work. *Intensely.* Wanted me to sell the agency and get into 'something more lucrative.' " He slipped his index finger under the strap of his watch and flexed the metallic band. "I tried to explain that the agency was, and still is, very important to me. That I didn't want to change careers." He shrugged.

Jamie drank some more of her wine. Funny. Try as she might, she couldn't imagine Flynn doing any other kind of work. Even though his investigative methods were a little unorthodox—and at times came close to being downright illegal—she knew he was very good at his job. More important, he *enjoyed* it.

Which was a helluva lot more than most people—herself included—could say about their jobs.

"By the time Marie filed the papers, I was relieved it was over. And I'd learned my lesson. If it's going to last, a relationship must have a solid foundation. It has to be built on mutual respect. Compatibility. The balancing of one partner's weaknesses by the other's strengths."

"The fine art of compromise," she said softly.

"Exactly." His gaze swept over her, lingering when it reached her mouth. "You also have to know what you want so you can recognize it when it comes along." He raised his eyes to meet hers. "Marie was looking for somebody on the fast track. I'm just not that type."

"So what type are you?" She leaned forward and rested her bare arm on the back of the sofa.

"Why don't you tell me?" His voice dropped lower. "I thought analyzing people was one of your strong suits."

She smiled. "All right."

She studied his face for a long moment, even though she'd already reached her conclusion. Just then, Stephen Flynn was a very kissable type. She'd start with his mouth, she decided. Then move to his chin. The curve of his earlobe.

Still smiling, she raised her gaze to his eyes. Desire burned there like emerald fire. *He wanted her.* And knowing that he did fanned the flame smoldering inside her.

He averted his gaze and reached for his wine, his fingers wrapping around the fragile glass like a drowning man to a life buoy. He raised the goblet and tilted it back, his long, dark eyelashes fluttering closed. Her gaze dropped

to his throat, entranced by the rise and fall of his Adam's
apple as he swallowed. When the glass was empty, he
placed it on the table and turned toward her. His expression was guarded, distant.

"It's getting late. I should call the office and—"

She pressed her fingers to his lips, stopping him.

"It can wait."

He didn't move. His eyes locked with hers. She slid
her fingers off his lips, then along his cheek, feeling the
stubble bristle beneath her fingertips.

"I haven't finished my analysis."

She smiled and raked her fingernails through the soft
strands of his hair. She leaned forward until their faces
were inches apart, then closer still until their lips met in
a tentative kiss.

He groaned and slid his hands around her waist, pulling
her to him. She could feel the heat of his body through
the lightweight cotton of his shirt, hear the wild thudding
of his heart. He brushed his lips against hers. Teasing,
tempting. Such sweet torture. She moaned and opened her
mouth to meet the thrust of his tongue. She tightened her
grip on his hair as he lowered her to the sofa cushions.
Closer. Yes. She wanted to be closer.

She arched her body to meet his, wanting to mold herself to him. Her tailored skirt was pulled up to her hips
in a tangled mess, exposing the tops of her thigh-high
hose, but she didn't care. She slid her stockinged foot
down the length of his trouser leg, pulling him closer,
needing him closer. He shuddered.

"Jamaica." He said it as if it were being torn from the
depths of his very soul.

She knew she should stop, but, heaven help her, she
didn't want it to end. Not yet. For once in her life, she
didn't want to think about the consequences. She only
wanted to feel.

She tugged his shirt free from his trousers and smoothed
her hands along his warm back, feeling his muscles tense
and undulate beneath her fingertips. She lightly raked her

fingernails down to his buttocks and back again. Teasing. Tempting. Sweet torture reciprocated.

He groaned and thrust his hips against her until she felt the unmistakable outline of his male hardness through his trousers. The kiss deepened, intensified, taking her to heights of passion she'd never known were possible. His touch left her breathless, weak; so dangerously, deliciously, out of control.

He shrugged out of his shirt and flung it aside, then began unfastening the clasp of her silk top. She fumbled with his belt buckle. It was as though they couldn't shed their clothes fast enough. As though, she thought, each knew that a moment's hesitation might break the spell.

She felt his hand slide over hers to grasp the belt buckle. He pulled back the prong and released the belt with a flick of his wrist. She undid the button, slid down the zipper and tugged at the pants. He pulled away for a moment, kicking off his shoes and trousers with reckless abandon. She heard one of the shoes land next to the television; the other slammed against the door to the den.

She felt giddy, light-headed. She tried to tell herself it was the wine, but she knew better. It was Flynn.

She unzipped her skirt and wiggled out of it, then tossed it aside. She pulled off her blouse and bra. They hit the floor next to the love seat.

He grabbed her hands, interlocking his fingers with hers, and pulled her up until her breasts pressed against his bare chest. The heat of his skin against her nipples sent shivers of anticipation racing down her spine. She opened her mouth and met the thrust of his probing tongue with equal abandon. Without breaking the kiss, he slid off the sofa to the floor, taking her with him. He shoved the coffee table aside with his foot to make more room. The empty wineglasses clinked, shook but remained upright.

She felt his hand move up her right leg until it reached the top of the stocking on her upper thigh. He slipped a finger under the lacy band and twisted it.

"These are hardly regulation attire for army generals,"

he murmured hoarsely. He kissed her inner thigh right above the hose. Her skin sizzled.

Her throat felt parched. "Really? But they're so practical. No-nonsense. Just like me."

His hands slid up to her panties. He slowly eased them off.

"Nothing like you. You're wild and exotic and beautiful. So damned beautiful."

He entered her with a deep thrust that she could swear she felt to the base of her spine. She cried out, pressing her fingers into the rocklike muscles of his shoulders.

She didn't notice the hardness of the floor's wooden planks. Or the fact that their clothes were strewn about them in wild disarray. She had a fever only he could cool. A hunger only he could fill. She wrapped her legs, still clad in the thigh-high hose, around him and matched his rhythm.

He groaned her name against the hollow of her neck.

She called out his as she arched to meet his next thrust.

The lovemaking was fierce, all-consuming. Passion rose, spiraling higher and higher, until it reached its peak. Then it shattered like a pane of glass exposed to intense heat, leaving them both spent and gasping on the living room floor.

ELEVEN

Resting her head against Steve's shoulder, lulled by the steady beat of his heart, Jamie slowly drifted toward sleep. She could feel the light pressure of his hand against her hair, the warmth of his breath against her cheek. She felt safer, more content, than she'd ever dreamed possible. If she could have been granted a single wish at that moment, it would have been to stay there, on the floor, wrapped in his arms forever.

From outside, Rex began to bark. Deep, insistent barks. The kind of barks it was difficult to ignore from a ninety-pound German shepherd. He pawed the patio door, his weight rattling the heavy glass in its casing. Steve stirred. Jamie sat up. A sharp knock rapped against the front door.

Her gaze flew to the door, then down at Steve. He struggled into a sitting position.

The knock came again. "Flynn?" The doorknob twisted. "It's Lou Abrams. Unlock the damned door, will ya?"

Cursing softly, Steve rolled to his feet and grabbed his pants. "Just a minute," he called out.

"What's he doing here?" Jamie whispered, looking around for her clothes.

"I left a message for him at his office, remember? I wanted to discuss the case."

"He has great timing," she muttered under her breath.

"Tell me about it."

Grinning, he tossed her skirt to her. She giggled and scrambled into her clothes as quickly as she could. She felt ridiculously like a teenager caught making out in the backseat of a car. And busted by a cop, no less.

"Flynn?" Abrams demanded again. He rattled the doorknob.

"All right, all right." Steve glanced at her. She'd fastened her bra and was pulling the silk top into place. She tucked it into the waistband of her skirt and nodded. She was as presentable as she could get in under a minute.

He slipped his shirttail back into his pants, gave her a quick kiss, then went to unlock the door.

"What the hell took you so long?" Abrams barreled his way into the living room without waiting for an invitation. "Didn't you hear me pounding on the door? I coulda woke the dead. Hello, Jamie." He stopped when he reached the sofa. He saw the wineglasses, the dimmed lights, the coffee table shoved to one side. Steve's bare feet. Her own. Abrams' eyebrows rose.

She felt herself blush.

Abrams looked from her to Steve. "Did I, ah, interrupt something here?"

Hiding a smile, Steve shook his head and flipped on the table lamp. "We were just . . . talking."

"Oh, yeah?" Abrams didn't look convinced. He glanced around the living room, then sat down on the sofa. He tossed one of Steve's socks onto the coffee table. "Nice place. Is it the maid's day off or what?"

Steve met Jamie's gaze and grinned. "The, ah, maid quit." He sat down next to Lou. "Look, I'm glad you could stop by." Steve's expression grew somber, his voice businesslike. "I need to fill you in on a few things."

Abrams pulled a pack of cigarettes from his shirt pocket

and tossed it on the table. "Well, I need to fill *you* in on a few things, too. Most of which you ain't gonna like."

Jamie excused herself and went into the kitchen to make a pot of coffee, trying to get her wits together. It was hard to shift mental gears, hard to shake the memory of their lovemaking, yet Steve seemed to do it with relative ease. She took a deep breath and smoothed her hair back into place. Still, there'd be time enough to savor the memories later, she consoled herself with a private smile. Right now the case took priority.

She could hear the conversation from the other room as the coffee brewed.

"I got a call from your office today about an Ynez Miranda," the lieutenant was saying. "Tony said Rothenberg had the woman's number in his office. So help me, Flynn, if you removed evidence from a murder scene . . ."

"Let's just say I found it in Rothenberg's office and leave it at that, okay?"

"You keep 'finding things' and we'll both be in trouble. I've already told you I won't put up with any more interference in my investigation, and I meant what I said. I also heard you went to see Evelyn Von Zant this morning. Why?"

"We think Rothenberg was arranging a private auction for the doubloon. If so, Von Zant could've been one of the buyers. I just wanted to ask her a couple of questions, feel her out."

"Yeah, well, Chief Bernsen crawled all over my ass about it this afternoon. The chief doesn't like it when his friends are inconvenienced by murder investigations. And he likes it even less when the investigation's being conducted by a P.I."

"She could have refused to talk to me."

"That's not the point and you know it."

Jamie filled three mugs with coffee, added the necessary condiments to the round metallic tray and carried it all into the living room. She placed the tray on the cocktail table and sat down on the love seat, directly across from the two men.

Abrams glanced at her. "Anyway, the Miranda woman's got an ex-boyfriend who looks like he could be our man. He's got the right credentials and he matched Jamie's description." He pulled out a large brown envelope from inside his jacket and removed two photographs. He leaned across the table with the first one. "Do you recognize him?"

She glanced at the photo. She felt the color drain from her face as it all came tumbling back. The cold, menacing smile he wore in the elevator. His threatening phone call. The pictures.

She reached for her coffee mug, drawing strength from its warmth. "It's him. It's the pirate."

Her hands trembled as she stirred in the creamer and the artificial sweetener. When she glanced up, she found Steve watching her, his face etched with concern. She forced a smile.

"The man's name is Raoul Dominguez," Abrams went on. "He and his buddy David Hines specialize in antiquities thefts. Mostly pre-Columbian art, although they've been known to branch out occasionally." He passed the second photograph over to Jamie. "Recognize this one?"

It was of an unfamiliar-looking brown-haired man in his late twenties. She shook her head. Abrams handed both pictures to Steve.

"If you know who they are, why haven't you arrested them?"

Abrams shrugged. "Gotta find them first. We know they were holed up in the Miranda woman's apartment, but they're gone now. Seems Dominguez and Miranda had this thing going for years. But they split, and she hasn't seen him in about six months. For the last three weeks, she's been in Texas visiting relatives. Sick uncle or something. Her landlord's spotted both Dominguez and Hines at the apartment, though."

"Have you talked to the Miranda woman?" Steve asked.

"Nah, but El Paso P.D. has. She's furious. Wants to press charges. Said she never gave him permission to enter her apartment, that he's a scumbag. I get the impression they didn't exactly part on the best of terms." Abrams took a few sips of coffee.

"And she has no idea where he could be hiding out now?"

"No."

Steve frowned and reached for his coffee mug.

Lieutenant Abrams lit a cigarette, then exhaled a thin ribbon of smoke. He leaned back against the sofa with a scrunch of leather. "Hey, at least now we know who we're looking for. I've got an APB out on Dominguez. When he surfaces, I'll bring him in for questioning. 'Course, the most I can charge him with right now is harassment, but if we pressed him, we might get lucky."

"The bastard threatened to kill Jamie. He did kill Gary."

"Give me evidence, proof, and I'll bust him. So far, all we really got is that he harassed her in an elevator. A smart attorney would tear the rest of it to shreds."

"But what about the shot he fired at us in the parking garage?" Jamie asked. "And the pictures?"

"Look, Steve said neither one of you got a clear look at the gunman. A glimpse of blond hair in a black limo and a feeling ain't enough for me to press charges, people. The D.A. would laugh me outta his office." He took a long drag on his cigarette. "I mean, come on. In sunny California, blond-haired men are a dime a dozen—bleached or otherwise. And there're probably more black stretch limos on the streets here than anywhere else in the country. Without license plates, they all look alike."

She exchanged a quick glance with Steve. Well, *that* was one comment they couldn't argue with.

"The good news is ballistics matched the bullets. The same-caliber gun was used to kill Gary. If we find the weapon on Dominguez, we got ourselves a strong case. As for the snapshots, proving they were taken with Dominguez's camera'll be tricky." Abrams looked around for an ashtray. "But I've got some people going through the dumpster over at the Miranda woman's apartment to see if Dominguez threw away the silver-nitrate backing."

Steve lifted his car keys out of a small glass bowl, then slid the dish down the table toward Abrams with a soft scrape of glass against glass.

"Maybe the boys down at the lab can provide a link between it and the snapshots of Jamie." Abrams flicked ash into the bowl. "What I'm really hoping is that Dominguez took a couple extra shots of Gary for his scrapbook. It'd make it easier to nail him once we haul him in."

She blanched. What kind of madman would want to keep such a macabre memento?

"The telephone number you lifted from Rothenberg's office'll provide another link, though the D.A.'ll probably toss it out as inadmissible." Abrams cast Steve a sidelong glance. "Of course, if I had the sheet of paper, I might be able to slip it into the evidence drawer and say it'd been misplaced."

"I doubt anyone'll buy your explanation once they see the sheet, Lou. The original note had been torn off the pad. I used a chemical compound to restore the wording from the indentations on the paper underneath." Steve shrugged and rose to his feet. "But I'll get it." He returned moments later with a cellophane bag containing the restored note and handed it to Abrams.

"What's this scrawled underneath the number?" Abrams peered at the sheet through the plastic. "A *V*?"

"That's what I thought at first. But it's probably a *Y*, as in Ynez, since it's her telephone number. My guess is he was transcribing the number when the killer struck."

Abrams slipped the cellophane bag into his jacket pocket. "Think Dominguez did it? Gave Rothenberg the number, mentioned that it was his girlfriend's place, then killed him?"

"Couldn't be," Jamie said. "We think Rothenberg wrote the note right before he was killed. And since Dominguez was in the garage shooting at us . . ."

"He couldn't have killed Rothenberg," Abrams finished.

"My guess," Steve said, "is Rothenberg's killer was his accomplice. After all, Rothenberg didn't have the contacts to find someone like Dominguez on his own. He'd have needed someone with underworld connections. I also think Rothenberg was upset Wednesday afternoon, maybe even on the verge of an all-out panic. According to my receptionist, he'd been phoning my office every fifteen minutes and was coming more unglued with each call. Maybe he didn't like the way things were going. When his accomplice arrived, they got into an argument."

Abrams picked up the thread of the story. "And the killer gave Dominguez's telephone number to Rothenberg to calm him down. Told him to call Dominguez if he had any problems with the way things had been handled." He grinned as if he found the theory amusing. "Yeah, it tracks. While Rothenberg was writing the number down, the killer lifted the paperweight. Bashed Rothenberg's skull in. No more argument."

Abrams took a last drag, then stubbed out the cigarette. "I'll pass your theory on to Beverly Hills P.D. They're cooperating in my investigation, but right now they're treating Rothenberg's murder as an unrelated homicide. And they have no suspects."

"Any prints?" Steve asked.

"None, other than Rothenberg's and a few old ones on the video recorder. The killer must've worn gloves."

Steve cradled his coffee mug in his hands and frowned.

"So what do we do now?" Jamie asked.

"Sit tight. Until Dominguez and Hines reappear, there's not much else we can do. They're our only lead."

The room grew silent for a moment, then Steve spoke. "I don't think we'll have to wait long. Dominguez and his friends appear to be . . . persistent. Someone's already contacted Jamie's boss in an attempt to track her down.'' He filled the lieutenant in on Jamie's phone call to her office.

"Washington, huh?" Abrams took a sip of coffee. "Gotta give him points for being clever. He leave a message?"

"No, but he knows I live in Baton Rouge, which means that I won't be safe until he gets the coin or is arrested." Jamie ran her palms along the goose-pimply flesh of her bare arms. "Steve's right, Lieutenant Abrams. Dominguez isn't going to back off."

Again, silence. The two men exchanged a glance, but neither spoke. Abrams lit another cigarette; Steve stared at the floor.

She straightened her shoulders. "The way I see it, we can't afford to wait until they reappear. We need to flush them out now so we can control the situation."

"Oh?" Steve said. "And how do you propose we do that?"

"Dominguez still thinks I have the coin. I'll offer to sell it to him and when he comes to collect, the police can grab him."

"Forget it. It's entirely too risky."

Lou peered at her over the tip of his cigarette.

She placed her mug on the end table and leaned forward. "What other choice do we have? The only thing we have in our favor right now is that Dominguez thinks I have the coin. We have no proof he killed Gary, nothing that will stand up in court, anyway. If we let Dominguez think I'm willing to sell the doubloon to the highest bidder, it'll flush him out." She had reverted to the tone of voice she used when making a sales pitch: smooth, persuasive and matter-of-fact. "Then I could arrange a place and a time for the exchange so that the police would be waiting. Maybe even get him to admit killing Gary."

"And what if he decides to kill you instead?" Steve asked.

"What if the next shot he fires at me is more accurate?"

Abrams exhaled a stream of smoke. "She's got a point."

Steve's head snapped around. "Now, wait just a minute."

"Hey, Jamie's right. We *don't* have a lot of options here. I think as long as the exchange was well covered, it'd work. Hell, it's at least worth discussing."

Steve's jaw was set in disapproval. He glanced at her.

"We have no choice," she repeated firmly.

Steve was quiet for a long moment; then he sighed and ran his hand through his hair. "So what'd you have in mind?"

They spent the next two hours mapping out their strategy. They would have Harry Chung put the word out on the streets about the doubloon's availability. And they'd also place an ad in the classified section of the local papers. Jamie thought the wording direct and to the point— "Attention, Mr. Washington: Have reconsidered your offer. Please contact to discuss terms. J.R."

Lou suggested they rewire Steve's phone so all incoming calls could be monitored and, with luck, traced. Steve agreed.

When Jamie went to bed at a quarter past eleven, Steve and Lou were still reviewing the specs for the phone line. She hoped they'd call it a night soon. With the plans they'd made for the next day, they'd need all the rest they could get.

She sank down on the edge of the bed, feeling a wave of exhaustion and fear wash over her.

Most of all, she hoped that when the time came, she'd be able to carry out her end of the plan.

She drew her knees up and wrapped her arms around her legs.

Right now, when she thought about what she'd just volunteered to do, she wasn't sure she could pull it off.

Not sure at all.

* * *

"We can protect her, Steve."

Lou leaned against the wall, near the juncture of the kitchen and the dining room. One end of his balled-up tie hung out of the pocket of his rumpled jacket. Dark stubble shaded his jaw; his eyes were bleary and bloodshot from lack of sleep.

Steve set the empty glass pot back into the coffee maker. "I've got a bad feeling about this, Lou. Really bad. All it'd take is one screwup, and the whole thing'd be over."

Lou studied Steve's face for a moment. "Look, I know I said I couldn't spare the manpower"—he averted his gaze and stared off into the dining room—"but maybe I can pull a few strings. We could move her into a hotel. Put her under protective custody. Work something out."

"Forget it. She's better off staying with me."

"You sure about that?"

"Of course I'm sure!" Steve started walking back toward the living room.

"Well, I'm not convinced." Lou placed his hand against the center of Steve's chest, stopping him. "You're in over your head, Flynn, and we gotta talk about it."

Steve scowled. "There's nothing to talk about."

"Hell, if it were just your tail on the line, that'd be one thing. But Jamie's depending on you to keep her safe, and you're getting emotionally involved. Don't try to deny it. A person'd hafta be blind not to see what's going on."

Lou met Steve's gaze. "Now, I'm telling you as a friend, distance yourself from this before it gets out of control." His hand fell to his side. "And before you both end up dead."

Steve closed his eyes. The memory of Jamie's body melding with his, of her nails raking down his back, flashed into his mind. He took a deep, ragged breath and opened his eyes. "It's not that simple, Lou. I'm falling in love with her."

The lieutenant stared at Steve for a moment, then shook his head. "You've got a bigger problem than I thought."

At eight A.M. the next morning, Jamie walked into the kitchen to pour herself a cup of coffee. Steve sat slouched in a chair in the dining room, his bare feet extended before him. Gunmetal gray sweatpants hung low on his hips, the drawstring secured in a lopsided bow. A stream of sunlight from the open patio drapes splashed against his bare chest. His hair was tousled, uncombed.

She'd never seen him look sexier.

She reached for the coffeepot. "Good morning." She tried to sound light, unaffected, but doubted if she succeeded. She was too aware of his masculinity to disguise her feelings.

And he was much too good at reading her thoughts, anyway.

"Good morning, Jamaica."

His voice was as gentle as a lover's caress. She felt her knees weaken, her stomach do a flip-flop.

She busied herself with her coffee, trying to squelch the memory of his body against hers. The thud of his heart in her ear. The warmth of his skin. The taste of his mouth.

The harsh scrape of chair legs against the planks of the wooden floor jerked her back to the present. She turned to see him walking toward her.

"We . . . need . . . to talk."

She met his gaze. The barriers were up again, she noticed with surprise, all his feelings neatly contained.

"I guess we do at that."

He placed one hand on the counter, his long, tan fingers splayed out against the formica top. He took a deep breath, like a swimmer about to dive into an icy pool. "Under the circumstances, I think it's best that you move into a safe house until this blows over. Lou's going to assign an officer—"

"Safe house? Wait a minute. When did all this come about?"

"Last night. After you went to bed."

"But why?"

His expression was unreadable. "Things could get . . . dangerous," he finished lamely. "It's just a precaution."

"But I thought we were a team." She forced a smile. "That we'd work on the case together. Besides, you said this was a safe house, that no one could find me here."

He didn't answer. He just stared at her, unblinking. As unfathomable as the Sphinx.

She tightened the sash on her terry-cloth robe and turned back to her coffee mug sitting on the counter. "Besides, I've been chased, shot at and generally terrorized." She picked up the spoon and continued stirring. "What more could they do to me?"

"A lot more."

His words sent a chill racing down her spine. She tapped the spoon against the rim of the mug. "I'm not afraid." Even as she said it, she knew he wouldn't believe her. She didn't believe it herself.

"Look, I thought I made it clear the other night that I'm tired of being a victim. That I'm ready, willing and able to do something about it."

"Jamaica, please—"

"Why are you trying to get rid of me?"

"I'm not . . ." He sighed and ran a hand through his hair. "You don't understand."

"Well, that's obvious, isn't it?"

A muscle twitched at the corner of his tightly clenched jaw. "I'm just trying to do what I think is best. For both of us." When she started to protest, he went on. "Damn it, Jamaica, I've been through this with my own people enough times to recognize the signs. Your defenses are down, vulnerability level high. You reach out for the one person who understands. And when it's over, somebody always gets hurt. After what happened last night . . . I just think it'd be better if you moved into a safe house, that's all."

She flushed. "Are you trying to say you think last night was a mistake? That you regret making love?"

Again he didn't answer.

She felt as though she'd been punched in the stomach. "I see." She turned away.

"Look, if the circumstances were different . . ."

"Of course." Her words were tinged with ice.

"Dammit, Jamaica, if I get distracted, I could compromise your safety." He grabbed her shoulders and turned her toward him. "We have *got* to get our priorities straight. We've got to put our personal feelings aside for a while. Concentrate on the case." A spasm of fear crossed his face and his grip tightened. "Jesus." His voice dropped lower. "If anything were to happen to you, I don't think—"

She wrenched herself from his grasp. "I couldn't agree more." Her voice sounded odd, almost like it belonged to someone else. "We shouldn't let a physical attraction rule our lives. Nor can we let it interfere with the investigation."

She leaned back against the counter, her arms folded tightly against her chest. "But running away from a problem is hardly the solution. We're both adults. We know what's at stake. I think we ought to be able to keep our relationship on a professional level from here on out, don't you?"

"Jamaica—"

"Well, I know I can. Obviously, if you feel you can't keep yourself under control . . ."

He stared at her for a long moment, then nodded curtly. "No problem." He moved past her toward the hallway. "I want to leave for the office in thirty minutes. You'd better get dressed." Then he walked away.

And she just watched him go.

By noon, the plan was in motion. The special equipment needed to trace Dominguez's call had been installed and was ready for use. The telephone number Jamie would include in the ad was for a vacant apartment in Century City; all calls would be forwarded to the house in the Hollywood Hills. It was just a precaution, Steve explained. In case Dominguez tried to track her from the number in the paper.

A quick phone call from Lou to the editors of the local dailies had gotten the classified ad in the Saturday edition of each. Steve spoke with Harry Chung, who promised one better. News of Jamie's plans to sell the doubloon would be on the streets by nightfall. With the trap laid, all they could do now was wait for Dominguez to take the bait.

And knowing they had to wait only added to the growing tension she felt between them. Steve might have been able to pretend they hadn't made love, but she couldn't erase the memory as easily.

She felt like they were walking through a mine field in the dead of night, each afraid to say or do anything for fear of the resulting explosion. Each painfully aware that one false step could spell disaster. Their conversations were awkward. Their silences, worse.

Even so, she found her gaze following him wherever he moved. It was as if she couldn't help noticing the fit of his jacket across his broad shoulders. Or the stubborn strand of hair that dangled over his brow. And his hands, so strong and capable.

But knowing such thoughts could only lead to trouble didn't ease her yearnings for what she knew she could never have.

Quite the contrary.

The knowledge only seemed to accentuate the feelings.

Shortly after lunch, the intercom buzzed on Steve's desk, interrupting his re-review of Gary's itinerary. He hit the flashing red button. "Yeah?"

"Steve? This is Paulsen," came the static-ridden reply. "I'm over in Research. The background checks on those employees at Brownell are starting to come in. Think you need to take a look at it. Couple of them are pretty interesting.''

For a moment he wasn't sure what Paulsen was talking about. Then he remembered. Brownell Chemical. Missing inventory. Suspected employee theft. He rubbed his thumb and forefinger across his eyes. With everything else that had been happening lately, he'd forgotten about the agency's other clients. Understandable, of course, but still inexcusable.

''I'll be right there.'' He rose to his feet and walked around the desk to where Jamie sat reviewing part of the case file. His gaze darted, almost as though it had a will of its own, toward her long stockinged legs now tucked discreetly under the chair. She glanced up at him expectantly.

''I've, ah, got to check something over in Research,'' he mumbled, dragging his gaze away.

Without waiting to hear her reply, he opened the door to his office and stepped out into the anteroom. He felt warm. Like the supply of fresh air had been shut off.

''Hold my calls for a bit, Mona,'' he said, moving past the desk. ''I'll be in Research if you need me.''

''Got it.''

He walked around the corner and down the hall toward the front of the office, raking his fingers through his hair. Hell, he was acting like a seventeen-year-old with a hormone problem. But every time he looked at Jamie, he was filled with memories.

Memories of the silkiness of her hair, the suppleness of her body. The way her breath came in little gasps and her face flushed when she was consumed with passion.

He squeezed his eyes shut. He never should have agreed to let her continue to stay with him. Never in a thousand years.

''Hey, Steve, wait up.''

He stopped outside Records Research and turned. Tony Robinson was hurrying toward the reception desk, a stack of files in his hand. Tony was young, black and fresh out of college. He'd graduated from UCLA the year before and was still accumulating the hours needed for his investigator's license. Until then, he was stuck with the routine assignments. The drudge work. Right now the loosened tie and missing jacket made it clear Tony had spent most of his morning buried under a mountain of paperwork.

"What ya got?" Steve asked.

Tony grinned. "The follow-up reports on those collectors. Looks like Harry Chung was right. Got some real 'Lifestyles of the Rich and Unscrupulous' stuff here."

"Good work. Just leave the reports in my office. I'll review them when I get through."

"Okay." Tony shifted his weight to his other foot. "I, ah, hear Hathaway and Ferris are sending out one of their East Coast execs to take over the gallery. That true?"

"Yeah," he said wearily. "We should be hearing from them today." And when the gallery phoned, he'd have to explain that the doubloon was missing. Hell, he had no choice. The forty-eight hours he'd asked from Lou were up. With Rothenberg dead, he couldn't put off the inevitable any longer.

"Do me a favor," Steve added. "Have Mona pull our insurance policy. Might as well see what I'm up against."

"Sure."

"And pick up the green folder on my desk. I want a complete check on Jim Rothenberg. See if he had any financial problems, that sort of thing. Also contact the phone company, get a listing of all calls made to and from his private line for the past two weeks—you may have to get creative, Tony. Pac Bell usually doesn't hand out that information without a court order. Whatever you do, just make it fast."

Tony grinned again, and turned away.

Steve grasped the door handle and paused. "But you'd better let Mona get the file," he added with wry amusement. "I don't think you should go into my office right now."

No answer.

He turned around. "Tony?"

The younger man was already gone.

"Damn." Steve hurried back down the hallway toward the executive suites. Maybe there was a chance he could catch Tony.

Before it was too late.

When he reached the waiting room, Mona glanced up in surprise. "What—?"

Ignoring her, he ran to the open doorway, then stopped.

Jamie stood behind the desk, her hands gripping the edge, her body tense. Tony stood in the center of the room, staring back. Neither one moved. Neither one spoke.

Then she whirled toward Steve. "Hotel security? *Hotel security?*"

"Jamie, I can explain . . ." he began, slowly advancing toward her.

TWELVE

"You can *explain*?"

Jamie balled her hands into fists. "You scare me half out of my mind, and then you lie to me. How can you explain *that*?"

Tony set the files on the desk and turned to face Steve. "Maybe I should come back later." He glanced at Jamie, then over at Steve again. "I'm really sorry about this. I never meant—"

Steve shook his head. "It's okay, Tony."

The man nodded and left the room.

"I *knew* something was screwy about your story." Jamie started pacing behind the desk. "Dammit, why didn't I *realize* you were lying to me? Hotel security guards don't carry guns."

"Look, I'm sorry Tony frightened you in the park. He was supposed to keep an eye on you, but when you ran, he overreacted. Just like I told you."

She stopped. "Then why'd you lie about his identity?"

Steve gave her a sheepish smile. "Hell, you were breathing fire, and I didn't want to get burned."

"I'm not in the mood for one of your jokes, Flynn."

The smile faded. "The only lie I told you was about

164

who employed Tony. I thought if you knew I was having one of my people follow you, it might upset you.''

''Well, you were right about one thing.''

''Look, I only did it to protect you.''

She almost laughed. ''Yeah, sure.''

''And to see if you were who and what you claimed to be.''

She stared at him in shock. ''You mean you thought—''

He didn't say anything.

''I see.'' She took a deep breath.

A look of pain crossed his face. ''Jamie, I—''

''No, it's okay. It's just a surprise, that's all. Finding out that I was the prime suspect in Gary's murder. I mean, after all, he'd driven to the hotel to see me, rather than complete his assignment. What else did you have to go on?''

Mona rapped on the open door. ''Here's the policy you asked for.'' She held a large manila file in one hand. Her worried gaze darted from Steve to Jamie, but she said nothing more.

''Thanks.'' He moved around the desk and took the file. Moments later, Mona left the room, closing the door behind her.

Jamie walked toward him, pushing the cuffs of her lightweight sweater up her forearm. ''That your insurance policy?'' she asked, glad for a change of subject.

''Yeah. With Rothenberg dead, I can't keep pretending the coin's been delayed. Especially when you're offering to sell it in the daily papers.'' He gave her a wry smile. ''When I tell the client, I'll have to notify the insurance company, and—''

''You haven't notified your agent yet?''

''I haven't notified anyone, remember? I wanted to wait until I knew more.''

''Steve . . .'' She shook her head in disapproval.

''Look, we have a seventy-five percent coinsurance clause on our policy. If I don't find the coin, I'll be out a quarter of a million dollars. I had to buy some time. See if I could find the coin. Now . . ." He shrugged.

She reviewed the situation. "Okay, first you have to notify your agent. If you wait too long, the insurance company may refuse to honor the claim. Period. Trust me on this. Insurance underwriters tend to frown on people who disobey their rules." She removed the file from his hand. "Ordinarily, you'd be in big trouble, but it won't matter much in this case. They would've denied the claim anyway."

"Why do you say that?"

"Jim Rothenberg is one of the prime suspects in the doubloon's theft. He, or rather the gallery, would be the claimant in the loss, which constitutes fraud to most insurance companies. At the least, they'll hold up paying the claim until the case is solved." She moved to one of the chairs. "Tell you what. Let me read the policy, see exactly what coverage you have in place. Then I'll phone your agent and report the loss."

He smiled softly. "I appreciate the offer, Jamie, but it's really not necessary. I don't want to burden you with my problems. I've done too much of that already."

"I don't mind. Besides, your agent is going to be miffed that you didn't report the claim right away. And handling irate insurance agents is something I have a lot of experience with."

Then she opened the file. As she had thought, the coverage was standard. The usual clauses and normal verbiage. A quick review didn't reveal any surprises. Minutes later, she reached for the telephone, casting a sidelong glance at Steve.

He sat behind the desk, staring at one of the files Tony had left earlier. His brow was furrowed, his mouth set in a frown.

She sighed.

She only wished Stephen Flynn were as easy to understand as a professional liability policy.

*   *   *

Saturday and Sunday passed with no word from Dominguez. Jamie and Steve had settled into a routine that was, at once, both comfortable and awkward. Comfortable because being together felt so natural. Awkward because each took especial care to avoid a closer contact with the other. It was, she thought, a little like trying to straddle a fence between heaven and hell.

Gary's company car, a gold Honda Accord, had been dropped off at the house on Saturday afternoon. Steve had decided to drive the Honda until the Acura's rear window—and the bullet hole in its dashboard—was fixed. Agency personnel had already gone over Gary's car twice without finding anything, but Jamie insisted upon searching under the seat and in the glove box for the missing coin herself. She knew catching Dominguez was only part of their problem. They still had to find the coin, and they were no closer to that now than when the whole thing had begun.

Her search turned up nothing.

Monday morning dawned with a thick yellow haze obscuring the skyline. One of the worst smog advisories in years was in effect, according to the morning news. The heat was oppressive, already stifling, before eight. Temperatures were expected to break the one-hundred mark by noon.

The telephone rang at 10:05.

Sixty seconds later—too little time for the phone company to pinpoint Dominguez's exact location—Jamie had agreed to meet Dominguez at Descanso Gardens, a botanical garden in Western Los Angeles county, at 11:30 the next morning. She'd promised to give him the doubloon.

In return, he'd promised to pay her one hundred thousand dollars . . . and allow her to continue living.

It was, she thought as she hung up the phone, a little like striking a bargain with the devil.

Heaven help them if anything went wrong.

At 11:15 the next morning, Jamie slowly paced around the clearing. Her hair was damp with perspiration; her khaki blouse was plastered to her skin from the oppressive heat. She followed the narrow, unmarked trail up the steep hill with her eyes. Nothing. She turned back and started pacing again.

Dominguez couldn't have picked a better spot for the rendezvous, she thought, scanning the dense underbrush on either side of her. Gone were the flowering azaleas and roses and camellias. Gone, too, were the lush palmettoes and burbling brooks. Here were only thick, impenetrable patches of briars and brambles. Gnarled tree trunks. And eerie silence.

She supposed she should be grateful, though. The nearby underbrush provided plenty of cover for Steve and the others. Although she couldn't see them—and she prayed Dominguez wouldn't either—it was reassuring to know that Lou and his men were less than fifteen feet away.

Steve was less than fifteen feet away.

She glanced at her watch. Ten more minutes until the meeting.

Ten more minutes of waiting.

She slipped her hand into her trouser pocket and felt the comforting warmth of the counterfeit doubloon. She rehearsed the plan, even though she and Steve had gone over it at least a hundred times back at the house. Once Dominguez made the overture to buy the doubloon, she'd give the signal. Steve and the police would rush out and overpower him.

It had sounded so simple, so easy, in the living room. Now, standing in the clearing, waiting for Dominguez . . .

A twig snapped.

She whirled around, her heart pounding. Dominguez shouldered his way down the hill toward her. He still wore the faded leather jacket, black gloves and dark aviator sunglasses. When he reached the clearing, a shaft of sunlight glinted off the reflective lenses, nearly blinding her. She shaded her eyes from the glare and waited. His right hand was in his jacket pocket, out of sight. He held a small leather satchel in his left hand.

He came to a stop six feet away from her and surveyed the area.

He smiled. "You follow instructions well, *chiquita*."

She swallowed her fear. "You bring the money?"

He laughed. "Yeah, I brought it." He dropped the satchel on the ground with a scrunch of dead leaves. "Where's the coin?"

"You'll get it when I see the money. Open the satchel."

Dominguez stared at her for a long moment, then shrugged. He knelt down to open the satchel.

Suddenly the underbrush to their left crackled; twigs snapped. Dominguez sprang to his feet, withdrawing a gun from his jacket pocket. Jamie saw a flash of navy in the underbrush and groaned.

"You bitch!" Dominguez spun around and pointed the gun's long barrel straight at her midsection. He drew his lips back in a scowl, his finger poised on the trigger. "You're gonna pay for this."

Her blood pounding in her ears, she waited for the explosion, waited for the ripping pain she knew would soon follow. Her own frightened face stared back at her from the lenses of his sunglasses. She noticed a thin line of perspiration form along his brow.

Then, inexplicably, Dominguez turned and bolted up the hill, plowing his way through the undergrowth.

"Go!" Lou yelled. The policemen rushed forward. "Go, go!"

She backed away, her hands pressed against her abdomen.

"Jamie, get down!" Steve called.

She nodded, but didn't move. Just then she didn't think her legs would work. Angry shouts filled the air, quickly followed by the crash of brambles and briars as the policemen thundered through the underbrush after Dominguez.

Knees wobbling, she made her way to a tree stump on

the other side of the clearing and sank down. She heard another shout, this one farther away, and glanced over her shoulder. She saw something flash through the underbrush from the trail further ahead: the unmistakable glint of sunlight against a large metal object.

More puzzled than frightened now, she twisted around to get a better look. No good. Then she climbed onto the stump, the hairs beginning to rise along the nape of her neck as a premonition took hold. Through the bushes and trees she saw a high wooden fence cordoning off the gardens from a ranch-style home. From what Steve had told her about Descanso Gardens, she knew several private residences were located adjacent to the park. And since the house lay in the direction Dominguez had been headed . . .

She squinted. A black stretch limo sat in the driveway.

"I knew it!"

She stretched a little higher, trying to make out the license plate.

"Jamaica!"

She jumped. Steve stood at the edge of the clearing, horror-struck. He shook his head and motioned her down. She waved him on and strained higher. She had to get the license plate number. It might be their last chance.

She made out the letters first. H-L-S. And a space, followed by two numbers. A 2 and a 6. Now, maybe . . .

Two strong arms encircled her waist and yanked her off the stump, pulling her back against a hard chest. Her feet dangled helplessly off the ground. One low-heeled shoe flew off.

"Son of a—!" She struggled to break the man's hold. "Put me down!"

"Shut up," Steve hissed in her ear. "Are you trying to get yourself killed?" He took a step backward and stumbled.

His knees buckled. She saw her lost shoe sail past her as he pitched sideways, taking her with him. They hit the edge of the clearing and rolled toward a thick patch of briars, heading straight for a hundred-yard drop. She screamed. They went over the edge, tumbling down the steep incline.

Briars scratched at her face like the sharp claws of an angry beast. Hard rocks pummeled her body, tearing clothing, slashing skin. She tried to bury her head in his chest, thankful now for Steve's firm grip on her waist. Images flashed through her mind. Still shots of her life, a thousand memories condensed into a handful of seconds. *So this is what it feels like to die.*

And then . . . blessed peace.

Dazed, she slowly raised her head, her breath held. He lay quiet and still beneath her, his eyes closed. His breathing was shallow but regular, she noticed with relief. She glanced around. They were in the grass a few feet from the main trail. Water gently cascaded over man-made rock formations in a nearby stream. A wooden sign posted near the stream pointed toward the Japanese tearoom, some twenty yards away.

Steve groaned, slowly flexing his arms and legs. His eyes fluttered open and he met her gaze. His expression grew worried.

"Are you all right?" He grasped her shoulders, his fingers pressing into her bruised flesh.

She winced. "I . . . think so."

He rolled her over onto the grass, his gaze never leaving hers. She noticed flecks of blood clinging to the myriad scratches zigzagging across his face, the tiny branches stuck in his hair.

His touch was gentle as he brushed damp strands of hair off her forehead. "Damn it, Jamaica, why couldn't you have stayed down, like I told you?"

She struggled to sit up. "I was trying to get the—"

Pebbles rattled along the trail from just out of sight beyond a cluster of palmettoes. The sound of footsteps followed. He mumbled a curse. He pushed her back down on the grass and flung himself across her before she could say a word. Then he drew his gun and swung his arms into position. She clasped his shoulder, feeling his muscles tense, and waited.

"Somebody's butt is gonna be in a sling over this," a familiar male voice cracked.

Exhaling her pent-up breath with a sigh, Jamie watched as Lou and a glum-looking uniformed officer came around the bend.

"The whole damn thing's a regular outing of the Keystone—"

The two men stopped short.

"Flynn? What are—? What the hell happened to you guys?"

She felt Steve relax, the tension ebb. He lowered his gun. "You might say we decided to take the express route." He eased himself off her and sat up. "You catch Dominguez?"

"Nah. He had a car stashed at one of the homes in the area. By the time we figured it out, he was already gone. We couldn't get the license plate, either." Lou turned to the officer and handed him the brown satchel Dominguez had left in the clearing. "I'll meet you back at the car."

The officer nodded, then left.

Lou peered down at her. "You okay?"

She pulled her torn blouse back into place. "I'm okay."

Steve scowled at Lou. "No thanks to you." He extended his hand and helped Jamie to her feet.

Lou's face grew solemn. "Look, I'm really sorry about what happened up there."

Steve shoved his Beretta back into its holster. "Sorry isn't good enough."

Lou reached into his shirt pocket for his cigarettes. "Save it, Flynn. I ain't in the mood."

"Well, that's too bad."

"I got the license plate."

She said it quietly, yet her voice sliced through the growing tension like a razor through foam rubber.

Both men froze. They turned to stare at her. "What?" they asked in unison.

She smiled. "I said, I got the limo's license plate."

Jamie closed her eyes and leaned against the side of the unmarked police car, feeling the afternoon sun beat down on her shoulders through the ripped fabric of her khaki blouse. What she wouldn't give for a soak in a warm tub right about now! Every muscle in her body ached, including a few she hadn't even known existed. Her brown trousers were muddy and torn, and as if that weren't bad enough, she was still missing her other shoe.

She sighed and opened her eyes. Steve stood beside the open car door waiting for Lou to get the results on the limo's license plate. It wasn't fair, she thought with a twinge of jealousy. While she looked a mess, their tumble down a briar-covered hill had only improved Flynn's good looks.

In fact, it had given him a rakish sort of charm she was finding very appealing.

"Yeah, I'm still here," Lou said into the police band radio. He flicked cigarette ash out the door. "Just sitting here growing older. Take all the time you need."

Steve looked up and met her gaze. He smiled.

She smiled back. The concrete warmed the soles of her bare feet. In the distance, a bird chirped merrily.

"Fifty-two twelve. Got it." Lou scribbled the information into his notebook. "Have a unit meet us there. We're rolling now." He replaced the mike and crawled out of the car.

Jamie moved to stand by Steve.

"Okay, here's the story." Lou dropped the half-smoked cigarette to the concrete, then stubbed it out with the heel of his scuffed brown shoe. "The car's registered to Heritage Limo. They got a couple hundred cars serving L.A. and Orange counties. Business, pleasure, whatever. I've sent a black-and-white over to their main office to check out the limo. You guys wanna follow me there?" He moved around the car to the driver's side. "It's over on Wilshire, about a block from Highland."

"Wouldn't miss it for the world." Steve reached into his trouser pocket for the car keys, then grasped Jamie's hand and started walking toward the Honda, some six feet away.

"Do you think we'll find Dominguez at Heritage Limo?" she asked, moving gingerly along the hot concrete.

He unlocked the car door. "You want my honest opinion?"

She didn't answer. She climbed into the car and dropped her lone shoe onto the floorboard, beside her shoulder bag. Steve slid into the seat beside her.

"Realistically, the most we can hope for is another lead." He started the car. "I know Rothenberg had several of his out-of-town clients picked up at LAX in limos. Part of Hathaway and Ferris's red-carpet treatment. Could be Rothenberg used Heritage and that's where he met Dominguez." He backed out of the parking space and drove through the gates of the Gardens.

"But I thought Rothenberg's accomplice contacted Dominguez."

"He probably did. But we also know Dominguez has been using a limo, probably the same one he was in today. We can't afford to ignore the possibility of a connection."

She nodded. He had a good point. "The thing I don't understand is why Dominguez still wants the coin. With Rothenberg dead, the underground auction ought to be canceled. Unless . . ." Her mouth curved down as she considered the situation. "Unless the accomplice already has a buyer lined up."

"Or he's intending to conduct the auction himself." Steve turned onto La Canada. "Either way, they've already killed two people to get the doubloon. I doubt they'll give up now."

They drove the rest of the way in silence. When they arrived at Heritage Limo, Lou stood in front of the garage conversing with an officer and a middle-aged man in grease-strained coveralls. Lou motioned them over.

"We got a problem," he said, coming straight to the point.

"What?" Steve asked.

The head mechanic gave Jamie's and Steve's states of disarray an amused once-over. The name "Denton" was stenciled across the right front pocket of his blue coveralls. A Dodgers baseball cap was pulled low over his lined forehead.

"The license plate doesn't match," Lou said. "Are you sure you got the number right, Jamie?"

"Of course I'm sure. H-L-S. Twenty-six. Just like I told you."

Denton shook his head. "And like I keep telling *you*, number twenty-six is in for repairs. There's gotta be a mistake."

"What kind of repairs?" Steve asked.

The man wiped his hand on a soiled rag he'd removed from his back pocket and shrugged. "Come on in and see for yourselves." He walked back into the noisy garage.

Lou told the officer to return to his unit and wait for further instructions. Then he, Jamie and Steve stepped inside the garage. Seven limos were in the shop, two more parked near the rear exit with their hoods open. Two mechanics were bent over a silver stretch, listening to the engine race. The clank of metal against metal filled the air, as did the stench of sweat and motor oil.

Denton stopped at the rear of the shop and pointed to a black limo up on a rack some five feet off the ground. "This here's number twenty-six. And like I been telling ya, this baby ain't been nowhere."

"What makes you so sure?" Jamie asked, walking around the car. Dominguez and Hines could have raced back here and put the limo back on the rack. They'd had a good twenty-minute head start. Then she felt the limo's hood. It was ice-cold.

"Mostly 'cause she ain't got an engine." Denton

pointed to the object in question, now resting on a wooden bench behind the limo. "She blew a rod out in Culver City last week, and we've been trying to rebuild the damn engine ever since. First we had to wait for the part to be shipped from the warehouse. Then we lost three mechanics with the flu. Believe me, lady, this car ain't been nowhere today."

Lou removed a cigarette from his jacket pocket and lit it. "Maybe you misread the number."

She shook her head. Impossible.

Lou glanced around the garage, then turned to Denton. "What about some of the other cars? Could one of your limos have been out about thirty minutes ago?"

Steve went over to the front of the car and examined the license plate. He ran his hands over the metal rim.

"No way," Denton replied. "Headquarters likes to keep track of all the vehicles. We got a sign-in sheet around back. First the driver's gotta sign the car out and give a destination; then he's expected to phone in every thirty minutes thereafter. No way anybody could've taken one out without authorization."

"What about for test runs?" Steve fingered the screws that held the license plate together. "On cars in for repairs."

Denton rubbed his chin thoughtfully. "I guess somebody could get one without signing for it. But there's no way Twenty-six could have gone out today. Not without an engine."

"How long does it take to put an engine in?" Jamie knew the question was ridiculous, even before she'd asked it. But she also knew what she'd seen from the clearing.

Denton guffawed. "You gotta be kidding!"

"Answer the question," Lou instructed. He flicked ash onto the oil-stained concrete.

"Two, three hours. Even if we had an engine ready to go, which we don't, it'd still take time to get it installed. Like I told you, I'm down three men."

"And what about a license plate?" Steve turned around,

holding the limo's plate in his hand. "How long would it take you to change that?"

"Hey, you can't do that!"

Steve looked at Lou. "Only two of the screws on this one have been tightened. You can see where the metal has been worn away around the outer rims. My guess is they switched tags with another limo to throw us off."

Lou examined the screws, then glanced at Denton.

"Okay, it's possible," Denton admitted grudgingly. "Somebody could've switched the plates—but I still don't know how anybody coulda driven off in a limo without being seen."

"Who has access to this car?" Lou asked.

"Any one of the mechanics—but, hey! I trust all my guys."

"Right." Lou stubbed out his cigarette. "So which one of your *guys* was assigned to work on this vehicle?"

Steve walked over to stand beside Jamie.

"Hey, Gil!" Denton called toward a man hunched over a limo a few feet away. "Who's been working on Twenty-six?"

Gil turned, a lug wrench dangling from his right hand. He wiped his forearm across his brow. "That's David's car. He's been working on it all week since Carlos called in."

"Where's he now?"

"Went home, I guess. Said his old lady was sick. Left 'bout fifteen minutes ago."

Denton turned back to Lou.

"You got an address on this David character?" Lou asked.

"Sure. Back in the office." Denton started walking toward the front of the garage. "You think David took one of the limos out for a joyride or something? Look, if he caused an accident, we're covered. They got all the forms up front. No problem at all."

"What's David's last name?" Steve asked.

"Haines. David Haines." Denton pushed open the door

to the small office. He walked over to a battered filing cabinet, flipped through several files in the top drawer, then removed a manila folder. "He's only been with us for six months, but he's a good mechanic. Never caused me any trouble."

"You got any pictures of this guy around here?" Lou asked.

"What does this look like? A Fotomat? " Then Denton snapped his fingers. "Hey! You know, I may have at that."

He walked over to a bulletin board near the door. Several Polaroid snapshots were pinned to the corkboard, along with work schedules and a yellowing notice about workers' compensation.

"A friend of his came by one day about a month ago. Tall Mexican guy. Blond hair. Had a new camera—one of those new Polaroids you see on TV." Denton removed a snapshot from the bunch and handed it to Lou. "The one in the middle is Haines."

Lou examined the snapshot for a moment, then passed it to Steve. Jamie glanced at it, but she knew what she would see. Denton's description of Haines's friend with the camera was all she'd needed to make her identification.

"Hines," she said.

Steve nodded. "No question."

Denton's expression grew worried. "Is David in some kind of trouble or something?"

Lou walked over to the desk and lifted the receiver. "Mind if I use your phone?" He punched in a series of numbers before the man could answer. "Yeah, this is Abrams. On that APB on Dominguez and Hines, send a black-and-white over to—" He read the address from the file. "Suspects to be considered armed and dangerous. Approach with extreme caution."

"Suspects? Hey, does somebody wanna tell me what's going on?" Denton's voice rose higher. "Just what's David supposed to have done?"

Steve slipped his arm around Jamie's waist. "He's wanted in connection with a double homicide."

"Ah, geez." Denton whipped his cap off. He ran his hand through his close-cropped gray hair. "That's all I need."

Jamie leaned her head against Steve's chest. "That's sort of how we feel about it, too."

Three hours later, Jamie curled up on the couch next to Rex as Steve hung up the receiver in the adjoining office and came out to join her.

"Hines's apartment was abandoned," he said wearily. "Looked like it'd been vacant for weeks. The police are checking it over, but Lou doesn't hold out much hope of finding anything."

"So now what do we do?" She raked her fingernails through the German shepherd's short, coarse hair.

He poured himself a cup of coffee and slumped down a few feet from her on the sofa. He extended his long legs to the cocktail table and crossed his feet at the ankle.

"We wait."

THIRTEEN

They were still waiting a week later.

Neither the APB nor an exhaustive door-to-door search of Dominguez and Hines's old neighborhood produced any new leads. No one had seen the two men since the day of the Descanso Gardens fiasco. It was, Jamie thought in bewilderment, as if they had slipped into an open manhole after leaving Heritage Limo and been swallowed up by the city. Lou theorized that the men had skipped town to escape the dragnet, but she wasn't reassured. She knew Dominguez was still out there. Watching. Waiting.

At Steve's suggestion, technicians in the police lab analyzed the satchel Dominguez had left behind in the clearing, but neither the bag nor its contents offered any clues to the pirate's whereabouts, or to the identity of Rothenberg's illusive accomplice, for that matter. In fact, the hundred thousand Dominguez had promised to pay for the doubloon turned out to be ninety-nine thousand short. Strips of paper cut to the same length as the currency had been sandwiched between crisp twenty-dollar bills. Lou said it just went to show you couldn't trust anybody anymore.

News of the botched exchange spread fast. A highly amused Liu Chin phoned that same evening to repeat his offer.

Steve declined, though less tactfully than he had the first time.

Jamie understood his reluctance to involve the underworld figure, but she was beginning to wish he would reconsider. Just then, they needed all the help they could get.

Steve's theory—a damned good one, she had thought—that Rothenberg had used Heritage Limo proved false. Hathaway and Ferris's records showed a long-term affiliation with Monarch Limo, a small firm based in Beverly Hills. Heritage confirmed the lack of a connection. They had no client records for either Hathaway and Ferris or Jim Rothenberg.

Even Tony's background check on Rothenberg came up empty. The murdered man had no debts, no apparent financial worries, at all. Which, unfortunately, translated into a lack of motive. Why would Jim Rothenberg risk his career—and his life—by stealing the Washington Doubloon? It didn't make any sense.

But then, none of it did.

On Wednesday afternoon, Jamie and Steve sat in his office at Flynn Security, reviewing the case file, hoping to find the one clue that would enable them to connect all the divergent dots. By now the facts and dates had begun to run together. Yet she knew they had to continue searching. Until Dominguez reappeared, tracking Gary's movements was the only avenue still open.

At three minutes past two, the intercom buzzed. They both jumped. Steve had left explicit instructions with Mona to hold his telephone calls.

He leaned forward and flipped the switch. "Yeah?"

"A Marcus Saritsky is on line-three," Mona said, a note of exasperation sounding in her voice. "He says he must speak with you. *Now*. I tried to put him off, but he won't cooperate."

Marcus Saritsky? Jamie lowered the paper she'd been reviewing. Saritsky and Jonathan McCabe were the two other collectors mentioned in Rothenberg's appointment calendar. She knew these men were interested in acquiring the Washington Doubloon, but she could only speculate on their involvement in an underground auction. McCabe had been "unavailable" every time they phoned his San Francisco office, as had the reclusive Saritsky in his Palm Springs estate.

"Thanks, Mona." Steve pressed the flashing red button. "Mr. Saritsky? Stephen Flynn. What can I do for you?"

He grew silent for a moment, his face maddeningly inexpressive. Jamie leaned forward, elbows on the desk, but couldn't hear any of the conversation. Damn. The call could be the break in the case they'd been waiting for, and she'd never know. For all the emotion Flynn displayed, he might've been listening to a weather forecast.

"Yes, of course," he murmured. "I'd be happy to. What time should—?" He scribbled an address on his notepad. "Fine. I'll see you then."

He replaced the receiver.

"Well?" she demanded.

He tapped his ballpoint pen against the desk and frowned, the lines deepening along his forehead. "Marcus Saritsky wants to talk to me about the Washington Doubloon. We meet him at his apartment in an hour."

An hour and a half later, Jamie sat stiffly on the edge of a high-backed, red velvet sofa in Marcus Saritsky's Beverly Hills apartment, slowly sipping her Earl Grey tea. She glanced at Steve, who was seated a few feet away, wondering if he was getting as impatient as she was. They'd been sitting in the drawing room for half an hour already with no sign of their host.

"This is ridiculous," she whispered finally. "Isn't he *ever* going to come out?"

Steve's cup clinked against the saucer as he set the china on the table in front of them. "Your guess is as good as mine."

He rubbed his eyes with his thumb and forefinger. He looked tired, she thought with concern. Tired and beaten.

"We'll give him another ten minutes. Then we'll leave."

As if on cue, the double doors at the rear of the room slowly opened. The stocky attendant who'd escorted them into the drawing room some time ago now pushed a wizened old man in a wheelchair toward them.

Jamie lowered her cup to the table, unable to tear her gaze away from Marcus Saritsky. She noticed his eyes first, piercing and as black as those of a hooded falcon. Even his nose, hooked at the tip, resembled the beak of a large, predatory bird. His eyes moved from side to side as if he were sizing them both up. From what she'd learned by reading the background check, he probably was.

Saritsky was a financial genius. He'd made his first fortune in the stock market in the early 1930s. A few years later, he had tried his hand at real estate, with similar results. His business moves, often considered foolhardy by his competitors, rarely failed. Since his much-publicized retreat to his fortified estate in the desert on his seventieth birthday, rumors of his failing health had abounded. According to more than one source, though, Saritsky's physical condition was the least of his problems. His eccentricities, once thought amusing, now bordered on the psychotic. The man had gone mad.

"Here. That'll do." Saritsky waved a bony hand as the wheelchair reached the sofa. The attendant locked the chair into place and began tucking a blanket around his employer's lap. Saritsky scowled. "I said, that's enough. You're not deaf, are you?" He slapped the attendant's hand. "Now go. Leave us. And I'd better not catch you listening at the keyhole, either."

The attendant bowed, his vacuous expression unchanged, and left the room, closing the door quietly behind him.

Saritsky looked at Steve. "Flynn? What the devil took you so long, man? I told you three o'clock sharp."

"Well, I— Sir?" Steve shot Jamie a confused glance.

Saritsky peered at the pocket watch pinned to his royal blue bed jacket. "It's 3:32. You're late." He shook his head. "Can't abide tardiness. Smacks of impertinence."

"Look, I don't know what you've been told, Mr. Saritsky, but we've been sitting in here for the past thirty minutes waiting for *you*. Your attendant brought us tea, and—"

Saritsky swatted his hand in the air, cutting Steve off. "What's that? You mean Jackson? Man's a damn fool. Can't trust a thing he says." He turned to Jamie. "Who are you?"

She smiled. "I—"

"This is my assistant, Miss Klindsmidt. She'll be taking notes."

Saritsky glared at Steve. "Can't she speak for herself? Never met a woman yet who couldn't talk your ear off."

Jamie caught a glimpse of Steve's expression—a sort of why-did-I-ever-agree-to-this look—and stifled a laugh.

She turned to the collector. "How do you do, Mr. Saritsky."

"Humph." Saritsky leaned back in his chair.

She felt her earlier tension fade. Marcus Saritsky was blunt and outspoken. Like a cowboy from an old-time Western, he shot straight from the hip. All things considered, she thought it a refreshing change.

Steve shifted position on the velvet sofa. "On the phone, you said you wanted to talk about the Washington Doubloon. . . ."

"Of course I did. Don't you think I remember why I called you?" Saritsky clawed at the blanket tucked around his waist, trying to slip a hand into his bed jacket. "Doubloon's a magnificent piece. You seen it?"

"We've been told it's one of a kind."

Jamie leaned forward, clasping her hands at her knees. She could tell that Steve's patience was wearing thin. If she didn't step in, they'd probably never learn anything from the collector.

"Rumor has it your collection is the best in the world,

Mr. Saritsky. Better even than the Smithsonian's. The Gloucester Token. The New England Threepence. A 1794 Liberty Silver Dollar. Tell me, Mr. Saritsky, is there any coin from that period you *don't* have?''

Saritsky peered at her again, as if seeing her for the first time. Then his face broke into a wide smile. ''Just one, Klindsmidt. But we'll soon take care of that, won't we?''

She returned the smile and waited for him to continue.

''I've worked all my life to build my collection. Traveled around the world three times. Been to Egypt to see an Arab sheik rumored to have a Silver Eagle I needed to round out a set—nearly got myself killed, too. You have to understand, Klindsmidt.'' Saritsky leaned forward, his expression intense. ''My collection means more to me than life itself. More than my children—damn ungrateful brats, the lot of them. Plan to leave every penny I have to charity just to spite them.'' He slapped his knee and let out a laugh. ''Love to see the looks on their faces when they hear the will. That'll teach them.''

She exchanged a cautious glance with Steve. He rolled his eyes heavenward, then looked away.

''Family's been trying for years to get my collection assessed,'' Saritsky went on, more seriously now. ''See exactly what I have, but I won't go for it. They don't fool me. Not one bit. They plan to sell it off, one piece at a time. Well, they're going to be in for the surprise of their lives. Yes, indeed.'' He settled back in his chair with a self-satisfied smile. ''Didn't spend all that time so the likes of Von Zant could get her hands on it, that's for damn certain.''

''Evelyn Von Zant?'' she asked in confusion.

''Woman wants my Fugios!'' Saritsky's hands gripped the armrests of the wheelchair. His face suffused with color. ''Been trying to get me to sell them to her for years. Won't do it, though. Never will. She's too much like her father for my tastes. Man's a human parasite, you know. Went to Europe after the war, brought home a fortune in stolen art treasures. What the Nazis didn't destroy, Peter Von Zant carried out.''

Steve cleared his throat. ''Mr. Saritsky, exactly why have you invited us here?'' He reached for his teacup.

Saritsky turned to stare at Steve. ''Haven't you been paying attention? I want to buy the Washington Doubloon from you.''

Steve stared back, the cup held in midair.

Jamie felt her breath catch.

''What . . . makes you think we have it?'' Steve took a sip of tea.

''Don't. But I do know it's your job to find it. Spoke to that fool who took Rothenberg's place. He told me so. Also told me the auction's been put off. Might never have one at all. Now . . . where did I put it?'' Saritsky fumbled in his bed jacket again.

''Mr. Saritsky,'' she said, hoping to clarify one final point. ''You had an appointment with Jim Rothenberg on Monday of last week. Had he promised to show you the doubloon?''

Saritsky shook his head, but didn't look up. ''Told me he couldn't show the doubloon. That it was going to be kept in a bank vault until the auction. He had some Higley tokens he thought I'd be interested in. Weren't even A-G Three, though. Could barely see the deer.''

She exchanged another glance with Steve.

''Why does that damn fool have to tuck it in so tight— aah.'' Saritsky pried loose a leather-bound checkbook from his bed jacket. ''All right, now. Enough beating around the bush.'' He turned to Steve. ''Flynn, what's your price for selling me the doubloon when you recover it? I'm willing to pay half a million, but not a penny more.''

Steve set the cup back in its saucer. ''It seems you've made a mistake, Mr. Saritsky. I'm a security consultant, not a coin dealer.'' He rose and started for the door. ''Coming, Agnes?''

''Flynn, don't be a fool. I could make you a wealthy man.''

Jamie gathered her purse and quickly stood. Steve had already retreated into the foyer. She heard him punch the button for the private elevator.

"Klindsmidt."

She stopped in the doorway and turned.

"Tell him I'll double any offer he receives."

"Mr. Saritsky . . ." She shook her head, not knowing what else to say.

"It's a seller's market, and I know it. I'm willing to be fair. Always have been. But I must have that coin. I can't take the chance they'll cancel the auction. I must—" His shoulders slumped and he fell back against the chair with a long sigh. The color faded from his face, like chalk on a sidewalk in a summer rain. Even his eyes lost their intensity. "I've waited all my life for the doubloon. The others don't appreciate it. Can't." His hand reached out, fingers curled in supplication; then it fell back against his lap. "Please."

She felt a wave of pity wash over her, pity for a man whose only remaining joy in life was a two-hundred-year-old gold coin.

"I'll tell him," she promised softly. Yet even as she said it, she knew that delivering the message would change nothing. If they found the coin—*when* they found the coin—it would be turned over to Hathaway and Ferris. What happened to the doubloon afterward would be out of their control.

Saritsky nodded, seemingly satisfied with her answer, and his eyes fluttered closed.

Then soundlessly, so as not to disturb him, she turned and walked toward the private elevator.

The drive home was quiet. Jamie could sense Steve's need for solitude without his saying a word, and kept her thoughts to herself. They'd both been hoping Saritsky would provide a solid lead. Instead, the collector had only raised more questions.

Why, she asked herself in growing confusion, had Evelyn Von Zant been promised a private showing of the doubloon and Saritsky refused one? If Rothenberg had been planning an underground auction, Saritsky surely qualified as the perfect bidder. As his offer to them demonstrated, his only concern was in acquiring the doubloon for his collection.

She frowned. Were they mistaken, then, about Rothenberg's plans for the doubloon? According to Harry Chung, only four collectors—Evelyn Von Zant, Marcus Saritsky, Jonathan McCabe and Kwon Liu Chin—wanted the Washington Doubloon badly enough that they'd resort to the black market in order to get it. Liu Chin had already been eliminated. He wanted an open auction, so his purchase of the doubloon would be well publicized. And if Saritsky were to be believed . . .

"We need to talk to McCabe," she said as they pulled into the driveway. "See if Rothenberg had promised to show him the doubloon."

"I've been thinking the same thing. We'll catch a commuter flight to San Francisco tomorrow." He shut off the engine and met her gaze. His mouth was set in a hard, grim line. "And he'll see us if I have to kick down his damned door."

Ten minutes later, Steve sat at the dining room table, perusing a copy of McCabe's dossier. Jamie set a mug of coffee before him, then reached for the transcripts on Gary's movements. She slumped in the chair across from Steve as Rex padded into the dining room. The dog looked expectantly from her to his master, then let out a loud sigh. He plopped on the floor beside the table and rested his head on his paws.

She took a sip of coffee. *The dog's right*, she thought with a frown.

It looked like it was going to be another long night.

At five minutes past eleven, she dropped her pen and groaned. This was getting her nowhere. Her head ached and her neck was beginning to cramp from bending over the table, double-checking the facts. By now she could've recited the information in the transcripts from memory—backward *and* forward—and it still would've done them no good. Flynn Security simply had no record of Gary's movements for the hour between his departure from the airport and his arrival at the hotel. He could've driven somewhere and deposited the doubloon, or he could've been trying to evade, then follow, the pirate.

Just now, she really didn't give a damn which.

"Okay, that's it for me," she said wearily. She closed her eyes and massaged her temples. "I've had too much fun for one day." Any more and she was liable to scream.

"Why don't you call it a night?" he suggested. "Go get some sleep."

"I think I'd better." She opened her eyes and met his tired gaze. Exhaustion tinted the skin under his eyes, deepened the lines along the curve of his mouth. His tie had been tossed onto the table sometime before, and the collar of his wrinkled shirt stood open. He was the one who needed to get some sleep, she thought worriedly. He looked ready to collapse.

"What about you?" she asked, trying to make her question seem casual. "If we're going to tackle McCabe tomorrow, we'll need to get an early start, don't you think?"

He shrugged, then returned his attention to the report. "I need to finish reviewing this dossier on Rothenberg. Probably got a good couple hours' work here."

She frowned. The damn records could wait.

Impulsively, she reached out and touched his shirtsleeve, feeling the warmth of his skin burn through the fabric. "Steve, you've *got* to get some rest." Her voice was quiet, yet the tone insistent. "You've been running yourself ragged over this case for the past week. If you don't slow down—"

"Hey, I'm fine." He looked up in surprise. "Just a little tired, I guess, but who isn't?" His fingers slid over her hand and squeezed. "Don't worry about me, Jamaica. I'll be okay." Then he flashed a weary smile and gently pushed her hand back across the table. "Now, why don't you go to bed? I'll see you in the morning."

Biting her tongue to keep from voicing another protest, she nodded and averted her gaze. They'd both agreed, she reminded herself, to keep their relationship on a strictly professional basis. Rules had been made, boundaries drawn. And right now she knew she was coming dangerously close to blowing it all. He didn't need—or want—any advice on how to live his life.

Especially not from her.

She pressed her palms against the table for leverage and stood. "Good night," she murmured softly. Then she turned and, without a backward glance, walked down the hall to her bedroom.

She awoke at 2:12.

Eyes wide open, she stared at the ceiling, listening to the low hum of the central air-conditioning unit. It wasn't like her to awaken in the middle of the night, she thought in annoyance. She usually slept straight through until morning. But awake she now was, and she knew without trying that she wouldn't be able to go back to sleep. Not with all the unanswered questions still running around in her mind.

"Damn."

She threw off the crumpled covers and reached for her robe. As long as she was awake, she might as well review the dossier on Rothenberg, see if she could find something Steve had overlooked. She doubted she'd have much success, but reading the case file was a helluva lot better than lying in bed, worrying about it.

When she stepped into the hallway, she saw a dim glow coming from the front of the house. *That's odd*, she thought. *Why are the lights still on?* She walked down the hall, turned into the kitchen and came to an abrupt stop.

Steve still sat at the dining room table, penciling comments into his spiral notebook. His shirtsleeves were rolled to the elbow. His hair was tousled, standing up in little tufts as though he'd been running his fingers through it in frustration. An empty coffeepot sat on the table before him.

She felt her spirits drop even lower.

"I thought you were going to bed after you finished reading that report on Rothenberg. It's already after two."

"Guess I got a little sidetracked." His voice was rough from too much coffee and too little sleep. He looked up and met her gaze. "I decided to review Von Zant's statement again. That led me back to Saritsky." He gave her a tiny smile. "So why are you up? I didn't wake you, did I?"

"No. I, ah, couldn't sleep." *From worrying about you.* She tightened the sash on her robe. "Did you find anything new?"

He tossed the pencil onto the table. "Not a damn thing. From what we were able to reconstruct, Rothenberg didn't deviate much from his regular routine the week before he died. He seemed nervous, but he always was like that just before a big auction." Steve pushed his chair back from the table with a loud scrape against the hardwood floor and stood. Frowning, he grasped the empty coffeepot and walked toward her. "And at this rate, I'm afraid we may never find his accomplice. It's been a week since the murder, and we don't even have a list of probable suspects."

He stopped at the sink, just inches away, and turned on the water. Quietly, she studied his face as he rinsed out the glass pot. His eyes were turned downward, the dark lashes casting shadows on his cheeks. A shock of hair tumbled across his forehead. Just then, he looked like a vulnerable little boy.

The sight was enough to break her heart.

Before she could stop herself, she had reached over and brushed the fallen hair back into place. "Why don't you go to bed? Let me take it from here."

He tensed as though she'd struck him. "I told you, I'm fine." He shut off the water. "Besides, this is my investigation. My responsibility. I can't walk away."

"Hey, I'm your partner, remember?"

Glass scraped against porcelain as he set the filled pot on the bottom of the sink. "You just . . . don't understand. We're running out of time."

She stared at him for a long moment. "That's your answer for everything, isn't it? That I don't understand." She felt a lump form in her throat. "Well, I *understand* far more than you think I do. I understand that you blame yourself for Gary's murder. That you're letting that guilt consume you."

He shook his head and started to turn away.

"Steve, please listen to me." She grabbed his arm. "There was nothing you could have done to prevent Gary's death. Nothing at all. You've told me time and time again that if Tony had taken the assignment, none of the rest would've happened. That Gary died because he tried to outmaneuver Dominguez and failed."

"I also told you I analyzed the risk factor." His eyes were filled with pain. "For Chrissake, Jamie, you know as well as I do that Rothenberg must've been planning to have the doubloon stolen all along. I didn't notice the warning signs, and that mistake cost Gary his life." He turned his head and stared off into the dining room. "And it nearly cost you yours."

"Steve . . ." she released his arm.

"Hell, nothing's changed. You're still in danger. You can't go home. You can't even tell your family where you are."

"I don't blame you for what's happened. I don't even blame Gary. He . . . involved me because he felt he had to. I've accepted that. I've had to. I may not like it, but it's a fact we can't change."

"Well, I can't accept it." He brushed past her and headed back to the dining room table.

"And I can't accept *this*! Not anymore. It's ripping me apart inside. Watching you punish yourself day after day for something you had no control over. Knowing there's nothing I can do to make it better. Knowing there's noth-

ing *you'll let me do*." She balled her hands into fists.
"Don't you realize what this crusade of yours is doing to
the people around you? To those who care about you?
Dammit, Steve, don't you know that I love you?"

The words seemed to echo through the quiet room. *I
love you . . . I love you.*

He turned to face her, startled green eyes meeting shattered brown ones. Seconds passed, each as long and pain-
ful as an eternity of silence. From around her came the
sounds of normalcy. The hum of the refrigerator. The plop
of a drop of water from the faucet into the coffeepot. The
click as the central air-conditioning unit shut itself off.

But not a sound from Steve. He just continued to stare,
his gaze unwavering in its intensity.

She turned away. She felt as though she were going to
cry.

"Jamaica." He said it so softly she barely heard him.
"Don't . . . go."

She shook her head, not trusting herself to speak. And
then she fled down the hall to the safety of her bedroom.

My God, she thought, hugging her pillow to her chest.
I really do love him. With all my heart and soul.

Why had it taken her so long to realize it?

Steve's fingertips rested against the cool wood of the
bedroom door for a long moment; then he slowly turned
the doorknob.

"Jamaica?"

She sat on the edge of the rumpled bed, her arms
wrapped around a pillow. At the sound of his voice, she
looked up. Her eyes brimmed with unshed tears.

Pain seared through his heart like a hot-bladed knife.

"I swear to God, hurting you was the last thing I ever
wanted to do."

She shook her head. "I walked into this with both eyes
open." Her voice was thick with emotion. "You told me
you wanted to keep things strictly professional. It's not
your fault."

The knife blade twisted. "I don't know how things got so complicated. So out of control." He walked to the bed and sat down beside her. "Hell, I've made a mess of everything, haven't I?" He tried to smile and found he couldn't quite manage it. She looked so fragile, so vulnerable.

"I guess I'm more of a rules player than you thought," he went on huskily. He touched her cheek, trailing his index finger down her chin. "I was trying to play it by the book. Do what I thought was best for both of us." His voice grew rougher. "I was wrong. Seeing you every day, sitting next to you, working with you and not being able to touch you. Having only the memory to cling to . . . God, that was worse."

"Steve . . ."

He tilted her head back with the crook of his finger, then brushed his lips against hers. Gently. Tenderly. He felt her tremble, the pillow fall to the floor. Then she slid her hands around his waist and up his back, holding him tight. It felt so good just being close to her.

"I can't make you any promises," he muttered hoarsely. "As long as Dominguez and his employer are out there, as long as the coin is missing, we'll have to take it day by day. It's not what you deserve, but it's all I can offer."

He felt her fingers fumble with the buttons on his shirt, then her warm hands slide across his chest.

"I'm not asking for promises."

Hunger filled him; a blind, aching need. He could have made love to her right then. As fast and furious as it had been the first time. But he knew she needed more. *He* needed more.

He untied the sash of her terry-cloth bathrobe, then eased it off her shoulders and down her bare arms. He raised her hands and turned them palm upward. He slowly kissed each finger, gliding his tongue from base to tip. Then he kissed her palms in the same way. A soft sigh escaped her lips.

He lowered her to the bed. He wanted to touch her. Taste her. Fill his senses with the magic of her.

He slipped the straps of her nightgown off her shoulders. The gown dropped lower, exposing her breasts. They were full, ripe; the nipples erect. He traced the curve of her breast with his finger, then followed the path with his tongue. She shivered and moaned his name.

He slid his hand up under her garment and pushed her legs apart. He could feel the heat. Feel the need. He touched her. She murmured something—a mad tumble of words he couldn't recognize but understood nonetheless—and arched toward him. He raised himself up to find her mouth. Her fingers entangled themselves in his hair. Her tongue probed his. The kiss was hot. Urgent. Desire raced through him, pounding through his blood, setting his nerve endings ablaze.

He pulled away for a moment to slide the gown down her hips and toss it aside. Then he undressed himself, his gaze never leaving hers. Her face was flushed. Her eyes shone with the same fire that smoldered inside him.

He entered her slowly, wanting to burn the moment into his memory. His heart thudded. His throat grew dry. Blood rushed through his ears, but he held back his passion. This was for her. His pleasure would come later.

He moved against her, building a slow, steady rhythm. It didn't take long until he felt her fingers tighten on his shoulder. Her body went rigid. Then she moaned, arching herself to meet his thrusts, crying out his name. He slid his hands under her hips and pulled her close. He felt her shudder, then relax.

He held her for a moment, listening to the rapid beating of her heart, the unevenness of her breath. Their bodies were slick with perspiration, yet his still burned.

Knowing his need, she kissed him, sliding her hands down his back to his hips and pulling him closer. Groaning, he thrust against her. Harder. She urged him on, returning the pleasure he'd given her a thousand times over, sending him to the brink of madness and back again.

"Say it," she gasped. "Say my name."

He shuddered from the power of the release. "Jamaica." It came out with a cry of suppressed longing, of paradise lost and found once more. "Jamaica!"

Sometime later, they moved into Steve's bedroom, where they made love slowly, languidly, in his king-size bed until their passion was spent. But long after he'd fallen asleep, Jamie lay awake, staring at the ceiling.

He'd made her feel wonderful, cherished. Whole again. Lord knew he was all she could ask for in a lover, and yet . . .

He hadn't told her he loved her.

She knew he cared for her. She could feel it in his touch, hear it in his voice. But she remembered what he'd said about his ex-wife, how he'd rushed into a marriage he'd quickly regretted. She wondered if she was forcing history to repeat itself, forcing him into a commitment he wasn't ready to make.

He stirred. "Jamaica," he murmured, his hand reaching out for her.

A wave of tenderness swamped her. She snuggled closer, feeling his arm encircle her shoulder, holding her tight. His heart thudded reassuringly against her ear.

Perhaps she was just kidding herself that they could have a future together, she thought and closed her eyes. But for tonight, she felt safe and loved.

Which was enough.

And so she slept.

FOURTEEN

Steve was awakened at nine o'clock the next morning by a high-pitched ringing that seemed to have the decibel level of a jackhammer running at full force. Without opening his eyes, he reached for the bedside table, grabbed the alarm clock and flung it across the room. The noise stopped.

Seconds later, the ringing started again, its sound of origin strangely unchanged.

"It's the telephone." The soft voice held a trace of wry amusement. "It's that large white object on your table. The one with all the numbers and buttons."

His eyes flew open. Jamaica lay beside him, her elbow propped up on the pillow, her cheek resting against her open palm. Her hair was mussed, her skin glowing. If possible, she looked even more beautiful than she had the night before.

He smiled and leaned over to kiss her.

The phone rang a third time

His hand reached out and fumbled for the receiver, knocking over an empty coffee mug in the process. It hit the carpeting with a thud.

"Flynn," he mumbled hoarsely a moment later.

"Steve? It's Tony. Did I wake you?"

Jamie ran her foot down his leg, slowly, sensuously.

"Tony, this better be good."

Tony laughed. "I just found out Jim Rothenberg sold counterfeit coins to a South American businessman about a year ago. Is that good enough?"

"Let's just say it has potential," Steve said, sitting up.

"Okay. Seems the client—a guy named Domingo Santiago from Brazil—wanted to turn a large sum of cash into gold coins. Specifically, American Eagles. As many as he could get his hands on. Most of Rothenberg's contacts were tapped out, so he had to resort to nonstandard markets. By the time he discovered the coins were forgeries, the client had already left town."

Steve rubbed his hand over his beard-stubbled chin. "How do you know Rothenberg never contacted the guy to straighten everything out?"

"Mainly 'cause he couldn't. The plane Santiago was on crashed in Mexico. No survivors. Rumor has it Rothenberg never contacted the family. Probably figured there was no point, since the coins were presumably destroyed in the crash."

"Okay, I'm impressed. Where'd you get your information?"

"Guy named Jerry Wong. He used to work for Isaac Gallagher down at A-West Collectibles—they're a front operation for the black market, mostly illegal antiquities sales. Gallagher's the one who sold Rothenberg the coins."

Steve frowned. "Isaac Gallagher. That name sounds awfully familiar."

"It should. It came up a few times in the background checks I ran on the collectors."

Jamie climbed out of bed and reached for Steve's football jersey draped across the back of the laundry hamper. "Isaac Gallagher sells stolen coins. Evelyn Von Zant makes most of her illegal purchases from him. It was in the report."

He grinned. "Beautiful *and* smart," he said, cupping the mouthpiece.

"So what's going on?" She pulled on the jersey.

He shook his head, then returned his attention to the phone. "How'd you find this guy, Tony?"

"That's just it. I didn't. Wong called me at the request of Kwon Liu Chin. Don't know what Liu Chin said to him, but it shook the guy up pretty bad."

"I can imagine," Steve said dryly.

"Anyway, Wong's willing to talk, even turn over some documents which he claims will back up everything he's saying. The only hitch is that we meet someplace private. He, ah, doesn't like crowds."

"Haven't met an informant yet who does." Steve rubbed his eyes. "Did he say anything else about the sale?"

"Just one other thing. Rothenberg was referred to Gallagher by one of Hathaway and Ferris's oldest clients— you get three guesses who."

"Evelyn Von Zant."

"Got it right the first time. Now *I'm* impressed."

Steve smiled grimly. "When do you meet Wong?"

"Eleven-fifteen. Venice Beach. At Papa Joe's Pizzeria. Place belongs to a buddy of mine. It doesn't open till after twelve, so we'll have lots of privacy—just what Wong wanted."

"I'll meet you there in two hours," Steve said and hung up.

"What was that all about?" she asked.

He reached for a pair of sweatpants, and briefly filled her in on the call as he got dressed. "The last thing Rothenberg would have wanted was for that story to get out," he concluded. "It would've shot his career to hell."

"So you think Gallagher blackmailed Rothenberg into divulging the doubloon's delivery schedule?"

He shrugged. "Best reason we've seen yet for Rothenberg's involvement in the heist."

She nodded. "You may be onto something. We need

to check that printout from the phone company. See if Rothenberg made any calls to Gallagher. If Gallagher *was* blackmailing Rothenberg, they'd probably have kept in close contact that last week."

"Good idea." He walked over to where she stood near the dresser. "You know, we'd cover more ground if we split up. Why don't you check the printout while I talk with Wong? We can compare notes over lunch."

"Okay."

"Great." He rested his open palm against the doorframe of the master bathroom. "Now I'm going to take a quick shower." He gave her a lopsided grin. "And try my damnedest to wake up."

She smiled, then reached up and kissed him, her lips soft against his bristled cheek. "Why don't I go make some coffee?"

He sighed. More precious words he'd never heard.

Thirty minutes later, Steve sped along the 405 Freeway, his mouth set in a frown. The more he thought about it, the less likely it seemed that Gallagher had been blackmailing Rothenberg. After all, Gallagher had broken the law himself by selling counterfeit coins. If news of Rothenberg's resale went public—as Gallagher would have threatened in a blackmail attempt—Gallagher would've been facing a jail term.

Which pretty much blew Steve's brilliant theory sky-high.

He reviewed the facts a second time.

Rothenberg needed American Eagles. When Von Zant heard about it, she referred him to Gallagher, a major supplier of stolen coins, *her* supplier. Gallagher sold Rothenberg counterfeit Eagles, which Rothenberg in turn sold to a South American businessman. Von Zant said Rothenberg had promised her a private showing of the Washington Doubloon, yet other collectors who'd made the same request had been turned down.

Evelyn Von Zant. Evelyn Von Zant. Everywhere he turned, the woman's name kept popping up.

SUNSET BOULEVARD ¼ MILE.

Maybe it was time he talked to her again.

He glanced at his watch. Nine-forty-five. Venice was a good twenty-minute drive. Tony would be at the restaurant at eleven; Wong, fifteen minutes later. It'd be cutting it close, but he might still make it to the meeting if he swung by Von Zant's Bel-Air home first.

He quickly merged into the far right lane and exited at Sunset before he could change his mind. Hell, at this point, what could he lose by questioning her again?

Suddenly Lou's warning flashed into his mind. *The chief doesn't like it when his friends are inconvenienced by a murder investigation.*

He smiled grimly. Looked to him like the chief would just have to get over it.

Less than ten minutes later, Steve parked in the circular driveway of Evelyn Von Zant's home. He turned off the engine and got out of the car, quickly surveying the area. Rays of golden sunlight struck the windows of the second floor, bathing the stately Tudor-style brick house in a warm glow. He lifted the brass knocker and rapped once on the double doors.

No answer.

Where was everybody? he wondered. He lifted the knocker to rap again, then stopped, as the proverbial light bulb flashed in his memory. It was Thursday. The staff's day off. The day Von Zant tended her prize-winning roses. He could knock on the door all morning long and she'd probably never hear him.

Letting the knocker fall back with a clatter against the door, he turned and walked toward the brick pathway, which separated the house from the four-car garage. In the distance he could hear murmured voices coming from the patio. Strange, he thought. He hadn't seen any cars around in front.

Seconds later, the stone patio came into view. Evelyn

Von Zant and a brown-haired man sat at the wicker-and-glass table, deep in conversation. The man turned in Steve's direction. It was David Hines.

Steve ducked out of sight, pressing his back against the garage wall. Breath held, he hazarded a quick glance toward the patio and relaxed. Von Zant and Hines were still talking. They hadn't seen him. But they would if he didn't get out of there.

He inched his way along the garage wall back toward the driveway, feeling the warm brick press through the fabric of his sports coat. His shoes made scarcely a sound on the spongy grass. His heart started to pound, his palms perspire.

Only one person had nothing to lose and everything to gain from Rothenberg's blackmail. Mother Teresa herself. Hell, she'd probably set Rothenberg up from the very beginning.

Nice bit of detective work, Flynn. Too bad you couldn't have figured it out sooner.

Coming even with the trellis, he darted around the corner to the driveway. He'd phone the police from outside the estate, he decided, then wait for backup. Without a gun, there wasn't much else he could do.

That was when he heard an ominous click-click, as though a semiautomatic were being primed. The sound stopped him dead in his tracks, two feet from the car. He slowly turned.

"Leaving so soon?" Raoul Dominguez smiled, his bleached blond hair gleaming silver-white in the morning sun.

He held a .38-caliber revolver in his right hand. Its long nose was aimed straight at Steve's chest. At a foot away, Dominguez couldn't miss.

"I'm sure Miss Von Zant would want you to stay a while longer. In fact, she'd insist upon it."

Still smiling, Dominguez raised the gun. Then he brought it down across the side of Steve's head, and everything dissolved into blackness.

Complete and total blackness.

* * *

"Damn."

Jamie tossed the computer printout of telephone numbers onto the cocktail table. Rothenberg had made a total of seventy-six calls in the two-week period before his death. Unfortunately, none of them were to Isaac Gallagher.

Frustrated, she slumped back on the sofa and sipped her coffee. She'd been so certain Gallagher had forced Rothenberg into helping them steal the doubloon. After all, Rothenberg's sale of counterfeit coins made a perfect case for blackmail. A golden opportunity, in fact. But considering the way the heist had turned out—and Rothenberg's emotional state after Gary's murder—it just didn't make sense for Rothenberg *not* to phone Gallagher. Not if Gallagher was blackmailing Rothenberg, that is.

She sat up straight, her fingers tightening around the warm mug. Maybe that was it. Maybe *Gallagher* wasn't the blackmailer. If Jerry Wong knew about Rothenberg's sale of counterfeit coins, other people could have as well.

She quickly eliminated Gallagher's employees as possible suspects. It would've been nearly impossible for them to do it without his knowledge. Besides, the blackmailer would've needed access to collectors, people with money to spend on the doubloon. Or—she glanced down at the dossier on Evelyn Von Zant—a strong desire to possess the coin herself.

Of course! Von Zant had introduced Rothenberg to Gallagher, so she must've known about the counterfeit coins. More important, she wanted the Washington Doubloon.

Jamie set the mug on the table and reached for the computer printout. If she remembered correctly, Von Zant's telephone number had come up several times on the phone log. What were the chances that—?

Rex jumped up on the sofa, trampling the open case file with his front paws.

She sighed in exasperation. "Not now, Rex. I'm busy." She gave the dog a firm shove.

After giving her his best wounded-puppy-dog look, he jumped off the sofa. His heavy tail swatted her purse as he sailed past, and the bag toppled off the table and onto the floor with a resounding crash. Rex yelped, then took off as though his life depended on it, which it might very well have.

"Rex!" She set the printout aside. Great. Everything that had once been inside her purse was now out. Wallet. Notebooks. Pens. Can of Mace. Half-eaten candy bar. She wrinkled her nose at the last item and placed it on the table.

She couldn't remember the last time she'd cleaned out her purse, but since everything was already out, she decided she might as well sort through it now. If nothing else, it'd take her mind off the case for a while.

She pushed the cocktail table back a few feet and plopped down on the hardwood floor. When she finished sorting through the mess, she unzipped the side pocket and removed a crumpled pack of sugar-free gum, three pennies and Steve's business card. She ran her fingertips over the raised lettering and smiled. Then she slipped her hand into the other pocket.

Her smile froze.

Something was lodged behind the lining of the purse.

Curious, she peered inside. Thanks to her habit of overstuffing the bag, the lining in the side pocket was ripped. She worked her hand into the slit and felt paper crinkle. Moments later, she pulled out a small white envelope.

She stared at it in confusion. The plain white envelope, no bigger than two inches by three, was made of a heavy bond paper. She could feel the outline of something flat and round inside, like a medallion of some sort.

Or a coin.

Her heart began to beat faster. She ripped open the envelope.

The Washington Doubloon, sealed in clear plastic, slid into her palm. She stared at it for a moment, awestruck. The coin's edges were frayed and most of the inscription was worn away. Only one leaf in Washington's olive wreath was visible. Even so, the doubloon was as magnificent as Marcus Saritsky had said it would be. Harry's counterfeit was good, no doubt about that, but it couldn't compare with the real thing. Jamie felt like she was holding a piece of history in her hand.

She flushed. A piece of history she'd have a hard time explaining to Steve just how she came by. When he found out she'd been carrying the damn thing around in her purse, he'd never let her live it down.

Carefully she set the doubloon on the table. At least now she knew what had happened. After Gary had made his check-in phone call, he must have realized he was in trouble. He'd slipped her the coin, then tried to lose Dominguez, rather than call for backup. When Gary had thought it was safe, he'd gone to the hotel to retrieve the coin, but Dominguez had reappeared. And since Gary hadn't had the coin on him and he'd been seen leaving a note at the reception desk for Jamie Royale . . .

She nodded. Yes, it all made sense now.

She glanced at her watch. Twenty-five till eleven. She could hardly wait for Steve to return from his meeting with Wong. First she'd tell him about her theory that Evelyn Von Zant was the blackmailer. Then she'd show him the coin—hopefully without having to explain exactly where she'd found the damn thing.

The phone rang.

She scrambled to her feet to answer it. "Hello."

"Jamaica?"

His voice sent a familiar warmth coursing through her. "I was just thinking about you," she murmured, twisting the phone cord around her index finger. "Listen, I think I finally figured it out. Gallagher wasn't blackmailing Rothenberg. Evelyn Von Zant was."

"I know." His voice sounded odd, distant.

"And I found the doubloon. You'll never believe where it was. I know I didn't." When he didn't answer her, she frowned and released the cord. "Really, Flynn. You could show a little enthusiasm here. I just cracked the case."

He sighed. "Don't listen to them, darling. Whatever they say, promise me you won't—"

His words were cut off by a sharp blow. She heard him groan, then a loud crash as the telephone hit the floor.

"Steve?" Her grip tightened on the receiver. *"Steve?"*

Silence.

Then she heard someone pick up the telephone receiver. "Your boyfriend can't talk right now, Jamaica. I'm afraid he's had a little . . . accident."

Her knees turned to rubber and she braced herself against the wall for support. "Please don't hurt him. I'll do anything you want. Anything at all. Just don't . . . hurt him."

"Then listen to me very carefully." Dominguez's voice was as cold as ice. "You've got thirty minutes to save your boyfriend's life. Bring the doubloon to Evelyn Von Zant's house in Bel-Air. Come alone and tell no one where you're going. You make it here in time, he lives. Arrive a minute late or bring the cops, he dies. Simple as that."

"How do I know you'll let us go when I give you the coin?"

"You don't." Dominguez paused. "But you got my word I'll kill him if you don't show."

"That's not good enough." She tried to make her voice sound confident and unafraid but doubted if she had succeeded. "I need a guarantee you'll let us both go. Otherwise the deal's off."

"Hey, you don't want to deal, fine with me. I'll just waste your boyfriend right now and we can forget the whole thing." She heard a clicking sound, as though he was loading the firing chamber of a gun. "The choice is yours."

"No! Please. I—I'll do what you want."

He laughed. "Yeah, I thought you might."

Then the line went dead.

Blinking back tears, she punched in Lou's number. Precious moments later, she slammed the receiver down. Lou was out of the office and couldn't be reached. She ran her fingers through her hair, trying to think. Walking into Von Zant's house without first notifying the authorities was suicidal.

But wasting time trying to reach them could get Steve killed.

She dialed Steve's direct line at Flynn Security, her mind racing. She'd take the Acura. Fortunately, the car window hadn't been replaced yet, so Steve was still driving the Honda. She rummaged through the desk drawer for the car keys. She found Harry Chung's counterfeit doubloon, looked at it for a moment, then stuffed it into her jeans pocket along with the keys.

"Stephen Flynn's office," Mona answered.

"Mona, it's Jamie. We've got an emergency. I tried to get in touch with Lou Abrams, but couldn't. Now it's up to you."

"All right, Jamie, take it easy. Try to relax and tell me what's happening."

"I don't have time to relax! Dominguez has threatened to kill Steve." She filled the secretary in on Dominguez's call. "I'm on my way to Von Zant's house now."

"No, no, absolutely not. Once Dominguez has the coin, you've lost your bargaining chip. He'll kill you both."

"But I don't have any choice." She glanced at her watch. "I'll try to stall until Lou gets there, but I don't know how long I can hold out. Tell him to hurry—and, for heaven's sake, to be careful. If Dominguez sees any police, he'll kill us. Now I have to go!"

She hung up and raced into the living room. She dumped her belongings into her purse and grabbed the Washington Doubloon off the table. She paused for a moment, comparing the real doubloon with the fake one she'd taken from Steve's desk. Then she slipped the original into its hiding place behind the tear in the purse's lining and tucked the fake coin back into her jeans pocket.

She ran through the kitchen to the garage, hit the button

on the wall to open the electric door, then jumped into the Acura. She pumped the accelerator wildly several times and turned the key. The car wouldn't start.

Calm down, she told herself. She tried it again. The car sprang to life. Murmuring a prayer of thanks, she shifted gears and backed out of the garage with a squeal of rubber on the concrete just as the garage door was about to close. Von Zant's house was fifteen minutes away.

And Dominguez had promised to kill Steve in twenty.

FIFTEEN

Steve sat slouched in a Queen Anne chair in Evelyn Von Zant's drawing room, his hands tied behind his back. Feigning unconsciousness, he worked at loosening the bonds on his wrists. Dominguez stood by the fireplace, smoking a cigarette. Hines, wearing a chauffeur's uniform, sat on the sofa, sipping a cup of tea. Steve knew the two men were waiting for Jamaica to bring the coin. He also knew, once she did, Dominguez would kill her.

And there wasn't a damned thing he could do about it.

He forced himself to relax, his body to go limp. It wouldn't do to let them know he was awake, he told himself. Right now it was the only advantage he had.

Slowly he flexed his wrists, moving the knot down to his groping fingers. He manipulated the rope and felt it give. He smiled. Knot tying obviously wasn't one of Hines's specialties. But then—he tasted blood from the cut on his lower lip and winced—Hines had probably figured the bonds weren't necessary. Dominguez had packed enough wallop in the last blow to knock out a bull elephant. If Steve hadn't ducked at the last minute, he'd probably have gotten a concussion. Instead, he had a throbbing headache and a busted lip from the fall to the floor.

He worked the first knot loose.

The doors opened and Evelyn Von Zant walked into the room. In her herringbone suit and sedate brown hat, she looked the familiar image of L.A.'s Mother Teresa. Kind. Caring. The much-heralded benefactress of the downtrodden. But appearances were often deceptive, he thought grimly. He now knew that behind Evelyn Von Zant's soft exterior lay a core of solid steel. What amazed him was that he hadn't seen it before.

"It shouldn't be long now." Hines poured her a cup of tea.

She frowned and sat down on the sofa. "It'd better not be." She spread a linen napkin across her lap. "I've got a committee luncheon with the mayor at noon and don't want to be late."

The Acura screeched to a stop alongside the Honda. Jamie killed the engine and grabbed her purse. Pulse racing, she jumped out, skirted the two cars and ran across the driveway to the double doors. Her thirty minutes were up.

She reached for the knocker when the front door suddenly popped open a crack. Startled, she looked up to meet David Hines's suspicious brown eyes peering out at her. A chauffeur's cap was pulled low on his forehead. He held a snub-nosed revolver in his right hand. He scanned the driveway to make sure she'd come alone, then opened the door wider without saying a word. He waved the revolver, motioning her inside the house.

Jamie ran a perspiring palm down her jeans leg and stepped through the doorway. The heavy door swung shut, leaving her in semidarkness. She waited for her eyes to adjust to the change in lighting.

"Follow me," he instructed in a flat, accentless baritone. Then he turned and walked across the dimly lit foyer, his soft-soled shoes making barely a sound on the parquet floor.

Feeling like a lamb being led to the slaughter, she obediently followed him across the entry hall—a blur of polished wood and gilded mirrors—to a pair of French doors. Hines jammed the gun into the waistband of his trousers, then turned the brass handle. He moved aside to let her pass.

Swallowing her fear, she stepped forward. She met his gaze when she crossed the threshold. Nothing. Not even a flicker of acknowledgment in his hooded brown eyes. His bland face might have been carved of granite for all the emotion he showed.

"Jamaica."

Her head snapped around.

Steve sat bound to a chair near the windows. Sunlight streamed through the heavy brocade draperies behind him.

She dropped her purse and rushed toward him. "Darling!"

"That's far enough." Dominguez stood by the fireplace on her left. His finger was poised on the trigger of a long-barreled gun aimed straight at her. The cold expression on his lean, tanned face assured her he had no qualms about shooting.

She stopped.

"Search her," he ordered.

She heard the doors close, then felt Hines come up behind her. His hands moved impersonally over her body, checking for a weapon. Then she heard him dump out her purse, scattering the contents on the hardwood floor.

"She's clean."

She kept her gaze riveted on Steve's face. His skin had a grayish tinge; his bottom lip was cut and bleeding. Every fiber of her being wanted to run across to him, but she dared not move.

"You shouldn't have come," he said.

The note of regret in his voice stabbed through her heart.

"Really, Mr. Flynn," Evelyn Von Zant chastised softly. "I'd have thought you'd be pleased to see Miss Klindsmidt again. I know we certainly are."

Jamie's gaze darted toward Von Zant. The woman sat on a high-backed sofa, drinking a cup of tea. She wore a tasteful brown suit and matching hat—standard attire for the well-dressed society matron. She gave Jamie a smug little smile.

Jamie clenched her hands. She glanced back at Steve. "Are you all right?"

"He's quite well," Von Zant answered. *"For the time being."* China clinked as she set her teacup in its saucer on the table. "Did you bring the coin?"

"You're not going to get away with this, you know."

"But, my dear Agnes, I assure you I already have." Von Zant's face hardened. *"Did you bring the coin?"*

Jamie glanced at Dominguez. He'd placed a boot-clad foot on the metal fireplace screen. The revolver rested on his thigh. Hines stood a few feet away. Both were watching her, waiting.

She took a deep breath to gather her faltering courage. Then she slipped her hand in her jeans pocket and removed the fake doubloon. She handed it to Von Zant.

"Aah." The collector stared at the coin in open adoration, like a child with an eagerly awaited Christmas gift. Her pale blue eyes danced as she lifted the doubloon by its edges and inspected the obverse. "Exquisite," she breathed.

"Is it really worth it?" Jamie asked, trying to divert the woman's attention lest she examine the coin too closely. "Is that piece of gold really worth the death of two men? All the pain you've caused their families?"

Von Zant lowered the doubloon. "What sentimental rubbish! Surely you can't expect me to show pity for two fools? They both got what they deserved." She ran her fingertips along the coin's surface. "Dodsworth decided to play hero, so Raoul accommodated him. When Jim got cold feet, he had to be eliminated as well."

"And so you killed him," Steve said. "Then you removed the tape from the video recorder to cover your tracks."

Von Zant turned to stare at him. "You're quite the little detective, aren't you, Mr. Flynn?" Her voice was edged with ice. Then she shrugged and placed the doubloon on the table. "Yes, I killed Jim. Regrettably, he gave me no choice. He wanted to call it quits and tell you everything. I tried to reason with him, but it was no use. So I told him he'd have to talk to Raoul, tell him his services were no longer needed. While Jim was writing down the telephone number, I picked up the paperweight. I remembered the video camera on my way out. Jim had shown me the security room shortly after he'd installed the system. He was so proud of it, you know."

Jamie rubbed her arms to ward off a chill. "You were blackmailing him, weren't you?"

Von Zant frowned. "Jim brought it all on himself. He allowed greed to compromise his principles." She reached for her teacup. "He needed a large number of American Eagles for a new client, a client who was willing to pay above the market rate. I referred him to an . . . associate . . . who could accommodate him. Jim knew the Eagles were probably stolen, but he didn't want to worry about the minor details just then.

"The amazing thing is that Isaac didn't realize the coins he'd sold Jim were counterfeit. He might never have known if one of his people hadn't run a microscopic analysis on the remaining Eagles. When Isaac read the report, he contacted Jim immediately. A professional courtesy, you see. To Isaac, of course, the solution was simple. Since Jim's client had perished in the plane crash along with the coins, there was no need to worry. Jim foolishly agreed to keep silent.

"Of course, when I pointed out the dire consequences his actions could have—and showed him the copy of the sales slip and analysis report I'd gotten from Isaac's office—Jim begged me not to tell a soul. He knew if his superiors at Hathaway and Ferris heard about the sale, he'd lose everything."

"So you forced him to help you steal the doubloon," Steve said quietly.

Von Zant sipped her tea. "I knew I'd have tough competition in an open auction. Marcus Saritsky would barter his soul to the devil for that coin, if only to prevent me from getting it. And Paul Murphey had the backing of the Metropolitan. So Jim and I made a deal. If he provided Dominguez with the doubloon's delivery schedule, I would destroy the information I had managed to acquire on his little indiscretion. No one would ever know. Unfortunately, when things got a little rough, Jim panicked."

"Do you really blame him?" Jamie asked. "With Dodsworth dead and Dominguez trying to kill me?"

Von Zant looked Jamie coolly in the eye. "Raoul only threatened you, my dear. If he'd intended to kill you, believe me, you'd already be dead. He wanted to persuade you to surrender the doubloon without causing any *permanent* damage. And his pictures did frighten you. So much so, you fled the hotel. Luckily for Raoul, you attended Dodsworth's funeral the next day. It confirmed our suspicions that Mr. Flynn had you under wraps somewhere. Raoul hoped the shot he fired in the garage would persuade you to surrender the coin. He obviously miscalculated."

Jamie felt a wave of nausea. The reporters she'd seen at the funeral, the flash of light—Dominguez had been taking snapshots for his grisly photo album.

"Then you show up here," Von Zant continued, "posing as Agnes Klindsmidt. I assumed you either didn't have any knowledge of the doubloon or were trying to outsmart us. Raoul convinced me it was the latter. He said Gary had admitted giving you the coin. Raoul told me we had to be patient. That, given time, you would cooperate. When you placed your advertisement in the paper, he thought you'd finally come to your senses, but you'd only intended to double-cross him. You made Raoul look very foolish, my dear. I don't think he's quite forgiven you for it."

Dominguez's foot slid off the fireplace grille and landed

with a thud on the hardwood floor. Jamie's gaze darted toward him. He flexed his black-gloved hand, crinkling leather. The subtle move sent a chill racing down her spine.

Von Zant glanced at her watch. "Dear me, how I do run on. Now I'm late for my committee luncheon." She reached for the doubloon. "David, would you bring the car around, please?"

Hines nodded and left the room.

"What about us?" Jamie asked hoarsely. "I kept my end of the bargain. You got the doubloon. Now let us go."

"Let you go?" Von Zant shook her head apologetically. "But that would spoil everything, wouldn't it?" She turned to Dominguez. "I trust you'll use discretion."

Dominguez's reply was a curt nod.

Von Zant smiled, then glided toward the door.

Once she'd gone, Dominguez turned to Jamie. His eyes were as cold and dark as the pits of hell. He motioned at her with the gun. "Come here."

She swallowed hard. She glanced at Steve. The rope that had once bound him now lay in a coil on the floor. How had he—?

He met her startled gaze and shook his head. She bit her lip and looked away. Slowly, she began walking toward Dominguez. She wasn't sure what Steve was planning to do, but she did know it might be their only chance for survival.

When she came even with the fireplace, Dominguez's hand shot out and grabbed her arm, yanking her toward him.

She gasped with pain.

"Miss Von Zant's right. I *haven't* forgiven you for setting me up."

She stared back at him. A ray of sunlight from the crack in the draperies struck the gold earring in his left earlobe. The tiny hoop flashed, sending out golden sparks whenever he moved. She felt the tension in his grip, noticed the taut muscles bunched at the corners of his mouth. He was as tightly wound as a child's top, but far more deadly.

He released her arm. "The funny part is I never wanted to hurt you, *chiquita*. If you'd just given me the coin, none of this would've happened." Then he brushed the gun barrel down her front. "Seems like such a waste, don't it?"

"You bastard," Steve growled. "If you're going to kill us, then kill us. Stop tormenting her."

Dominguez turned, lowering the gun. "Shut up!"

Jamie took an instinctive step back. Her foot hit the metal stand of fireplace instruments.

Dominguez whirled at the sudden sound.

Steve lunged out of the chair. He hit Dominguez broadside and they toppled over, grappling for the gun. Her mouth opened in a scream, but no sound came out. Her vocal cords were frozen in fright. Almost without her being aware of it, her hand reached down and touched the cold iron of a poker. Her fingers tightened around the handle.

She couldn't tell who was winning. Steve and Dominguez were roughly the same size, yet Dominguez had the advantage of superior strength. But Steve was fighting for his life.

The gun fired once, the bullet lodging harmlessly in the ceiling above the windows. She removed the poker from the stand. Then Dominguez landed a sharp uppercut to Steve's chin. The blow knocked him back toward the chair. He stumbled and hit the floor. His head drooped.

Dominguez slowly raised the revolver. He took careful aim. His lips were curled in an evil, twisted smile. "Watching you die is going to be a pleasure."

"No!"

She wielded the poker like a baseball bat. It struck Dominguez's forearm just as the gun fired. He screamed in pain and dropped the revolver. She swung again, feeling metal contact with bone and sinew. Dominguez fell to his knees.

The drawing room doors burst open. She spun around.

"Freeze! Police!" Lou and a host of blue uniforms rushed into the room.

She squeezed her eyes shut. Moments later, she felt a warm hand slide over hers. "Jamaica?"

The poker slipped from her trembling fingers and fell to the floor with a clatter.

It was over, she thought with relief. The nightmare was finally over.

The next two hours were a blur of police reports and flashing cameras. Dominguez had been patched up by the paramedics and carted off to jail where he, Hines and Evelyn Von Zant would stay, Lou assured Jamie, for a long, long time. The press had descended on the police station with the frenzy of sharks on the scent of fresh blood when news of Von Zant's arrest on murder and conspiracy charges—during the middle of the mayor's luncheon, no less—hit the airwaves.

Steve was in his element during the press conference. Jamie thought—a strictly biased opinion, of course—that he cut quite a dashing figure with his various bruises and bandages, looking sort of like a sexier Humphrey Bogart after cracking the big case. For the sake of public relations, he gave most of the credit for solving the case to Lou, who, not to be outclassed, insisted it had been the result of teamwork.

It had been easy for Jamie to slip away during the commotion. Easy to climb into the Acura and drive back to the house. What hadn't been so easy was making the decision to return to Baton Rouge.

By the time Steve came home, her suitcases were packed and sitting in the living room.

"Hey, what happened to you?" He slipped his arms around her waist and gave her a hug. His bottom lip was still bruised and swollen; a bandage was taped over the scrape on his upper cheek. But the shadows that had shaded his eyes, the heaviness of spirit, had lifted. His demons were finally laid to rest.

"When I looked for you after the press conference, Lou said you'd told him you were going home." He glanced at her suitcases lined up near the front door. His smile faded. "I didn't realize he meant to Baton Rouge."

"My flight leaves at eight." She tried to make it sound casual, like it was no big deal, but inside she was falling apart, crumbling like a dried leaf when you squeeze it too tight.

She eased out of his arms, needing to put some distance between them. "Lou said as long as I come back for the trial, there'd be no problem."

"So you're going? Just like that?"

She shrugged. "The case is solved. Von Zant is under arrest. Dominguez and Hines are out of operation. We even found the coin. There's no reason for me to stay."

He met her gaze. "Isn't there?"

She flushed. "Besides, I have a job, remember? Commitments."

He closed the distance between them in two long strides. "You hate your job. Hell, you were planning to quit when you attended the insurance conference. And if you're worried about your cat, call your super and ask him to have K.C. shipped out here. I'm sure Rex would enjoy the company."

She looked into his eyes and tried to smile. "You make it sound so simple."

He touched her cheek. "It is." His hand slid down to her neck, the tips of his fingers lightly ruffling her hair. "It's excruciatingly simple."

"So I stay another day. Maybe two. Then what? We both know I'll have to leave eventually. And I know the longer I stay, the harder it'll be to go when the time comes."

"Jamaica—"

"We've been living in limbo for the past two weeks," she went on, trying to ignore the tingling warmth of his hand against her skin. "But now we're back in the real world. We have to face certain facts. You told me so yourself. If a relationship is going to last, it has to be built on a solid foundation. Shared interests. Common goals."

A flicker of pain crossed his face. "And you don't think we have that?"

She felt as though her heart would break. "I do, but . . ." She let her voice fade away.

He stared at her for a long moment. "When I said I rushed into marriage with Marie, I meant we hadn't taken the time to get to know one another. That the only thing we shared was a strong physical attraction. It's not that way with you and me. Sure, we've known each other only a short time, but we've crammed a lifetime into those days." His hand slowly stroked her neck. "It's been long enough for me to know that I want you in my life. Today and tomorrow. For always."

Her eyes filled with tears. "Do you really mean that?"

"I love you, Jamaica." He kissed the top of her forehead. "I probably have since the moment I saw you walking across that hotel lobby. Probably will till the day I die. I know the past two weeks have been rough. You've been through hell. We both have. But you love me. I know you do. We can make this work. Just give me a chance to prove it to you."

"Take all the time you need." She slid her arms around his waist and held him close. She'd learned a long time ago not to argue with the results when they were in your favor.

Sometime later, he pulled away. "I suppose you'll want a big wedding," he teased.

She nodded. "My mother started planning it the day after I was born."

"So we're talking Dodger Stadium here. Ten thousand people or so."

"But I'd settle for a small church wedding. A few friends. Family . . . That way we'd have more time for the honeymoon."

He grinned. "You know, we could start on the honeymoon now, if you're afraid we'll be pressed for time."

She punched his arm.

He cleared his throat. "There is one thing we should get straightened out before we book the chapel," he said, folding his arms against his chest and trying to look stern. He failed miserably.

"Oh?"

"It's about your purse. Back at the station, you told Lou you'd found the doubloon behind a tear in its lining. Is that true?"

She felt her cheeks redden. "I think the important thing to remember here is that we found the coin, not necessarily where."

"Uh-huh." He walked over to the cocktail table and picked up her shoulder bag with two fingers. He dangled it in front of her. "Start talking."

"What's to talk about? Sometimes I overstuff my purse and the seams give."

"Sometimes? How about all the time? I seem to remember your pulling out staplers and magazines. The last time I checked, you even had a bottle of wine stashed in there."

"A very tiny bottle," she corrected with a grin.

"*And* an umbrella."

She walked over to where he stood. "Can't we discuss this later?" she asked, running her hands up his chest to his shoulders.

"No, I want to hear more about this torn seam of yours. Give."

"Are you sure?" She leaned up and kissed him on his throat, his chin, the edge of his jaw.

"Perhaps," he said huskily, dropping the purse on the table. "you could persuade me otherwise."

And she did just that.

SHARE THE FUN . . .
SHARE YOUR NEW-FOUND TREASURE!!

You don't want to let your new books out of your sight? That's okay. Your friends can get their own. Order below.

No. 144 OUTSIDE THE RULES by Linda Hughes
Jamie and Stephen play a dangerous game with high stakes and no rules.

No. 20 CHEATED HEARTS by Karen Lawton Barrett
T.C. and Lucas find their way back into each other's hearts.

No. 21 THAT JAMES BOY by Lois Faye Dyer
Jesse believes in love at first sight. Will he convince Sarah?

No. 22 NEVER LET GO by Laura Phillips
Ryan has a big dilemma. Kelly is the answer to *all* his prayers.

No. 23 A PERFECT MATCH by Susan Combs
Ross can keep Emily safe but can he save himself from Emily?

No. 24 REMEMBER MY LOVE by Pamela Macaluso
Will Max ever remember the special love he and Deanna shared?

No. 25 LOVE WITH INTEREST by Darcy Rice
Stephanie & Elliot find $47,000,000 *plus* interest—true love!

No. 26 NEVER A BRIDE by Leanne Banks
The last thing Cassie wanted was a relationship. Joshua had other ideas.

No. 27 GOLDILOCKS by Judy Christenberry
David and Susan join forces and get tangled in their own web.

No. 28 SEASON OF THE HEART by Ann Hammond
Can Lane and Maggie's newfound feelings stand the test of time?

No. 29 FOSTER LOVE by Janis Reams Hudson
Morgan comes home to claim his children but Sarah claims his heart.

No. 30 REMEMBER THE NIGHT by Sally Falcon
Joanna throws caution to the wind. Is Nathan fantasy or reality?

No. 31 WINGS OF LOVE by Linda Windsor
Mac & Kelly soar to new heights of ecstasy. Are they ready?

No. 32 SWEET LAND OF LIBERTY by Ellen Kelly
Brock has a secret and Liberty's freedom could be in serious jeopardy!

No. 33 A TOUCH OF LOVE by Patricia Hagan
Kelly seeks peace and quiet and finds paradise in Mike's arms.

No. 34 NO EASY TASK by Chloe Summers
Hunter is wary when Doone delivers a package that will change his life.

No. 35 DIAMOND ON ICE by Lacey Dancer
Diana could melt even the coldest of hearts. Jason hasn't a chance.

No. 36 DADDY'S GIRL by Janice Kaiser
Slade wants more than Andrea is willing to give. Who wins?

No. 37 ROSES by Caitlin Randall
It's an inside job & K.C. helps Brett find more than the thief!

No. 38 HEARTS COLLIDE by Ann Patrick
Matthew finds big trouble and it's spelled P-a-u-l-a.

No. 39 QUINN'S INHERITANCE by Judi Lind
Gabe and Quinn share an inheritance and find an even greater fortune.

No. 40 CATCH A RISING STAR by Laura Phillips
Justin is seeking fame; Beth helps him find something more important.

No. 41 SPIDER'S WEB by Allie Jordan
Silvia's quiet life explodes when Fletcher shows up on her doorstep.

No. 42 TRUE COLORS by Dixie DuBois
Julian helps Nikki find herself again but will she have room for him?

Meteor Publishing Corporation
Dept. 493, P. O. Box 41820, Philadelphia, PA 19101-9828

Please send the books I've indicated below. Check or money order (U.S. Dollars only)—no cash, stamps or C.O.D.s (PA residents, add 6% sales tax). I am enclosing $2.95 plus 75¢ handling fee for *each* book ordered.

Total Amount Enclosed: $_____.

___ No. 144	___ No. 25	___ No. 31	___ No. 37
___ No. 20	___ No. 26	___ No. 32	___ No. 38
___ No. 21	___ No. 27	___ No. 33	___ No. 39
___ No. 22	___ No. 28	___ No. 34	___ No. 40
___ No. 23	___ No. 29	___ No. 35	___ No. 41
___ No. 24	___ No. 30	___ No. 36	___ No. 42

Please Print:

Name _____

Address _____ Apt. No. _____

City/State _____ Zip _____

Allow four to six weeks for delivery. Quantities limited.